MEDICINE WHEEL

a novel by
RON SCHWAB

Poor Coyote Press
PO Box 6105
Omaha, NE 68106
www.PoorCoyotePress.com

ISBN: 1-943421-14-5
ISBN-13: 978-1-943421-14-5

In memory of my father, Doc Schwab,
a dedicated country vet, an avid reader and,
in my eyes, a five and a half foot giant

MEDICINE WHEEL

SPRING 1885

1

THAD'S KNIFE BLADE split the soft flesh of Harold's scrotum, and he squealed like a pig, struggling to escape the inevitability of his fate. Quincy Belmont tightened his grip on Harold's legs as the one hundred pound patient fought frantically. Thad's fingers grasped one testicle, and he tugged and sliced it free of the connective tissue, and then grab, tug, and slice again, and Harold could no longer declare himself male in the true sense of the word. It took less than a minute to complete the surgery.

Quincy released the husky, black and white spotted porker from the vise of his clamped knees, and Harold staggered stiffly away to join his wounded comrades, the bright scarlet of fresh blood dripping from between his hind quarters.

"You shouldn't let them get so big, Reverend," Thad chided. "It wouldn't be so hard on them, and we wouldn't have to wrestle with them like this."

Thad had been castrating Quincy's hogs for five or six years now, and he knew his scolding was a waste of time. Every three or four months he would have fifteen to twenty boars to cut, and they'd always be overweight—one hundred pounds or more. Half the size, or even smaller, would have been better, easier on both the handler and the surgeon and, certainly, less stressful for the animal.

"I do the heavy work, Dr. Locke. You shouldn't complain," he replied.

He was right, of course. And Quincy thrived on hard work, seemingly impervious to the muggy heat that turned the Flint Hills into a steaming cauldron this mid-July day. J. Quincy Belmont looked like a giant, leaning back against the thick, cedar planks of the hog pen. A barrel-chested man with shoulders like a heavily muscled bull, he was probably several inches shorter than Thad's own six feet, but he seemed taller somehow. If there were fifty men in a room, Quincy would stand out—and it would not be because he was a colored man. He imposed an undeniable presence that drew loyalty from his friends and followers and a serious uneasiness from those who were hostile to his race. He spoke with a deep, baritone voice in words precisely enunciated with a slight Bostonian accent. He never failed to say what he meant or to mean what he said.

As Thad cleaned and gathered up his instruments, Quincy picked up the bucket which had been the receptacle for the harvested testicles. The big mongrel dog that waited outside the pen began to dance and bark eagerly. Quincy plucked a bloody nut from the bucket and tossed it over the fence. The dog leaped and caught the morsel in his jaws before it hit the ground.

"I guess we won't miss one," Quincy said. "Rachael will make a feast from these. One reason I like to get a little growth on the boars before we call you over."

As Thad climbed over the fence, Quincy announced, "Rachael says you are staying for dinner." It was a command not an invitation.

Thad pulled his watch from a front trouser pocket. It was a bit past noon, which was confirmed by the sun's rays shining from midway across the southern sky. One of Rachael's spreads was worth tolerating the uneasiness that poisoned any comfortable conversation with Quincy.

Before Thad joined the Belmont family for dinner, he watered his Appaloosa gelding, Cato, and tossed him a bit of prairie hay offered by Quincy. He even gave Thad a small can of grain as a treat for the horse and suggested a spot in the shade where Thad might hitch his old friend. Quincy was not an unkind or selfish man, Thad thought, but it just seemed the preacher could not help being wary of him and that the jury was still out on where he placed Thad on his ranking of men.

As Thad grained Cato, he surveyed the Belmont farmstead. It was dominated by a two-story limestone house constructed of the rock that provided the natural floor of much of the eastern Kansas Flint Hills. It was a comfortable home with several fireplaces and an iron wood cooking stove to ward off wintry blasts, and the thick stone walls cooled the house nicely during the heat of summer. A hundred feet or so west of the residence was a small stone barn, not far from which stood a sturdy smokehouse that sent forth the enticing smell of smoking hams and bacon that sweetened the air. The hogs that Quincy did not market found their ways to the smokehouse to satisfy a seemingly unquenchable demand in this cow country that was desperately short of pork. Quincy was on his way to being a wealthy man, and every year the Belmont farm added more of the little A-framed huts for the growing herd of brood sows and their litters of pigs.

Quincy wore many hats: a livestock man, a commercial meat producer, a skilled blacksmith who manufactured quality knives— including some of Thad's custom-made surgical instruments—and a preacher with a ballooning flock. He had carved his place in the Flint Hills after his discharge from the Tenth Cavalry buffalo soldiers in 1868 while they were stationed temporarily at nearby Fort Riley. He was called to the lime-caked hills, he claimed, but he coupled his call with good business sense by purchasing this quarter section not more than five miles north of Manhattan, the growing county seat of Riley County, Kansas. It didn't hurt that Fort Riley, a thriving military post, lay something over fifteen miles east of Manhattan and provided an insatiable demand for bacon, hams and other pork products.

"Thad, time to eat. Come on up." The friendly, feminine voice came from the house porch, interrupting Thad's reverie. He looked up and saw Rachael waving, and he returned the wave and headed up to the house.

2

THE BELMONT GIRLS, attired in dusty work garments, were already seated at the long oak table when Thad entered the dining room. They looked up at him, almost in unison, with wide, welcoming smiles on their dusky faces, dark eyes appraising him with interest. Thad suspected that white guests were not commonplace in the household and that white diners were even more rare.

"Good afternoon, ladies," Thad said. "Thank you for allowing me to join you."

Elizabeth, the fifteen-year-old, replied, "We're honored, Dr. Locke. Mama told us you were coming. We so wanted to watch you castrate the boars, but Papa didn't think it was a proper sight for young ladies. Silly, but you think?"

Thad was not about to challenge Papa's wisdom. "That's your Papa's decision. It's not for me to say. I'm sure he has his reasons."

"Well, we've been scooping pig poop all morning, and Papa doesn't seem to find that too uncouth for our sensibilities."

Elizabeth was on the feisty side and not unknown to challenge her father's authority, not unlike her older sister. Serena would be twenty-seven now, a dozen years older than the spirited Elizabeth. Clarissa, who was two years younger than Elizabeth, and Susanna, who was two years younger than Clarissa, had always seemed more subdued and obedient. But who knew what a few more years might bring?

Rachael entered the room with a huge platter of—no surprise—ham, basted with a tasty-looking reddish sauce, and spared Thad further queries concerning his opinions about Quincy's edicts. "We're so happy you could join us, Thad. Aren't we girls?"

The girls smiled on cue, shaking their heads in the affirmative and rolling their eyes.

"It's my pleasure, Mrs. Belmont. I wouldn't pass up the opportunity."

"Thad, my name's Rachael. Please don't make me feel like an old woman."

"No, ma'am. I wouldn't want to do that. You're sure not an old woman, I mean—"

The girls giggled.

Quincy entered the room and took his place at the other end of the table. Rachael left for a moment and returned with bowls of sweet potatoes and green beans. As she took her own chair next to her husband's, she said, "You may go ahead with the blessing, Papa."

Quincy surveyed the table to confirm that all were in praying mode and commenced. "Heavenly Father, we ask that you bless this food we are about to receive. Please take note of our special guest this noon. I am informed that he is a seldom and reluctant churchgoer. Help him find the path to salvation that he might someday share with us the joy of everlasting life. Take care of this family and direct us in the way of righteousness. Amen."

Thad looked toward Rachael for direction, but her eyes were fastened with anger on her spouse. Momentarily, she turned to Thad and shrugged helplessly. She nodded to Elizabeth to pass him the ham platter. Rachel got up and returned with a tray of hot biscuits and a bowl of honey, and their attention was quickly diverted to the feast.

Silence settled on the dinner table until Elizabeth spoke. God, how she reminded Thad of Serena with her intelligent, coffee-brown eyes and the tawny skin, favoring her mother's Seneca lineage. "Dr. Locke, Mama says you're a real doctor. Is that true?"

"I'm a veterinary surgeon. That's a real doctor, but I take care of animals. What your mama means is that I was trained as a medical doctor, and I am also licensed to help people."

"I don't understand."

"There were no veterinary schools in this country until one was established at the Iowa State Agriculture College a half dozen or so years ago. Before that time most veterinary surgeons were either self-taught or learned their skills by working with another vet. Some attended medical colleges. I went to the University of Pennsylvania medical school."

"Really? Did you have to go to school a long time?"

"Two years, after finishing high school. I understand the curriculum requires three years now. When I was there, we took two years of lectures and had to pass an oral examination before we were turned loose on the public. In other words, we took courses in the theory and practice of medicine and studied anatomy, surgery and midwifery, but we never practiced on a live person before graduation. I do treat human patients sometimes in case of an emergency, but the first baby I helped birth was literally the first baby." I smiled and winked, "Of course, I didn't tell the mother. It might have frightened her. I did have the advantage, though, of having helped cows and sows give birth long before I went to medical school. Pulling baby pigs isn't that much different than delivering human babies, actually."

"That's kind of scary," Clarissa said, her eyes wide.

"There's not that much difference between animals and people. Except animals don't talk back and seem to appreciate more what you do for them. Well, not always. I've been stomped by an ungrateful bull or cow a few times."

The kids laughed, and after that, conversation loosened up. Thad received a good quizzing about his animal—and people—adventures while Quincy glowered in silence, although he forgot himself a time or two and betrayed some interest in what Thad had to say.

After putting away double helpings of Rachael's apple cobbler, Thad tendered thanks to his hosts and received a solemn nod from Quincy and broad smiles from the girls who had been given afternoon work assignments by their father. Rachael took his arm and led him out onto the porch and strolled with him to fetch Cato.

"It was so nice to have you join us, Thad. The girls thoroughly enjoyed your stories. Elizabeth says she wants to study to be a veterinary surgeon when she finishes high school."

"There's no shortage of work for a vet, but she'd better not be dreaming of great riches. I wouldn't change the life for anything, though."

Her expression turned serious as she watched him saddle Cato. "I was embarrassed about Quincy's blessing, Thad. It was rude. I'm sorry."

"There's no better man. I guess he was just trying to save my soul." Thad grinned and took her hand. "I may be a lost cause, though. I regret that he barely tolerates me."

"He respects you, Thad. He truly admires your skills, and you wouldn't believe how much pride he takes in the surgical instruments he fashions for you."

"There's a profit to be made in developing and producing top quality veterinary instruments. I have some ideas I'd like to discuss with him if we can carve out a bit more comfort between us."

"Just be patient with him. I'll broach the subject with him."

He decided to take a chance and abruptly shifted topics. "How's Serena?"

Rachael appeared neither surprised nor unnerved by the question, but Thad could tell she had already rehearsed a reply in her mind. "She's doing well, Thad. Very well." She offered a sad smile, and her eyes moistened a bit. "I'm sorry. You know I can't say more."

3

AFTER LEAVING THE Belmont place, Thad headed back to the Lazy L, the half section owned by him and the Manhattan Bank. The small ranch property lay about four miles—as the crow flies—southeast of the Belmont farm, and Thad ran a cow herd of about twenty-five Herefords there—not near enough to make a living, but they helped assuage his addiction to the cattle business. The grass would have carried two or three times as many cow-calf pairs, but he didn't have the cash or credit to fully stock the place yet.

He had built a four-room limestone house with a little windowless lean-to for an emulsion room—to facilitate a serious photography habit—on high ground. He had set aside one room with a separate entrance for storage of his veterinary instruments and supplies and had installed a crude oak table for treatment of the occasional small animals that were brought in for care. Unfortunately for his business, very few folks in the Flint Hills would spend a half dollar to fix a dog or a cat's broken leg or to patch up one of the creatures who had got the worst end of a fight with a bobcat. A bullet was more likely the poor animal's sentence.

Cato knew the way home, and Thad gave him his lead, although he thought about turning down the trail toward the Big Blue River Valley and making the climb to the medicine wheel. He had not been over that way for almost a year now, and it was probably just as well, since it usually sent him brooding about Serena. It had been eleven years now, and their story, he thought, was like a novel chopped off in the middle of a chapter. Maybe it was the unfinished part of it that haunted him so much and kept him from moving on.

He wondered what had become of her and why the family was so secretive about Serena's whereabouts and what she was doing. Of course, his only contacts with the Belmonts were professional ones that did not lend themselves well to casual inquiries. Would he ever see Serena again? He concluded that it was unlikely, and, perhaps, for the best.

SUMMER 1874

4

THADDEUS JACOB LOCKE, a sandy-haired, rangy six-footer, sat tall in the saddle astride his three-year-old Appaloosa gelding at the top of a scalped ridge overlooking the Big Blue River Valley. It was the first day of June, his mother's birth date. He knew that because Aunt Nancy, his mother's sister, had reminded him at breakfast. It saddened him just a bit, but he was not deeply troubled, because he had never known his mother, Deborah Locke, who had died giving birth to him and his sister, Hannah, 19 years ago, come July 4.

The Appaloosa, Cato, whinnied and danced restlessly. The horse was generally a calm beast just short of docile and had been given to Thad by his older brother, Cameron Locke, who ran the only Appaloosa herd in the Flint Hills. Cato had been gifted to the young man because of the horse's gentleness, since Cam Locke, a former Confederate cavalry officer, had long since given up on honing Thad into a first class rider.

Thad's eyes were fastened on puffs of dust a quarter of a mile north tracking a deer path that threaded its way along the steep, rocky slopes below. At first, he assumed the creature stirring up the powdered lime was a doe fleeing some real or imagined threat, but then he decided the form was human. He reached into his saddle bags and pulled out the old seaman's telescope the Judge had given him and twisted it into focus.

The creature was indeed human. Moving swiftly and gracefully over the trail as though swept by the wind, a young woman raced along the path. She was scantily dressed in what appeared to be a short buckskin kilt and a sleeveless shirt, and her black hair was tied back with a yellow ribbon in what he'd heard some ladies call a pony tail. She ran with determination and seeming intensity, as though she was in a rush to get somewhere before a deadline.

She had engaged his curiosity, and he followed her with the telescope as she angled downhill toward the Big Blue River Valley. Suddenly, she stumbled and catapulted forward, landing face first in the trail rut. She was deathly still for a moment before she tried to lift herself up and then collapsed again.

Thad dismounted and began leading the gelding down the treacherous shale footing of the slope, keeping his eye on the fallen runner as they inched their way toward her. She was sitting upright now, he noted, clutching her shin or ankle. As he approached, he yelled, "You okay, ma'am?"

She looked up but did not reply.

He released Cato, confident the Appaloosa would not stray and approached the young woman, stopping when he saw the wary look in her dark, defiant eyes. He was momentarily speechless as he got a closer look at the runner. Her face was smudged with dirt and her nose was skinned and dripping blood—and she was the most incredibly beautiful female he had ever encountered. She had flawless, bronze-toned skin and thick black lashes framing coffee-brown eyes, and her form was lithe and slender, almost boyish, but not quite. He couldn't tell for certain, but he guessed she wouldn't stand more than a few inches over five feet.

"You're staring at me," she said.

His face flushed. "Not my intent, ma'am. Can I help?"

She probed her ankle gingerly. "Who are you?"

"Thad Locke, ma'am."

"The lawyer family?"

"Yes, ma'am. My father and my brother practice law in Manhattan."

"What are you doing out here?"

"I live a few miles south of here . . . with my aunt and uncle. It's a complicated story. I was riding out this way and was up on the ridge when I saw you take a tumble. Thought I should come down and check. Can you get up?"

She started to rise but then winced and sat back down. Tears glistened at the corners of her eyes. He didn't know what to say. She seemed a bit contrary, but she was obviously hurting more than she was letting on. He decided to disregard her testiness. He gave a low whistle toward Cato, and the horse abandoned his grazing and trotted back.

He plucked a canteen from his saddle horn and dug in his saddle bags, pulling out a few clean, well-worn white shirts and a small bottle of rubbing alcohol. He returned to the young woman's side, knelt down beside her, and began ripping the shirts into strips. "What's your name?" he asked.

She hesitated, watching him with curiosity. "Serena. Serena Belmont," she replied softly.

"Kin to the Preacher Belmont?"

"His daughter. Do you know him?"

"Heard of him. Never met him. Lay your head back and press this against the nostril. Bleeding's already slowing." He handed her a piece of cloth, moistened another rag, and began wiping the blood and dust from her face, his fingers moving gently and deftly over the scraped nose. He applied some alcohol to the scrapes. She flinched, he noted, but didn't complain.

"Please don't tell me you're a doctor. You can't be much older than I am."

"I'll be nineteen in a month. But I'm as close to a doctor as you'll find within ten miles from here. I've been helping folks around here with their cows and pigs and cats and dogs since I was a kid."

"Some might say you're still a kid . . . of course, you're two years older than I am. By the way, I'm not an animal."

"I noticed." He turned away. "Now, let me take a look at that leg."

He took the muscled calf of her slender right leg in his hands, and his fingers probed and traced over the shinbone.

"Now just a minute, mister," she protested.

He ignored her objections and squeezed her ankle.

"Hurt?"

She grimaced. "Yes, it hurts."

"Grit your teeth. It's going to hurt some more. Try to wiggle your ankle . . . slowly."

She winced and tears came to her eyes. "I can't move it any more. It feels like it's locked in place."

Thad slipped the moccasin off Serena's foot and ran his fingers over the top and under, pressing the soft flesh firmly. "No pain in the foot is there?"

"No, not much."

He turned his attention back to the ankle. "I don't feel a break, but it could be a 'green stick.' I doubt it, though. More likely a nasty sprain. I'll wrap it for support and get you home to your folks, and they can decide if you need to see a sawbones."

"What's a green stick?"

"It's a break in the bone where the two ends haven't moved out of place . . . sort of a clean break, where the bone isn't pressing against the skin or punched through it."

"You're scaring me. I can't have a broken ankle."

"Well, you can, but I'll bet you don't." He took a long strip of cloth, centered it on the bottom of the foot, pulled the ends behind her ankle, and wrapped them around the leg before crossing the ends and looping them through the starting lengths. He pulled tight and tied. "This will give you some support, but you'll need to keep your weight off the foot for a week or more. Now we've got to get you home. I'd say your place is about three miles as the crow flies. I know you can run. How do you do on a horse?"

"I can ride well enough. But we only have one horse."

"Then we'll have to share."

Thad gave two sharp whistles, and the Appaloosa moved in close. He reached down and grasped Serena's hand firmly. "Okay, now you need to pull yourself up and see if you can put some weight on the foot."

He helped her up, and she pressed her foot to the rocky pathway. Her sharp gasp betrayed her pain. Abruptly, he lifted her into his arms and swept her mid-shriek her onto the horse's saddle. He grabbed the saddle horn and, putting his booted foot into the stirrup, lifted himself less gracefully onto the horse's rump and settled in behind her, arms wrapped gently around her slender waist.

"What the hell do you think you're doing?" she asked, clutching his wrist in an effort to push him away.

"I can't ride free-handed, ma'am, and I'm not so noble that I am going to lead this horse all the way back to your place. There's no way you're going to walk that far, so you can either take the reins and I'll hold on to you or you can hang onto the saddle horn, and I can lean forward and handle the reins. Either way, we're going to be in close company for a spell." The choices were no loss options from his standpoint. He did not find the nearness of this dark beauty the least unpleasant.

She looked over her shoulder, her dark eyes, less suspicious and hostile now, fastening on his. "I'll handle the reins."

5

THE MID-AFTERNOON sun had suddenly turned blistering, and the terrain had become rugged as they climbed the shale slope. Notwithstanding his previous vow to ride, Thad had dismounted and was walking beside the horse and solitary rider. He caught sight of a small cluster of young cottonwoods a hundred yards or so to the northwest. He broke the uneasy silence that hovered over him and his traveling companion. Pointing in the direction of the trees, he said, "I could use a spot of shade and a break. That's not far out of our way. Likely a spring or stream there."

Serena nodded her approval and nudged Cato toward the cottonwoods. As Thad had predicted, the trees were near a stream that meandered and snaked its way over the limestone creek bed and through the Flint Hills on its journey to the Big Blue. "At the pace we're moving, I'd guess we have an hour or a bit less to your folks' place. Let me help you down and we can unwrap your ankle and you can soak it in the cold water. It's starting to swell, and that should help some."

This time she cooperated without protest and leaned from the saddle, resting her hands on his shoulders as he lifted her by the waist and eased her to the earth. He placed her down next to the stream under the shade of a cottonwood branch and then unwrapped the ankle. "It'll be worse tomorrow," he observed, "but if you keep soaking it in cold water and step very carefully for a week or so, you'll be fine."

She slipped her foot into the water and after a few moments gave a sigh of relief. "Maybe you do know what you're talking about."

He returned a wry smile. "You need some water and I wouldn't drink it out of here. I have three-quarters of a canteen left, if you don't mind sharing. Sorry, ma'am, but I don't have any drinking glasses."

Cato was quenching his thirst downstream, and Thad retrieved the canteen and handed it to Serena. "You can have first swig, ma'am."

She accepted the canteen and he sat down beside her, keeping a respectful distance between them.

"You may call me 'Serena' if you like."

"I like," he replied, "if you'll call me 'Thad.'"

She smiled. She actually smiled, revealing perfect white teeth, of course.

"Here, Thad, your turn," she said, passing the canteen back.

He drank sparingly, and they passed the canteen back and forth several times like two old cowboys sharing a jug of moonshine. "Why haven't I seen you before?" he asked.

"We don't exactly move in the same society."

"I don't move in any society. My sister and I stayed in Manhattan with the Judge—that's my father—while we went to high school, and I broke for the ranch whenever school was out . . . but I've seen your folks with some tiny girls in town. You weren't with them. I'd have remembered."

She looked off into the distance. "I really don't live here. I come to see Mama and Papa and my sisters for a few weeks in the summers, but then I go back to school. I'm staying longer this year. I just got back, and I'll be with my folks another month or so."

"Where do you go to school?"

"Washington D.C. You'll never remember the name. It's called the 'Institution for Education of Colored Youth.' Papa's sister—my aunt—teaches there, and I live with her." She turned and looked directly at him. "You have noticed I'm colored, haven't you? A Negro?"

This was a challenge of some kind, and he sensed that his relationship with this young woman hinged upon his response. The Judge always told him "walk straight and talk straight, and you'll stay out of trouble." He figured that was just another way of saying it's best to tell the truth. "Well, yeah. I'm not blind. I wasn't sure when I first saw you . . . never gave it that much thought. I figured as much when you said your folks were the Belmonts." He shrugged and smiled, "You've noticed I'm Scottish, haven't you?"

"I don't understand. I can't tell what you are."

"Actually, I'm only one-fourth Scottish. I've also got parts of Irish, French, Swiss, German, a pinch of Mexican and God knows what . . . maybe a bit of African way back. The Judge always says the Lockes are pure-bred mongrels."

"That's an oxymoron."

"Wow. And she uses big words, too. What kind of a cow is an oxymoron?"

With a look of feigned exasperation, she said, "It's a contradictory state . . . you're making fun of me."

"Look for your sense of humor. I'm sure it's around here someplace. You're way too concerned about who's what. I'm guessing you're as much mongrel as I am. Anyway, that's for idiots who care to worry about."

"You're really serious, I think."

"Now, one question before we get on our way. How did you end up in Washington?"

"Papa came from near Boston. He was a free Negro descended from several generations of freemen. Mama is Seneca, although some places she'd be called a half breed since only her mother was Seneca and her father was some kind of a white man . . . I don't know if he was a mongrel or not. To make the story short, Papa was blacksmithing on her father's farm when he met Mama. They fell in love and got married over the objection of Mama's father. She was more or less disowned and they moved to Pennsylvania, where I was born. Papa started another blacksmithing business and, according to Mama, was doing very well when the war came along. Then he took Mama and me to Washington to stay with Aunt Clara while he went off with a Yankee infantry unit."

"But I've been told he was a buffalo soldier. They were cavalry."

"Papa was good with horses, working in blacksmithing the way he did, and when the war ended, and Congress set up the Negro army regiments, he enlisted with the Tenth Cavalry. Sometime while he was in the Indian Territory he caught religion, and when his enlistment ran out a few years later, he left the Army and came back to Washington to just pick up where he left off. Mama and I hadn't seen him for more than seven years. I didn't even know him."

"And then he brought the family to Kansas."

"He brought Mama to Kansas. He wrote her at least once a month all those years he was gone, and I guess that was enough to stoke the embers of love she had for him. By this time I'd been going to the Institution since I started school, and I didn't want to leave Aunt Clara to go off in the wilderness someplace with this gruff, scary man. Papa insisted I go with them. Mama had a private talk with him. I stayed with Aunt Clara."

Thad took her foot and started re-wrapping the ankle.

"I can't believe how I've rattled on. I've probably bored you silly. I don't usually talk much at all to strangers."

"We're not strangers now, and I find nothing about you boring. But I'd better be getting you home." He helped her to the horse and lifted her into the saddle.

"You're one of those responsible types, aren't you?" she teased.

He shrugged. "Most of the time, I suppose. I try."

The canteen had been emptied well before they approached the Belmont farmstead. Thad's legs felt sore and rubbery. Too much time on his ass, he thought. They had moved in silence for the last fifteen minutes, almost, it seemed to him, with a joint sense of foreboding. Thad knew there was nothing to physically fear, but he was terrified at the thought of just dropping Serena at the Belmont place and not seeing her again. Finally, he pulled up his courage, looked up at her, and broke the silence. "I want to talk to you again. I'm going to come by in a few days and see how you're getting along."

Panic flashed in her eyes. "No, you can't. You must not. Please."

"I wouldn't stay long. Just to know you're okay."

"I'll meet you someplace."

"When? Where?"

"A week from today. Noon. Where you found me. I'll bring something to eat. I'll show you where I was headed when I fell. Don't come to my home. I will be there." She hesitated. "Will you?"

"You can count on it."

SPRING 1885

6

KIRSTEN CAVELLE LAY on the cedar-planked floor of the single room that served as the dining and living area of the small ranch house. Except for her boots, Kirsten was fully clothed in her well-worn denims and heavy flannel shirt, but she was still cocooned in several blankets to ward off the early-March night chill. Only the top of her head ,with its short-cropped chestnut hair, emerged from her nest. The few remaining embers in the fireplace were dying, and the only light remaining in the room came from the streaks of moonlight that shot through the two small windows. Henry, her huge, gray tabby tomcat was snuggled against the small of her back, snoring softly.

Killer, her shepherd cow dog, slept next to the fireplace a few feet away, trying to soak in the last remnants of any warmth, even though the fire had been a token one to chase an evening chill. It was kind of a sad state of affairs, she thought, that her best friends in this rugged country were her furry companions.

She heard her husband, Maxwell Brannon, stirring in the bedroom, which she had refused to share for several months now. He refused to give up his claim to the bed, and she had made up her mind that she was finished with the mean drunk. She had met with Cameron Locke, the lawyer, about a divorce, and he had assured her she had grounds as a result of Maxwell having beaten her savagely the night before she abandoned the bedroom to him—not to mention his nightly drunkenness. The ranch was titled in her name, and Locke promised he would file the divorce papers tomorrow morning and procure a restraining order that would boot Maxwell out of the house by nightfall. This would be her last night bedding down on the floor.

"Kirsty! Get your ass in here now," Maxwell bellowed.

"Go to hell."

"I mean it. I've had enough of this shit."

Kirsten heard Maxwell stumbling across the bedroom floor, and momentarily, the door opened. Henry disappeared, and Killer retreated to a haven under the kitchen table. She untangled herself from the blankets and struggled to her feet. "Go back to bed. Stay away from me."

She could not see his eyes, but she could feel them glowering at her through his drunken haze. He was a big man, at least six feet, four inches, and he weighed close to two hundred eighty pounds. With his ample beer gut, he was a far cry from the muscular, young cowboy she had married four years ago when they were both twenty-two. Over five feet, nine inches, Kirsten was taller than most women and many men she encountered. Lean and sinewy, she could wrestle cattle with any man, but she knew in physical combat she was no match for Max.

Max staggered into the room. "I said I've had enough of this shit. You're my wife, and I've got fucking rights. And I'm claiming them right now."

"I'm done being your wife. I've seen a lawyer. Now leave me alone, you drunken asshole."

Suddenly, he charged her like a raging bull. She turned to run when his shoulder rammed into the small of her back and she crashed to floor with Max on top of her. His fingers latched onto her short-cropped hair and yanked her head back so abruptly she felt her neck crack. "Now, bitch, I don't give a shit what you're dreaming up with some shyster. You're my woman, and you're going to come to our bed and spread your legs like a proper wife."

He slammed her face into the floor and released her head before moving off of her and clumsily struggling up from the floor. While she lay motionless, he kicked her sharply in the ribs and she groaned and, for a moment, blacked out from the excruciating pain.

When her senses returned, she sprung up and started to race for the Colt six-shooter that was suspended in its holster from a wall peg near the door. She was pulled up short, however, when Maxwell's hand closed around her wrist and jerked her back.

"You bitch. I think you'd use that gun."

"You're damned right I would if you don't leave me alone. Go back to the bedroom and stay away from me. We'll talk about this in the morning when you're sober."

His fist hammered into the side of her nose, and then releasing her wrist, he attacked her ferociously with both fists, pounding her face and body relentlessly until she blacked out and her legs crumpled and she sunk to the floor.

Her next awareness was of Maxwell's string of expletives as he fumbled with the buttons of her shirt and finally, in one sweep, ripped them off. She realized then he had already pulled off her britches and was now tearing at the undergarments. He had evidently dragged her into the bedroom. She was disoriented and she tried to shake off the pain that throbbed in her skull and to clear the fog as he finished yanking off her remaining garments. Naked on the bed now, she saw his shadowy figure standing there as he unbuttoned his undershorts before they slid down his legs. He stood between her and the doorway; there was no escape.

He knelt above her now, his knees pried between her thighs. She wanted to drive her knee into his balls, but her legs seemed made of straw, so her hand found its way to the target, grasped and squeezed. Max howled in agony, but drove a fist into her throat, and she reflexively released her grip. Then his teeth sank into her breast and he tore at the flesh like a badger engaged in mortal combat.

She faded from consciousness briefly again, and when she came back she could feel his thrusting and found it no longer mattered. She heard him sigh when his release came, and when he pulled away and dropped onto the bed, she remained still and silent, wondering vaguely if there was any place on her body she did not hurt. She decided her feet were free of pain.

In a matter of minutes, he was snoring. That had been the pattern of their conjugal relations for almost two years now. He was on and off and asleep in a matter of minutes, leaving her to her own imagination for satisfaction.

When she was certain he was asleep, she got out of bed and slipped quietly from the bedroom. She could hear Killer whimpering from beneath his hiding place under the kitchen table.

"Thanks, Killer," she said softly, "for nothing."

She retrieved the Colt from its holster and made her way through the dark room back to the bedroom. She stood next to Max's side of the bed and lit the oil lamp on the bedside table.

"Max," she said. He did not respond, so she spoke louder. "Max, wake up."

He rolled over and looked up at her. "Now what? Can't you see I'm sleeping?"

"I've got something for you, Max." His eyes widened in terror for just a moment before she squeezed the trigger.

She walked out of the room and returned the gun to the holster before lighting another lamp and finding a robe to toss over her naked body. Only then did she become aware of the blood dripping from her face and the red mass that was saturating the cotton robe.

She turned back to the entrance door and opened it. "Killer," she commanded, "fetch Chet." The dog crept cautiously from beneath the table and then rushed for the open door and disappeared.

Kirsten suddenly felt lightheaded and faint, stumbled to the nearby rocking chair and sagged into it exhaustedly. Her strength was ebbing, and now she just wanted to go to sleep and make the hurt go away.

"Oh my God in heaven!" came the high-pitched voice from the doorway.

Kirsten's eyes opened and through the haze saw her wiry, diminutive foreman and only full-time ranch hand. "I'm not feeling too perky, Chet. Can you find some rags and maybe get a half bucket of water from the pump. A shot of whiskey would be nice, too, if Max hasn't sucked it all up."

The white-haired cowboy moved as fast as his gimpy leg would allow and began searching through the kitchen drawers, plucking out a handful of dish towels. He limped over to Kirsten's side.

"Jesus Christ, Kirsten, you look like you were run through a slaughter house, I don't know where to start. Your left brow seems to be bleeding worst."

"Hand me a towel. I'll press it on the cut while you get the water. First, check the cookie canister for a whiskey bottle."

The cowhand retrieved the half-full bottle and set it on the floor beside the chair before he hurried back outside to fetch the water. Killer crept into the house and joined his mistress, whining worriedly. She patted him softly on the head. "You did good, Killer. You got Chet." She picked up the whiskey bottle and flinched when she pressed it to her bruised and swollen lips. She took a good swig, and the burning sensation in her throat perked her up a little, but the taste was unpleasant. Why the hell Max would dedicate his life to drinking this crap was beyond her.

Chet returned with the water, and she wet a cloth and gingerly began to dab at her face. The coolness revived her some, but her touch triggered waves of pain. Meanwhile, with her other hand, she kept a cloth pressed to the slice on her brow.

Chet looked on helplessly. "Ma'am, I knew there was trouble. Killer was kickin' up a terrible fuss outside the bunkhouse and nearly scratched his way through the door. What happened here?"

"Max beat the shit out of me. That's what happened."

"Your . . . uh . . . chest seems to be bleeding something fierce. Did he knife you?"

"No." She decided not to elaborate and embarrass the old cowboy.

"Where is Max?"

"He died. He's in the bedroom."

"Oh Jesus." Chet began to shuffle his feet nervously. "Ma'am, I'm sorry, but I'm at a loss here. I want to help, but I ain't much of a doctor, especially for women folks. You're going to have to tell me what I should do."

"I'll be okay for a while. Do you know where Cam Locke's place is?"

"I sure do. About three miles southeast of here. Less as the crow flies."

"I want you to saddle up and ride as the crow flies as fast as you can. Tell him what's happened here. Then do whatever he asks."

"But I can't just go off and leave you like this. You could bleed to death."

"And what are you going to do about it?"

"Well, I can do something if you'll tell me what you want done,"

"Chet?"

"Ma'am?"

"Can you stitch a chewed up tit?"

"I'm on my way."

7

CAMERON LOCKE HEARD what seemed to be a frantic pounding on the thick door of their expansive two-story, stone house. He rolled out of bed, pulled on his undershorts, groped for the oil lamp on the table next to the bed and lit it, turning the glow up only a bit, so as not to awaken Pilar. She had apparently been oblivious to the knocking as she slept in naked, sated bliss on the opposite side of the bed. Oh, well, she'd damn sure earned her rest.

He slipped his Army Colt from the holster that hung from the peg next to the bedroom door and made his way down the stairs that led to the entryway on the main floor. With only brief pauses, the knocking continued. When he reached the door, Cam yelled, "Who is it?"

"Mr. Locke? It's Chet from the C Bar C."

Cam opened the door and lowered the revolver. He stepped aside, waving the cowboy in. "God, Chet, it's just after four o'clock. What's going on?"

"Miss Kirsten's had the livin' shit beat out of her. Bleedin' like a stuck hog all over the place."

Cam closed the door and turned and hollered up the stairway, "Pilar, I think you're going to be needed. Get dressed for riding and rustle Myles out of bed."

He swung back to Chet. "What happened?"

Chet shrugged, "I don't rightly know, Mr. Locke. Miss Kirsten sent Killer—that's her dog—to get me up to the house, and when I got there she was sittin' in her rocker, blood runnin' down her mashed up face and soaking up her gown at her . . . her chest."

"Her chest? Was she shot? Or stabbed?"

"Uh, no sir. Think she was bit or something. Talked about being chewed on."

"You're not making sense, Chet, but we need to get over there. What about her husband?"

"Think he's dead. That's what she said."

"What happened to him?"

"Don't know about that neither. Miss Kirsten just said he died. I didn't see him."

Pilar Locke moved quietly down the stairway, followed by a sleepy-eyed Myles Locke, their fourteen-year-old son, who showed no enthusiasm for being awakened at this early hour of the morning. Cam turned to his wife, a slender Mexican woman who was seven years younger than his own forty-two. She was a stunning beauty even at this hour of the morning, Cam thought. Damned if he wouldn't like to take her back upstairs for another go. He quickly shook off the thought.

"Pilar, can you come with me? I think you may be needed at the C Bar C. Kirsten Cavelle may be in a bad way. Myles, get dressed and saddle up and make a beeline for your Uncle Thad's. Tell him I said to get his ass over to the Cavelle place and that it's for a human patient not a critter. Apparently, the lady's been badly beaten."

The black-haired boy's eyes were instantly alert and he wheeled to head back upstairs to get dressed, Pilar not far behind. "I'll be out of the house in five minutes, Dad."

"And, Myles?

"Yeah, Dad?"

"Tell your Uncle Thad to bring his photography gear. Tell him I said it's very important. And you stay with him to help carry whatever he needs."

"I'll help him however he wants."

He turned back to Chet. "Chet, I need you to ride on in to Manhattan. Find the sheriff and let him know what's happened. No hurry. Don't run your horse into the ground. Do you understand what I'm saying?"

The grizzled cowhand cocked his head and looked at Cam with a glint in his eyes. "If there's one thing I'm damned good at, Mr. Locke, it's movin' slow. Manhattan's a good eight mile ride, and I'll probably have to rest my mount. Might even get lost with the dark and all."

"Thanks for everything, Chet. Now I'd better get dressed and head over to Kirsten's."

8

CAM AND PILAR rode side by side, their Appaloosas, his gelding and her mare, forced to pick their way in the darkness up the rocky slopes that rose eventually to the C Bar C ranch buildings. Cam took comfort in having Pilar nearby. Her quiet competence was always calming, and he marveled sometimes how, after sixteen years of marriage to this woman born and raised in a great hacienda on the Texas side of the Mexican border, she was as exciting and beautiful and beguiling to him as when he first met her on his way home from the war.

Pilar had been only fifteen then, and he had been a young cavalry captain, reeling yet from bitter defeat, when he stopped at the Sanchez ranch to see the fine Appaloosa stock bred and raised by Pilar's father, Guillermo Sanchez, the only herd Cam was aware of outside the northwestern United States. Sanchez had invited him to stay over a few days, and the tired soldier took him up on it. During the stay, he had encountered the dark-eyed beauty whose visage haunted him all the way home to Kansas.

"Ben and Sarah were sleeping soundly when I left the house," Cam said. Ben was their seven-year-old and Sarah was eleven.

"Yes. I stopped by the bunkhouse and told Cookie we were riding out. He said he'd get up to the house and be there when they awaken."

Cookie was an old scraggly-bearded trail cook who cooked for the seasonal wranglers and year-round hands, as well as the Locke family. Everybody on the ranch at any given time took their meals in the dining room of the big ranch house, so Cookie more or less ran the domestic side of the household with Pilar's occasional assistance.

Pilar, of course, had saddled both of their horses by the time Cam got to the barn, and they had ridden hard and fast until they neared the C Bar C and the terrain turned rough. They finally reached the more level ground of the ranch site and galloped into the yard and dismounted.

Cam knocked softly on the door before opening it and entering the house. He immediately saw Kirsten slumped in the rocking chair, either unconscious or sleeping. He rushed to her side. "Kirsten. Kirsten."

She did not reply.

Pilar pushed him aside and, pointing to the bucket next to the rocker, ordered, "Get some fresh water from the well."

When Cam returned and set the bucket down, Pilar took one of the cloths Chet had left behind, dipped it in the water, and began to bathe Kirsten's battered face. Then she started to open the robe and examine the chest wound, which was the obvious source of so much of the blood. "Go away," she told Cam.

Cam began surveying what he thought of as the slaughter house. He spotted the open bedroom door and peered in. The sun was beginning to rise and some of its rays sifted in through the window, sprinkling some light on the bed. He walked over to the bedside. "Holy shit," he whispered, as he met the glassy stare of Maxwell Brannon's dead eyes, separated neatly by a bullet hole seeping only a trickle of blood. "He died all right."

When Cam returned to the living area, Kirsten was regaining

awareness. Pilar had washed some of the blood from her face and retrieved another robe, but blood was still leaking through the fabric. Her face was swollen and red, waiting to morph to purple and blue, with a gash on the chin and a nasty slice on her left brow, he noted. Her nose seemed lopsided.

He moved closer. "Kirsten, can you talk?"

"I can talk, but I don't feel too sociable at the moment," she murmured groggily.

"Don't talk; just listen. My brother Thad's on the way. He should be here soon. He's a physician, and he'll tend to your injuries."

She looked to Pilar, who nodded reassuringly.

"Okay, I guess. I can't patch it all myself . . . but the only Dr. Locke I know is a vet."

Cam replied, "It's complicated." He changed the subject. "The sheriff likely won't be here for a few hours. I've been in the bedroom. Maxwell's dead."

"I know that. I—"

"Stop. You say nothing about this in the presence of anyone. I'm the only person bound by confidentiality. Pilar, my brother, or anyone else can be forced to testify to anything you say. You and I will talk later, when no one else is present. Understand?"

"I do." She met his eyes evenly.

"The sheriff's a good man, but he will want to ask you questions."

"I won't answer."

"You've got it."

There was a commotion outside, and soon Thad walked through the doorway. He nodded at Pilar and Cam and then went directly to Kirsten's side. "I'm Doctor Locke. Remember me? I was on your place to castrate some bull calves last fall?"

She looked up at him warily. Then she glared at Cam. "This is the brother you said was going to look after me? He's a damn horse doctor. I don't think so."

Cam saw he had a client on the verge of rebellion. "He's a licensed medical doctor, Kirsten. He graduated from a fine medical school . . . the University of Pennsylvania. Top of his class." He had no idea what kind of a scholar Thad had been but decided it had a convincing ring.

"Well, shit, why not? I don't much care who works me over at this point." She leaned back in the rocker resignedly. "Have your way with me, Doc."

Thad set his big leather bag down. "Pilar, will you help me? Cam, you can wait outside."

"I'm getting used to getting kicked out of here. Let me know when you're finished. And when you're done, I want you to take a look at her husband."

"Her husband?"

"Former husband. Don't worry; he's not going anyplace."

Cam started out the door and then paused. "I'm going to want some pictures, too."

"Pictures of what?"

"Her."

"Get out."

9

"MA'AM, I THINK we need to take a look at the chest wound first."

"I figured as much."

Maybe he should bind up her mouth first, Thad considered. She was going to be an annoyance very quickly, he feared.

"There's fresh blood showing through your robe, and we need to stop the bleeding. Have you seen the wound, Pilar?"

"Yes, and it needs attention."

Before Kirsten could object, Thad's fingers deftly pulled the top of the robe back to expose the wounded breast. It looked like she'd got it caught in a meat grinder. "Knife?" he asked.

"Teeth."

He looked at her in disbelief.

"Teeth," she repeated.

"Pilar," Thad said. "We're going to need some boiling water before I do my work. Could you ask Cam or Myles to get a fire going in the wood stove?"

"I'll Call Myles in. Cam's in another world thinking about his case. He's worthless in dealing with mundane tasks when he's absorbed in a case."

While Pilar and Myles worked at getting a fire going, Thad explained the procedure with Kirsten. "You'll need some stitches above your eye and on your chin, but they'll wait. Your breast has a nasty wound. If you look, you'll see that your nipple was nearly amputated."

She looked down at her breast. "Oh shit. What a mess. The son-of-a-bitch about ate it off. I don't have more than a mouthful anyway, if you haven't noticed."

"I haven't," he lied.

"Liar."

She might be small-breasted, he thought, but her breasts suited her lean, hard body that seemed devoid of wasted flesh. She had an interesting face, he recalled, more angular than soft with a generous sprinkling of freckles across the bridge of her nose. Of course, none of this could be seen through her battered and swollen face now. All in all, she was a striking woman, not one who bore Serena's flawless beauty but an eye-turner nonetheless. He compared every attractive woman to Serena, and they always came up short. After this many years, he supposed this was a flaw in his own character.

"Doc, you were going to explain things to me."

"Uh, yes. I'm going to stitch up your breast. It will take some time, and I'd like to do the surgery with you lying flat. Could we use your bed?"

"It's occupied."

He hesitated and looked at her quizzically.

"My late husband's using it."

It seemed like everybody was talking in nonsensical riddles tonight. "We can use your dining table. It's a little short, but I suspect you're hurting so much you won't notice if your feet hang over the edge a bit."

"It looks like it's all chopped up down there. Have you done this before?"

"Many times. I've sewn up dozens of cow teats. Same thing,

more or less."

She looked at him incredulously. "You are not serious?"

"I'm very serious. Now, as soon as the hot water's ready, we're going to move you to the table, and Pilar's going to wash the wound. Then I'm going to apply some cocaine hydrochloride to the injured area to dull the pain. It's usually very effective on open wounds, and you shouldn't feel much, if anything. When I'm done stitching the breast, I'll take care of the eye and chin wounds."

In a matter of minutes, Kirsten was stretched out on the table, wrapped like a mummy in a sheet pulled back just enough to expose her left breast. After Pilar washed the injured breast, he gently applied the cocaine solution. Many women would have been mortified, he thought, but Kirsten Cavelle seemed stoic and had turned quiet, possibly recognizing this was not a good time to distract him. He took one of the small curved needles Quincy Belmont had fashioned for him, strung the surgical thread through the eye, slipped it in a dish of the boiled water and began the tedious suturing.

"Am I hurting you?" he asked.

"Nothing compared to my damned head."

"I have some acetylsalicylic acid pills I'll give you when we're finished. They're not readily available yet, but they're very effective and not addictive like many of the pain killers being used."

"Don't ask me to pronounce that, let alone spell it."

"Some doctors are starting to call it 'aspirin' but I was trying to impress you."

"Impress me by not messing up my knocker, Doc."

"It will be better than it was . . . and bigger." He would never have talked to another patient like this, but this woman seemed to invite verbal combat.

"Jesus. Then you'd better work on the other one, Doc. You may be starting a whole new career path."

He chuckled. "I don't think there's much demand for that specialty in the cattle business."

When he was finished with the mangled breast, he stood back and studied his work critically. The bleeding had been abated, but the woman still carried a sorry looking chunk of flesh, crisscrossed now with intersecting stitches. It would be bruised and swollen for some days, but the nipple should survive, and he didn't think he was leaving any repulsive deformity.

He turned his attention to the wound above the eye and the chin gash. These he stitched quickly, and then he gingerly probed the engorged flesh that cocooned her nose. "It's broken," he said, "but it's not terribly out of alignment. If you don't re-injure it, I'd expect it to heal without leaving much damage . . . a small bump, at the most."

"Okay, Doc, thanks for the patchwork. Are we finished now?"

"I'd say so. I'm going to leave you some salve that you should apply to your breast wounds twice daily. It will help with the healing and the pain. You can use it on your face, too,"

"Is the stuff for people?"

"Well, it works fine on people, but I use it mostly for sore and injured cow udders. It softens the tissue."

She rolled her eyes. "Of course, I suppose I'll be mooing soon."

He smiled. "That's optional."

Pilar tapped Thad on the shoulder. "Thaddeus, I must speak to Cameron a moment. I shall return shortly."

Pilar quickly departed out the door.

"Well, Doc, now what?"

"First, you might like to get off of that table." He held out his hand, and she gripped it and leveraged herself to a sitting position and scooted to the end of the table.

"Sit for a bit before we try to move you to the rocking chair."

He retrieved a tin cup of water and handed it to her, and she downed it quickly. "That was better than your medicine, Doc."

"You can have more soon. You lost an awful lot of blood. I don't know how you can sit up."

"How much are you going to charge me for all of this work?"

"Well, it's your water. I won't charge you for that. And Cam's the one who invited me to this party, so I guess I'll send him a bill for five dollars."

"Five dollars! You must think I have a gold tit."

She left him momentarily speechless, and then their eyes met and he realized she was just needling him. This was a woman who could endure great pain and humiliation with her humor intact. He found himself liking her in spite of her rough manner and salty speech. "My charges are the same for all kinds of critters. Now, Miss Cavelle . . . or is it Mrs. Brannon?"

"Kirsten."

"Very well, you may call me 'Thad' if you wish."

"I think I'll stick with 'Doc.' That tag fits best. My God, what else can you call a guy who's two kinds of doctors?"

He grinned at her, shaking his head. "I'm honored to be ordained 'Doc' by you. Now, let me help you off."

The door opened and Cam and Pilar walked into the room. "Wait a moment, folks. We have something to discuss," Cam said.

"She'd be more comfortable in the chair. Wait until we move her."

"She may need to be on the table."

"Why?"

"Pilar says Mrs. Brannon was injured in her private parts."

"Kirsten?" Thad turned to his patient.

"First, tell the law wrangler I'm not 'Mrs. Brannon.' I never went by that, and I sure as hell won't be now."

"We'll talk about that later," Cam said, "but Thad needs to look at your other injuries."

"Jesus, I'm just hurting some. No blood. I'll be fine. I don't think he needs to be gawking at my muffin. That's kind of my last shred of dignity. Pilar took a look. Isn't that enough?"

"As my wife, she would be highly suspect as a witness."

"The doc's your brother. That's not suspect?"

"You have a point, but folks trust doctors . . . not that they should . . . and he would qualify as an expert witness."

"He's a muffin expert?"

"Please, Kirsten, I'm advising you as your lawyer to cooperate. It may be critical to proving you were raped."

"Raped? How many men in these parts would say a man would ever be guilty of raping his wife?"

"This man. And I hope to convince a few others by the time I finish with a jury . . . if there is one."

Kirsten sighed in resignation and slid back on the table. "Oh, shit. Go ahead Doc. Take a gander, but make it damn quick."

Cam left the room, and Thad made a brief examination, assuming that a married woman was unlikely to have suffered serious internal damage in the absence of bleeding. He noted deep scratches on the inner thighs and red marks likely left by brutal fingers that would look worse in a few days. Pilar had obviously washed the injuries, and Kirsten could apply some of the salve. There was nothing life threatening, but she had obviously been forced to submit to her husband's assault. When he concluded his examination, he stepped back. "You can sit up now. I'm sorry, Kirsten, if you found any of this unpleasant or humiliating. We're finished now."

"Not your fault, Doc. Your brother's kind of a ruthless son-of-a-bitch, but that's not a mark against you . . . and I want the ruthless son-of-a-bitch on my side."

On cue Cam opened the door and re-entered the room. "Now we need some pictures," he announced.

Thad and Kirsten looked at him in joint astonishment.

"Pictures of what?" Thad asked.

"Her injuries. I would have preferred to have them taken before you did your work, but I figured you'd get stubborn about it."

Thad bristled. "Damn right I would have, and I'm not inclined to take any now."

"We've got to. We're talking about critical evidence. Thad, take my word for it: your tintypes could save her life."

"It's okay, Doc," Kirsten said. "I guess you're a photographer, too. I can't wait to see what other talents are yet to be revealed. You're not a law wrangler, also, are you?"

He smiled wryly. "No, but everybody else in this loco family seems to be." He turned to Cam. "There's not enough light to get any decent tintypes in here."

"Sun's coming up now. You can move out on the porch . . . but first, Thad, I want you to take a look at her husband." He nodded toward the bedroom, and Thad followed.

This can't be happening to me, Thad thought. This whole situation is beyond insane. Nonetheless, he joined Cam in the bedroom and took a look at the corpse. "You're wanting me to render a diagnosis? He's dead."

"That's indisputable," said Cam. "Don't touch him."

"I don't want to touch him. But why not?"

"I don't want the sheriff or coroner saying we tampered with the body."

"Okay, no tampering. Now what did you want me to see?"

"What would you say is the cause of death?"

"That looks like a bullet wound between the eyes to me . . . but I wouldn't want to say for sure without touching him."

"Suicide maybe?"

"I don't see a gun . . . unless he put it away after he shot himself."

"You're going to be a helluva witness for the defense."

10

THE ROCKING CHAIR had been moved out on the small porch and Kirsten rocked slowly, her fingers tentatively testing the swollen flesh that nearly swallowed her eyes. She watched curiously as the doctor-vet-photographer set up the tripod and anchored the black box and something that looked like a bellows to the top. This guy was pretty much all business, she decided. He'd shown flashes of a wry sense of humor when she had baited him earlier, but most of the time he was focused on the task in front of him.

Dr. Thaddeus Locke was a ruggedly handsome man, trim and muscular from the work of a profession that demanded physical as well as mental agility, tall but not quite as tall as his older brother, who stood a good six feet two inches. His piercing gray eyes he had in common with Cam Locke, and they were both sun-bronzed, and given their sandy hair, she figured they were naturally of lighter complexion. Dr. Locke, she guessed, would be more comfortably anonymous in a crowd. Cameron Locke would always be the center of attention in a room and would love every moment of it.

"Kirsten, we're ready to start, and I'll get this done as quickly as I can," Thad announced, as he moved his equipment in closer to the porch. He turned to Cam and Myles who were leaning on the hitching post, watching the proceedings with interest. "You two make yourselves scarce. Pilar, I'd like you to stay near Kirsten. We'll try to do this in a way that protects her modesty as much as we can."

Cam put his arm around his son's shoulder and headed for the other side of the house. "This is the last time I'm moving out of the way today. When I come back, I'll be giving the orders."

Pilar laughed. "He does like to be in charge. And he is when he's working. We have a different management arrangement in our home."

"You really love each other, don't you?" Kirsten asked.

"Yes, we do. And we're best friends."

"Must be nice."

"Now, we're going to do the face shots first," Thad said. "The light's fine here, but if I get closer than five or six feet the picture will blur out. Kirsten just look right into the camera. I know you're suffering pain, but make an extra effort to look like you're suffering. I have a hunch Cam would like that."

So the doctor had a devious side, too. Perhaps he was not the innocent she perceived him to be. She squinted her eyes a bit more and forced the side of her mouth to droop some.

"Perfect."

He took several more photographs from different angles. "Now, as for the breast, Kirsten, you will decide how much you're willing to expose, and Cam can go to hell if it doesn't suit him. Remember, if I know Cam, he wouldn't hesitate to put the tintypes in front of a jury . . . all men . . . if it comes to that."

She pondered the issue for a moment. Talk of a jury suddenly hit her with the seriousness of her situation. She shrugged. There wasn't anything provocative about her chewed-up breast. She pushed back her robe just enough. "Doc, you've got the whole udder for one minute. But forget about taking any pictures of my muffin."

Just as Thad took the last of the tintypes, Cam came around the corner of the house. "Riders on the ridge. Three, I'd guess. They'll be here in ten minutes. Thad, get your photography equipment out of sight. Pilar, would you help Kirsten back inside? I'm going to walk out and meet the riders and slow them up a little." He called for Myles. "Myles, you're needed out here. Take the rocker back in the house."

"Do you want me to stay?" Thad asked.

"Yeah, you're a witness now, so the sheriff is going to have questions. You can't do us any harm."

Kirsten and Pilar were in the doorway. "Wait a minute, ladies. Kirsten, remember, you answer no questions unless you see me nod. Otherwise you don't remember. Groan a little and start to faint if the sheriff pushes too much. Pilar, have you ever run into Sam Mallery anyplace?"

"I have never encountered him."

"You don't speak English very well. Understand?"

"*No comprendo.*"

11

THAD JOINED PILAR and Kirsten in the house and claimed a chair near the dining table while they waited for Cam and the sheriff. Myles had pulled up a chair for Pilar next to Kirsten's rocker before he made a hasty retreat out the door with the timid dog, Killer, who had apparently taken a liking to the boy. After a few silent moments, Thad was startled by a furry creature landing in his lap. He looked down and saw an enormous gray tabby with yellow eyes staring back and appraising him carefully. He reached down and scratched the cat's ears gently, and the animal snuggled closer and began a throaty purring.

"I'll be damned," Kirsten said. "Doc, meet Henry. He generally doesn't take to men. He detested Max. Of course, Max kicked him around when his mood turned foul."

"Glad to make his acquaintance."

As he stroked his new friend, Thad surveyed the room. He was surprised to see a wall of books, which he had not consciously noticed previously, framing the doorway leading to the bedroom. Thad had never met Maxwell Brannon, but it was difficult to imagine the man who had brutalized this woman as a serious reader. On the other hand, he had a hard time visualizing the rough-talking cowwoman with her nose in a book. Strike the profane language, though, and she was well-spoken, and he had certainly found it true that first impressions often deceived. The thumping of footsteps on the porch caught Thad's attention, and he felt Henry tense, but the feline made no effort to leave his spot.

When the door opened, two sharply contrasting men followed Cam into the house. The first was Sheriff Sam Mallery, a tall, thickly-built, and barrel-chested man with wavy white hair partially covered by his dusty, crumpled Stetson, and a brushy mustache. He was trailed by a much younger man with black, perfectly combed and parted hair and wearing a gray tweed suit. County Attorney Frank Fuller was a bit overdressed for the occasion, Thad thought, but he had never seen Fuller with a rumpled appearance anywhere. Standing next to Mallery, the lawyer, who would have to stand up on his toes to reach five and a half feet, looked almost birdlike, but Thad knew that most ladies found him a handsome bird and that many would like to take the young bachelor home.

Fuller without doubt knew Pilar, so she would have to forget her little act. She likely wouldn't have fooled him anyway. Cam had commented on more than one occasion that Fuller was one smart lawyer, "almost as smart as me," his brother had once declared, only half in jest. But what was Fuller doing out here? From the way Thad understood the system the county prosecutor rarely got involved this early in a criminal investigation. The sheriff must be uneasy about the case—a woman's involvement, perhaps.

The sheriff doffed his hat when he saw Pilar and Kirsten. "Ladies." His eyes locked on Kirsten. "My God, Mrs. Brannon, what happened here?"

Kirsten looked at Cam, who had slipped between the sheriff and Fuller. Thad saw Cam respond with a barely perceptible nod.

"And where's your husband?"

"See for yourselves, gentlemen," Cam interjected. "He's in the bedroom." He stepped back and let the visitors go into the bedroom.

Thad heard the sheriff exclaim, "Jesus Christ." After that the voices went soft, and he could hear only their secretive mumbling.

"When they come back out," Cam spoke softly to Kirsten, "answer no questions about what happened to Max. If they want to ask about what he did to you, it's okay to answer unless you see me tug my ear."

Finally, the sheriff and county attorney returned from the bedroom. Fuller looked at Cam. "I take it, Cam, you're representing Mrs. Brannon?"

"I am."

"Do you mind if I ask her a few questions?"

"Try one, and then we'll see."

Fuller walked over to the table where Henry and Thad were sitting. "Excuse me, Doctor." He stepped past Thad and grabbed a chair and slid it over next to Kirsten and sat down beside her. "Mrs. Brannon, where did this alleged beating by your husband take place?"

"Out here. In this room. It was in front of the fireplace. He started out using words not fit for a lady's ears, and then he commenced beating on me."

Thad wondered what words were not fit for Kirsten's ears. This was not a stupid woman.

"Something must have triggered the altercation. What happened that caused your husband to start beating you, assuming that's what happened?"

Cam tugged his ear, and instantly Kirsten clutched her stomach, commenced to moan and fell forward in her chair. Thad plucked Henry off his lap, set him on the floor and moved to Kirsten's side, as Fuller got up and moved his chair out of the way.

"Kirsten, what's the matter?" Thad asked.

"I think it's my ribs," she groaned, "where he kicked me."

Thad probed her ribs gently with his fingertips.

She shrieked with pain, her eyes closed and her head flopped down limply on her shoulder.

Cam interceded. "That's all, Frank. My client will have nothing else to say at this time. You're welcome to speak with anyone else . . . Mrs. Brannon is off limits." He turned to me, "Thad, would you check her out while Frank and the good sheriff speak with Pilar?"

The county attorney glared at Cam suspiciously, and then asked Pilar if she would join them at the table.

Thad felt Kirsten's pulse and it seemed fine, and then he placed his hand on her forehead to see if there was any indication of fever. At that moment she opened one eye and winked. Her obvious ruse annoyed him, and he just looked at her disgustedly before he got up and told Cam. "She'll be okay, but I strongly suggest she have her bowels purged; it might be character building."

Cam frowned at him disapprovingly, but did not respond.

"I'm ready to head home," Thad said. "Can you get your lawmen to speed things up?"

An hour later Thad had finished his interview with the law. They were not pleased that he could tell them so little. He was not a witness to any of the previous night's events, and he could only relate the facts relevant to Kirsten's injuries and verify that, yes indeed, Max Brannon was as dead as you get. He knew nothing about the circumstances, and, no, Kirsten had told him nothing. He was assured they would want to interview him further and that Dr. Horace Kleeb would be sent out that afternoon to confirm Thad's diagnosis of Brannon's condition and to make a detailed analysis. Thad assumed that Kleeb would be sober by that time and suggested he be accompanied by the undertaker, Simon Longtree, as the corpse would be ripening quickly.

Before Mallery and Fuller departed, they met at some length with Cam on the porch. Meanwhile Kirsten made a remarkable recovery.

When Cam returned, he promptly took command of the gathering. "Kirsten, you're not going to be placed under arrest pending further investigation. But Frank Fuller will likely file charges at some point. He's just trying to figure out the politics of the situation first. A battered and beaten woman and a dead husband . . . he has to calculate where public opinion is going on this and lay the groundwork for what he's going to do."

"And what's he going to do?" Kirsten asked.

"Well I'm going to have another chat with him tomorrow, but you have to face up to the possibility he's going to charge you with the murder of your husband."

Kirsten's face blanched, and her eyes widened as if the possibility of legal charges had not even occurred to her.

"Murder?"

"Yes."

"But why?"

"Kirsten, your husband's stretched out on the bed in the next room with a bullet between his eyes. It's understandable that the sheriff and prosecutor might suspect he did not do that to himself." Kirsten started to respond, but Cam raised his hand. "Stop. No more discussion. What you and I talk about is protected by attorney-client privilege. Pilar and Thad may be subpoenaed as witnesses, and they could be required to testify about our conversation. Remember? We discussed this earlier. I am the only person you discuss this situation with. Understand?"

"I understand."

"Good. You will be coming home with Pilar and me immediately. You will not return here until I say so. The sheriff's sending out a deputy to watch the place, and the coroner and undertaker will be here this afternoon sometime."

"But there's work to be done here, and I have a meeting tomorrow with Clem Rickers about buying a half section."

Cam's temper flared. "Kirsten, get your head screwed on here. Murder's a hanging offense. Your life is at stake. Another half section of land isn't going to do you a damn bit of good if you're swinging from the gallows."

She had evidently blocked her dilemma out of her mind now, and she turned to Thad. "Doc, can you take Henry home with you? I think he's taken a liking to you. He doesn't care much for Chet. Killer gets along fine with Chet, though, and he'll be fine here."

How could he say "no"? Thad replied reluctantly, "I guess so."

"And Doc, I was going to get ahold of you today about Clem's place. I've got an idea."

Thad was bewildered now and was saved by Cam. "Enough," Cam snapped. "Pilar, Chet and Myles are bringing up the buckboard from the barn. Would you grab some blankets and see if you can make up a bed in back for Kirsten. I'll hitch our saddle horses to the rear and we can ride up front."

Cam turned to Thad. "Myles will help you get your gear home —"

"And Henry," Kirsten interjected.

Cam sighed. "And Henry. Why don't you ride over for supper tonight and you can check on Kirsten."

"We can talk about Clem's place then," Kirsten said.

12

THE NEMESIS SAT alone at a wobbly table in a dark corner of the tavern, nursing a warm beer as he watched the after-work crowd stream into the filthy barroom. They were a worthless lot, drunks and other riffraff, all well-suited to the run-down, uncouth environment, he thought. Certainly, he would not ordinarily frequent a place like this. He lowered himself to enter the premises only when the black mood set in, so he would be unlikely to encounter any of his colleagues or would-be friends. His only real friend had been ruthlessly murdered last night by his crazy bitch of a wife.

He generally found Father here, and he would find understanding, and Father would tell him what he must do. He waited and remembered.

His mother and father had been arguing in the barn on their small Missouri farm, and the Nemesis had been drawn to the structure's half-open doorway by the angry shouting. His parents had just returned from a shopping journey to the village that prospered not far from the farmstead.

He saw Father slap his mother, and she responded in kind, which further enflamed Father's rage. "Slut," he yelled, "I saw you making eyes at that storekeeper, and then you buy up half his dry goods. I can't afford you. I told you when we went to town we wasn't buying nothing but foodstuff."

"I used egg money I saved up. It was my own to do with as I pleased. And if you can't afford me, let me go, and I'll take the boy with me."

This sent shivers down the fourteen-year-old boy's spine. He adored Father and understood that a woman's job was to serve. Father had told him many times over the years that his mother was not an obedient wife. His mother had always seemed gentle and loving to the boy, but she was sometimes mean and insolent with Father. Now that he was beginning to notice such things, he was aware that she would be thought quite pretty by most men. At thirty-three years of age, she was fifteen years younger than Father, and this may have increased her husband's watchfulness.

Father suddenly turned and marched to the barn wall and plucked off the bullwhip that was hanging there. His wife's eyes widened in terror, and the boy backed away as he saw his mother running for the door. The whip cracked like a rifle shot, and just before she reached the door it coiled about his mother's neck like a black snake. Father yanked on the whip and dragged her back into the depths of the barn toward the hay piled there. The boy saw Father tearing at his mother's clothes until she stood whimpering and naked in front of him, and he saw his mother's bare breasts for the first time in his memory.

The whip cracked again, carving a thin red line across his mother's breast. She screamed pitifully. "No, no, please no. I'm sorry."

"You have no money of your own. Submit to your own husband as to the Lord. Do you understand?"

"Yes, I understand. Forgive me," she begged. The boy almost felt sorry for her, as he heard the whip crack twice more.

Then he saw Father drag her deeper into the shadows of the barn and unbuckle and drop his britches. Father fell into the straw and mounted his wife as she sobbed and wailed. The boy watched, mesmerized as his

Father's white buttocks moved up and down with each thrust, until he became aware of his own excitement and stepped away from the barn window and unbuttoned his trousers and quickly spilled his seed.

Then he peeked back into the barn and saw Father standing and fastening his trousers and then coiling the whip as he took it back to the hook on the barn wall. He didn't notice his mother until she ran full force at Father with the pitchfork, driving the long, rusty tines into his middle back and kidney.

The Nemesis picked up the unmistakable scent of stale sweat intermingled with tobacco, and he knew Father was near. He pulled out a chair, for he knew Father's gimpy leg made standing in one place too long difficult. He ordered another beer but did not put it at Father's place on the table. It might seem strange to observers.

Momentarily, he felt Father's presence and turned his eyes toward the empty chair, listening intently for his voice. Finally, Father spoke with a raspy voice in a near whisper. "We haven't spoken in some months, Son. You must be troubled."

"Deeply, Father. My best friend . . . my only true friend . . . was murdered in his own bed by his evil bitch of a wife last night."

"You know this to be true?"

"A deputy sheriff told me. He was at the ranch home and saw Max Brannon dead in his own bed with a bullet between his eyes. They said there was an argument . . . just like with you and Ma . . . and she must have shot him while he slept."

"Do you know this woman?"

"I met her several times in business situations. She was not obedient. To the contrary, she would not share ownership of the ranch she inherited, and she treated Max like a common cowboy. She was bossy and nagged at him constantly. He drank sometimes to escape his misery, and we met in a saloon . . . not in this shitty place . . . and became fast friends. I, of all people, would understand the pain that can be inflicted by a disobedient woman."

"Yes, of course you would."

He did not feel comfortable telling Father that he and Max Brannon had been whoring buddies, often spending long weekends at the Junction City bawdy houses, occasionally sharing the same whore for a full night of frolic. He never understood Max's penchant for whores, given that his woman was strikingly handsome and unconsciously seductive and alluring. If he had not known her for what she really was, he might have been quite attracted to her himself.

"I feel such hate and contempt for this woman, Father. I must avenge Maxwell Brannon's death. What should I do?"

"Yes, you must avenge. But you must be very careful. Who knows of your friendship with Max?"

"No one. A few may have seen us sharing drinks at a saloon . . . or having lunch on occasion . . . but the depth of our friendship would have been unknown. For the sake of respectability much of our association took place outside of this community."

"Has this witch been arrested?"

"Not yet. The investigation is still underway. The deputy believes it is just a matter of time."

"Then you must wait and see if the law acts."

"But I want to punish her."

"You must wait. Be patient. There will be opportunity. I promise."

"Father," he said with near panic, "I will need to speak with you again . . . soon."

"I will be here when you need me. You have been a fine boy."

SUMMER 1874

13

THAD COULDN'T REMEMBER a longer week in his short lifetime. He had been baffled by Serena's reluctance to have him stop by the Belmont farmstead. They had been welcomed by three stair-step little girls who had raced to meet them as they came into the farmyard. They followed with excitement, calling for their mother as they approached the house. The remarkably youthful-looking Rachael Belmont, once assured of her daughter's condition, had been effusive in her appreciation, had instructed the oldest of the three girls to fill the canteens from the well, and had insisted he wait while she fetched ginger cookies from the house for him to snack on during his ride home.

Reverend Belmont had shown up at the sound of the commotion in the yard, shook his hand firmly and thanked him for helping Serena, and then asked him if he had been saved.

"I . . . I don't understand," Thad had responded.

"Accepted Jesus?"

Thad had been momentarily speechless and responded awkwardly, "Oh, I think Jesus is just fine."

The preacher had stared at him incredulously. He looked to Serena for rescue, but she just gave an impish smile and, with her mother's help, turned and hobbled off to the house.

"Well, goodbye, Sir," Thad had said.

"May the Lord be with you, young man."

Thad felt foolish now about how he had handled the encounter with Serena's father. He wondered for a moment if Serena, after watching the clumsy country boy display his eloquence, would show up for their agreed rendezvous. He pulled out his watch. Ten minutes until noon. He looked off to the north in the direction of the Belmont farm. No sign. Then he cast his eyes to the southwest and saw a rider approaching.

He watched until Serena, astride a buckskin mare, came into view. When she arrived and dismounted, he noticed instantly that her attire was sharply changed from their first meeting. She still wore moccasins, only a thicker sort, but today she was dressed in washed-out dungarees and a baggy, long-sleeved cotton shirt. A battered, wide-brimmed straw hat was pulled down over her head, nearly covering her forehead. And he thought she looked absolutely stunning.

She smiled. "Am I on time?"

He looked at his watch. "Two minutes ahead."

"I sneaked out a couple of slices of Mama's fresh-baked bread . . . I love bread and she sort of expects that anyway . . . and picked up a small slab of ham we can cut up and found a few apples in town. It's not much, but we won't starve. Can you wait an hour to eat?"

Food wasn't close to being on his mind right now. "I can wait as long as you want. You were in Manhattan?"

"I couldn't tell Mama and Papa I was meeting you . . . well, not Papa anyway, and Mama doesn't like to keep secrets from Papa. Even if she suspects, as long as she doesn't know for sure, she doesn't feel like she's keeping a secret. So I said I was riding into Manhattan for the day to see if they had any school things in the shops. I'm always visiting Fox's Bookstore, although they don't seem to be too friendly to colored folks . . . until you show your money for a book."

"Your father wouldn't approve of us meeting?"

"You met him didn't you?"

"I guess he wouldn't."

"I'm a grown woman, in case you hadn't noticed. Mama was married by my age. I can do what I please. I just don't want a big squabble with Papa during my short stay."

"Follow me," she said, mounting the buckskin.

As they eased the horses carefully along the steep trail winding down to the Big Blue Valley, Serena pointed to a rocky butte rising like a giant molar from a forested shroud of oak and ash to the east. "That's where I was headed."

"To the mesa?"

"Yes. We'll have to climb when we get there. We can tie the horses in the shade near the spring at the base of the bluff. There's tallgrass for them to graze on."

"What about your ankle?"

"Almost as good as new . . . if I have trouble, you can carry me."

He squinted one eye in disbelief. "You're not serious, I hope."

"You were so chivalrous when I was hurt. You're no longer the knight in shining armor?"

"I'll carry you."

She laughed. "You probably would. Don't worry; I'll be fine. You're way too serious sometimes."

Spring 1885

14

FOR PROPRIETY'S SAKE Thad insisted on Pilar's presence when he examined Kirsten in Cam's study. It had been less than twenty-four hours since Maxwell Brannon had rendered the beating, but Kirsten's recovery was remarkable. There was no indication of infection in the head and face wounds. Upon a cursory examination of the breast, he determined that the wounds, while still ghastly-looking, had not worsened and the bleeding had been sealed.

"Are you experiencing much pain?" he asked.

"Not a lot. When it gets too bad, I take the aspirin. It does work, Doc."

"You're fortunate I had some. It's rather hard to come by, and my inventory of human medications is a bit skimpy."

Her face was swollen and had turned to a massive blue and purple, but her ribs, while deeply bruised, seemed to have withstood the blows quite well. He knew that rib injuries could be particularly painful and long-lasting, but she walked with little stiffness and no complaint. Tough lady.

After the doctoring they joined Cam and the kids at the supper table, where Pilar and Cookie had put together a spread of beef ribs, mashed potatoes and refried beans, the latter evidently a concession to Pilar's Mexican heritage. The valiant Cam was actually something of a fussy eater and not that fond of Mexican food. Pilar spoiled him most of the time. A delicious flan followed the main course, and Thad noticed Cam was not discriminatory when it came to dessert. Thad would have enjoyed a bit more time with precocious, eleven-year-old Sarah and Ben, who was four years younger with his father's flair for the stage, but Cam rose from the table and suggested Thad and Kirsten join them in the study.

Assembled at Cam's massive oak desk, Cam said, "I've arranged for Dr. Roberts to come out here tomorrow to examine Kirsten. We need a second evaluation of her injuries in the event her case goes to trial."

"I understand that," Thad said. "I assume you're aware the bruising will be more vivid tomorrow?"

"The thought had occurred to me."

"She's doing remarkably well for what she's been through. Someone will need to remove the stitches in a week or so."

"Pardon me, gentlemen," Kirsten interrupted, "I'm in attendance at this little meeting, and I don't appreciate the two of you talking about me like I'm a dumb monkey, and Cam, you can get your ass out of here . . . I want to talk some business with the Doc."

"You asked if you could have a meeting in the study, so I just assumed—"

"Wrong assumption. I don't want to pay for your time for this business. If we need a lawyer, we'll talk to your father."

Cam was obviously baffled and somewhat taken aback. Thad knew he was not accustomed to this lack of deference, and he could sense the racing of his brother's mind, probably coming to the conclusion he had a loose cannon of a client, who would need to be disarmed soon. But not now. Cam got up. "Let me know if you need me . . . but I won't hold my breath."

Cam closed the door as he left the room, and Kirsten turned to

Thad, "I pissed him off, didn't I?"

"I would say so."

"He's so damned bossy."

"I'd strongly advise that you listen to him when it comes to your case."

She nodded. "I will. I just want him to know that he's not going to lead me around like a mindless idiot. I had six older brothers, and I learned early you have to push back sometimes with the male species."

"It appears to me you learned very well."

"Well, I guess I'd better get down to business."

"I have to admit I'm a little curious."

"It's about Clem Rickers' half section."

"You mentioned that." Thad knew all about the 320 acres, which included nearly 40 acres of Big Blue bottomland with rich, fertile soil that was hard to come by in this hilly, rocky country. The south quarter section was all prime, tallgrass prairie, a rancher's paradise. The crop land was all located in the north quarter along with a bit less than sixty acres of grass. The balance of the north quarter was essentially trees and wasteland with a few nearly impassable bluffs, one of which flattened out into a broad mesa that had a special meaning to him.

"You know the place?"

"More or less."

"Clem wants to sell the land pretty bad."

"He hasn't owned it more than four years. Why does he want to sell?"

"He doesn't own any other land within five miles. With all the fences going up, that's a long way to drive cattle to and from pasture every season. He didn't even run cattle on the grass this season and didn't plant a seed on the crop ground."

"I did notice that. I thought it was strange. You can't turn a profit that way."

"The old fart's past eighty. He came out to this country with the Free-Staters almost thirty years ago. He loved the Flint Hills, but his wife hated it here and went back to Ohio, taking their two nearly grown daughters with her. He let all but one or two of his hands go, and he's cutting his operation way back."

"So, what do I have to do with this?"

"I want you to partner with me on the land."

Thad eyed her suspiciously. "Why?"

"I worked out a deal with Clem before Max . . . passed away. I haven't told Cam about this . . . I know I'll have to . . . but Clem agreed to sell the whole thing for twenty dollars an acre. Close to robbery, but the south boundary's less than a mile from my home section, and I figured someday I could link it all up."

It was an old story. Ranchers weren't land hogs; they only wanted the land next to them. "I still don't see where I fit."

"After selling off some of the yearlings and adding the rest of some money my dad left me, I could only come up with half of the $6,200. I think I could have taken out a mortgage for the other half, but Max would have had to sign the note and lien papers. He said he wouldn't do it unless I put his name on the home section and another three hundred acres I own. I told him he could go to hell. I finally gave in and said we could own the Rickers land together. He refused and said it was all or nothing. That was the first time he beat the shit out of me."

"You do need to tell Cam about this. I'm not a lawyer, but I'll bet Frank Fuller would love to know about this."

"I'll talk to your brother first thing in the morning. But I came up with this idea that I'd talk to you and see if you'd be interested in going partners on the deal. We'd split the land some way."

"The bottomland's on the north quarter . . . and the waste and buttes."

"Well, shit . . . take the south, but the south's closer to my place. I just figured we'd each have the parcel that's closer to our home places. And I'm not a farmer. I don't give a damn about the bottomland."

"If . . . and I say 'if' we partnered, I'd want the north quarter section, so we don't have differences on that score."

"You're nuts. You'd be taking all the wasteland and the bluffs."

"And I'd have the bottomland."

She looked at Thad suspiciously and was silent for some moments. He met her gaze. "What?"

"You said you knew about Clem's land 'more or less.' I think it's 'more.'"

"Alright," he replied, "I do know something about the properties. And I like the bottomland. I'd lease it out on shares and get a cash crop to help pay for the place. And I don't have enough cow-calf pairs yet to stock the pasture . . . I'd rent it out to you if you wanted."

"At least you're starting to make some sense, Doc. But you're still dancing around the truth. Please, don't piss on my leg and tell me it's raining."

Thad sighed and shrugged. The woman was nothing if not insightful. "Okay, I'm not trying to take advantage of you."

"I never thought that."

"I was just embarrassed to tell you my real reason for wanting the north quarter . . . it's the buttes."

"You're serious, I think." She cocked her head to the side,

looking at him quizzically.

"I've spent some time at the top of one of the buttes over the years . . . a breathtaking view. I always thought I'd like to own it."

"That doesn't make business sense, but, of course, you're not telling me most of the story, whatever it is. But I'm pretty sure it's none of my business. I wouldn't mind seeing it sometime, though."

Thad was non-committal. If Kirsten Cavelle wanted to see the view, she was on her own.

"So," Kirsten asked, "will you work with me on this deal if you can take the north quarter? I'm getting the parcel I want. I just want grass to fill up with Red Angus. My pastures are overstocked right now."

"Have you discussed this with Cam?"

"I mentioned it. He thought I was insane to be even thinking about this right now. And he said it wouldn't look good if it came out I was buying land right after I supposedly murdered my husband."

"That thought had occurred to me."

"I've got a plan."

Thad wasn't certain he wanted to hear it. This woman was moving way too fast for him. She was beyond strange. He sighed— she seemed to leave him sighing a lot, he noted—"Okay, I'll bite. What's the plan?"

"You buy the entire half section. When this is all over, I'll buy the south quarter from you. I'll advance the money for my half. It will be a loan, and you can give me a note"

"I can't give you a mortgage if the bank makes the loan, and you don't want anything on the public record. You won't have any security. You're taking quite a chance. How do you know you can trust me to pay the note or sell to you later?"

"You've seen what happens to men that mess with me."

He looked at her in disbelief.

"Oh shit. Don't look at me like that. I'm joshing. You take things too seriously."

"I need to think about this. I don't have any cash, and I'd have to find a lender. I assume you have your money lined up?"

"Yes, I've got some inheritance from my dad left, and then I was going to have to sell off more cattle than I wanted anyway to pay your brother some up-front fees. Makes me wonder if he thinks I'm going to be around to pay his bill when they're done with me."

Thad didn't say so, but he wondered if she was going to be around to finish her part of the land deal and what would happen if she was not.

"Well, I have to look into all of this. Give me a few days and I'll let you know either way . . . are you certain Rickers will sell the land to me?"

"As long as he knows I'm out, he'll sell to you. He just wants to get the deal done."

"You will run this by Cam?"

"Yes, first thing in the morning. One more thing."

"What is it?"

"How's Henry?"

Thad smiled. "He's fine, but he's taken over my office. Thinks he's in charge. I can't sit down or he's settled on my lap."

"Bastard. He's loyal to his next meal."

15

THE NEXT MORNING Thad was rousted out of bed before five o'clock with a pounding on his door. One of Jasper Shortridge's young hands informed him that a first-calf heifer was having trouble calving over at the Circle JS. He lifted Henry out of his bed in spite of the cat's protests, fed him a hunk of sausage, and then tossed him outside. Thad figured he could do some mousing the rest of the day and earn his keep. He didn't seem inclined to abandon the place.

Thad kept a half dozen saddle bags in his home office, each stuffed with supplies for specific veterinary tasks, and he grabbed the obstetrical bags before he saddled Cato and joined the cowboy, whose name he learned was Luke, and headed for Jasper's. He was not all that pleased when Luke told him the heifer was calving in one of the pastures about five miles southeast of his ranch house but was relieved to learn that the patient was tied to a scrub oak tree. He decided he should just be glad they had her roped and tied.

When he arrived, Jasper, a stocky, fair-skinned rancher in his mid-fifties, who seemed to have a perpetual sunburn, was pacing back and forth like an expectant father. His son, Junior, a younger version of his father, sat Indian-style in the grass nearby, puffing slowly on a just-rolled cigarette.

Thad dismounted, nodded at the ranchers and walked over to the heifer. She was still on her feet and strong enough yet to strain against the rope. He noted she was a Hereford, but small and bred too young. Jasper ran a sloppy operation when it came to keeping young breeding heifers separated from the bulls until they were proper age and size.

"I need a tail holder," Thad said.

Luke ran up and grabbed the heifer's tail, hanging on tight as she commenced kicking. The tail holder helped by pulling the tail to the side and giving the vet a better view of the animal's vulva so he could make an initial appraisal of the problem. More important, he helped by controlling the heifer's rear-end and, with some luck, deterring a few kicks—a vet's shins tended to be perpetually bruised.

Thad saw two small hooves peeking through the swollen flesh of the vulva. He would usually expect to see the beginning of the calf's nose at this stage—his guess was that the head was turned back, blocking exit from the womb. "Do you have a place close by where you can get some clean water? Do you have a bucket?"

"No on both counts, Doc."

Thad stripped down to his waist and retrieved some short chains with narrow links Quincy Belmont had fashioned for him, as well as a bottle of bean oil he'd been using for lubricant lately. Quincy had also devised some cylindrical handles, each with a hook welded midway between the ends. Applying a generous helping of the oil to his hands, he moved in behind the heifer. "Hang on to that tail like your life depends on it, Luke."

"I'll do my best, Doc."

Junior hadn't moved since his arrival, although he had rolled and lighted another cigarette. Jasper, on the other hand, watched the proceedings intently. "You going to get me a live calf, Doc?" he asked.

"I don't know. I think the calf's head is turned back and that's not good. And Mama's not much more than a calf herself. You're letting these heifers get bred too damn young, Jasper. You're begging for calving trouble."

Unfazed by Thad's scolding, Jasper asked, "What's this going to cost me?"

"Two dollars."

"Shit. I'll go you double or nothing for a live calf."

"You're on." Thad began working his oily fingers into the heifer's vagina and she reared and kicked, missing him by an inch. To his credit, Luke held on to the tail and soon had her under control. Thad's arm was quickly buried to the elbow, his fingers probing, functioning as his eyes in the dark cavern. He began pushing the calf back the way it came, leaving some room to latch onto the nose and, both hands working now, got purchase and straightened the head.

The calf moved forward and the nose and front feet poked through the vulva. The heifer strained and pushed mightily, bawling loudly with pain several times. Thad could see the route out for this calf was just too narrow. In spite of slick and bloody hands, he quickly hitched the chains to the front feet, and then hooked the handles onto the ends of the chains. "Junior, we need some muscle over here."

"Shit, I'm not no good at this stuff."

"Junior," his father yelled, "Get your fat ass off the ground and lend a hand."

Mumbling to himself, Junior got up and stumbled over to the cow. Thad put the handles in his hands. "You just hold onto these and keep the chains taut, and put your weight into it and pull when I say so."

He put some more lubricant on his hands and began to slick the vulva and lower vagina to help ease the calf's journey. He knew that one way or another he'd get this calf out, but he'd about given up on a live birth. Suddenly, the chains went slack. Thad turned his head and saw Junior lying face-down on the ground. He had fainted dead away.

Jasper grabbed his son's legs and dragged him out of the way and moved into Junior's spot, picking up the handles, which Thad re-hooked to the chains. "He has trouble with blood sometimes. Helluva thing for a cattleman."

"Pull," Thad said, "Steady, but hard as you can." He kept working his fingers around the calf and felt it coming inch by inch. He got a grip on the legs and helped with the tugging. All at once, the calf shot out like a ball out of a cannon, knocking both Jasper and Thad to the earth. Thad jumped back up and drug the calf off Jasper's legs and began clearing its mouth of the mucous and afterbirth and then pumping its rib cage vigorously. It coughed and took a few breaths.

"Release the mother . . . she's got work to do here," Thad said to no one in particular.

By this time Junior was on his feet and helping his father release the heifer. Thad grabbed his simple instruments and got out of the way. They all stood back and watched as the heifer scrutinized this creature that had caused so much pain. There was instant forgiveness, and she went over and began to lick her baby as it gathered the strength to get to its feet.

"It's a heifer calf," Thad said. "If we'd had a big bull calf, we would have been at this for hours yet. And by the way, Jasper, you owe me four dollars."

He didn't argue. "I'll get a draft to you next week."

There was no reward, though, like bringing a live, baby calf back from the brink of death.

16

IT WAS STILL early in the morning, so Thad returned home to wash up and change clothes, deciding he needed to look respectable if he was going to make a visit to the banker. He didn't see Henry but didn't worry any. The tomcat seemed perfectly capable of looking after himself. He grained the three horses and turned Cato and the pregnant mare out to grass, saddling up the sorrel mare and nudging her south toward Manhattan.

Aunt Nancy's and Uncle El's place was on the way, and Thad stopped by to get Uncle El's thoughts on his plans. Aunt Nancy thought he could do no wrong—and he never wanted her to think otherwise—and he considered Uncle El very wise, even wiser than the Judge when it came to things ranching.

The three sat down at the kitchen table after Aunt Nancy had set down a pot of coffee and a plate of spice butter cookies. This had been a ritual of many years, for this was the home in which Thad and his twin sister, Hannah, had grown to adulthood. He figured Aunt Nancy had reached her fifty-fifth birthday now, so that would put Uncle El at sixty years. They hadn't changed all that much. Aunt Nancy was still a trim handsome woman with only a few streaks of gray in her almond-brown hair, and her twinkling, blue eyes radiated the same enthusiasm for life. She was a quiet woman, almost always calm and collected. To be near her was to feel warm and loved.

Uncle El, with white, short-cropped hair and sun and wind burned skin, looked a bit older than his age, but barrel-chested and thick-shouldered, he was still a fit and vital man. The crow's feet at his eyes dug deeper when he smiled, which was often. He and Aunt Nancy were a team in harness. They stood firm together when they were raising Hannah and Thad, he remembered—no sense trying to play them off of each other. They were best friends first, lovers second, Uncle El once told him. "That's the recipe for a good marriage and a good life, Thad." He hoped to have that someday, but it didn't look like it was coming anytime soon.

"You're up to something, Thad," Aunt Nancy said, "Why don't you just tell us?"

Thad told them about the Rickers land, leaving out the part about Kirsten's involvement in the deal. He doubted if Uncle El would have approved of the little side agreement, and he likely would have shot some holes in it. Thad didn't feel right about the subterfuge, but he owed confidentiality to Kirsten. He admitted to himself this could be part excuse.

From the way he was looking at Thad it was evident that Uncle El thought he wasn't getting the whole story, but he wasn't the snooping kind. He certainly must have wondered where his nephew had come up with the cash for half of the purchase price.

"It's a big chunk of land to take on," Uncle El said, "but you've got nice equity to start with. The price is probably top of market, but by the time you're my age the value will triple or more. And when it comes to land, they don't make any more of it and it's always there . . . not going to run away from you." He looked at Aunt Nancy, and there was some silent communication between them.

She nodded and said, "It would be fine with me, El."

El said, "We'd loan you a thousand, if you'd let us."

"I couldn't—"

"Nan and I had talked about this a week ago. Times have been good and we've set aside some money. I'm done buying land, and we agreed that if you came up with a use for it at the right place we'd offer a loan. I think this is the right place. We'd charge you one percent interest and take a second mortgage on the land . . . after the bank's lien."

"I don't know what to say."

"Yes and thank you," Nancy teased. She was sitting beside Thad and reached over and gave him a hug.

"Yes and thank you. I'll only need a third from the bank. I don't see how they'd turn me down for a loan on the balance."

17

THAD STAYED FOR lunch with his aunt and uncle and then rode in to town to talk with a loan officer at the bank. When he got to the bank and entered the small lobby, he was pleased to see that both of the loan officers were available. He preferred to deal with Corbett Avery, one of the Manhattan Bank's junior vice-presidents. Avery had been with the institution only a little over a year but had always been congenial to work with. Nigel Baker, the other junior vice-president, a slight man with slicked-back black hair and a thin mustache, had a slightly longer tenure with the bank, but Thad had always found him a bit standoffish, if not unfriendly, although he had never tried to do serious business with the man. Baker nodded at him, though, as Thad walked past him toward Avery's desk, and he returned the nod.

Avery got up to greet Thad as he stood in front of his desk. He had a round, cherubic face with a ruddy complexion and was a man of average height who packed extra pounds about his mid-section, but he was not obese. He was a man who could quickly put a stranger at ease and he reached out his hand and gave Thad's a firm grip. "Good afternoon, Thaddeus," he said, "sit down. You look a bit grim. I hope I can help with that."

Thad supposed he did look a little grim. He had procured a number of loans, several from Corbett Avery, who was only a few years older than himself, but borrowing money was never a casual occasion from his standpoint. He knew loaning money was the bank's business and that the directors were always looking for good loans, but he still hated asking for money and had not yet become comfortable with debt. He doubted he ever would. "I'd like to speak with you about a real estate loan," he said.

Once again, Thad selectively told his story. Kirsten's money was some he'd saved up. He didn't have to lie about the money he was getting from Uncle El and Aunt Nancy, but he felt like something of a criminal. Of course, as long as the bank held a first mortgage to secure its loan, the source of the remaining funds was none of the lender's concern.

"You could have paid off your other real estate loan with the money you'd set aside," the banker observed. "Would have saved some interest."

"Yes, I suppose I could have."

"You know, Clem Rickers banks here, too."

"Uh, no."

"Yes. He spoke with Nigel the other day . . . said he was working on a deal with Kirsten Cavelle or Brannon or whatever her name is."

Shit. "Yeah, well, she's had something come up." He realized that must have sounded mighty stupid.

"Yes, I hear your brother, Cameron, is representing her."

"I can't say." Thad could feel the perspiration gathering on his forehead.

Corbett Avery smiled broadly, "I understand. Well, I have to get board approval, but I don't see any problem with the loan. Come back in when you've got a signed contract with Rickers."

They shook hands, and when Thad started to leave he realized Nigel Baker was staring at him. When their eyes met, he quickly turned away.

18

THE NEMESIS ENTERED the three-room clapboard house he rented from the next door neighbor, a craftsman who had built the structure himself. Dusk was dying and easing into nightfall, but he did not light the oil lamp. Instead he tossed his coat on the flowered settee and sat down in the oak rocker that had been his father's and began to rock rhythmically, first very slowly and then faster and faster.

His mother immediately sent him running to the sheriff of their sparsely populated, rural Missouri county. They resided less than a mile from the county seat, and the boy returned soon with the sheriff and a deputy. By this time she had covered her obscene nakedness, but without hesitation she bared her neck and back and even the cleavage or her ample breasts to display the evidence of her punishment. The sheriff was a kindly old man, who was beguiled by the young, bitch woman, and he quietly set aside further investigation and declared that Father was killed in self-defense. Father was buried on a barren knoll in the town cemetery with only the boy, his mother, the undertaker, and a babbling preacher at the graveside.

His mother settled quickly into a life without Father, but life was hell for the boy. He did not suffer for want of food or the necessities of life, but he missed Father terribly. And the pain heightened when he came to understand how his mother was providing for their livelihood.

He despised his mother, and he nearly vomited when her gentlemen callers visited and stayed the night. He listened to the creaking of the bed and the sighing and groaning of its occupants. Eventually, he punched a tiny hole between his and his mother's room that he might witness for himself the perversions that took place in her room, which smelled of fornication, reeked of it. And when the visitors joined her, never more than one a night and sometimes the same man for as long as a week, his eye could not resist the summons from the hole in the wall, and he would watch, mesmerized, with his hand gripping and pumping his erect phallus as they coupled in raw nakedness and did other unspeakable things with each other.

And, finally, hours into the night, when he was exhausted and sated, he would collapse on his own bed, sick and consumed by his mother's wickedness in giving so freely of those pleasures to other men that she denied to her own husband.

He slowed the rocking of the chair, as he smelled the approach of Father.

"Father, are you here? I feel your presence."

"I am here, son. Rest easy. I am always nearby."

He looked over at Father's special place on the near end of the settee and knew he was seated there. "Father, they have not arrested the woman. She is still free, flaunting her disobedience, secure in the thought there will be no retribution."

"Patience, son. Have you received any confirmation that the authorities are not going to act?"

"No. The sheriff and county prosecutor are being very secretive. Speculation is rampant in Riley County. Some have talked of bringing the bitch to justice on their own if officials fail to act. Most believe she is guilty, but a few, mostly women, insist no charges should be filed. The county is divided, more against her than in favor, but politics make this treacherous ground. I am ready to act."

"It has only been three days. You should be patient. One week. You must wait one more week. Then, if she is not arrested, you may avenge your friend. In the meantime, watch her when you can. Learn her ways, where she goes and when. Can you do that?"

"I will try."

19

It was a Saturday morning in the Flint Hills, although for ranchers, Saturday was no different than any other day—especially in the spring. Calves didn't hold off being born over weekends, stock still had to be tended to; fence needed fixing and folks had to be fed. Some farmers and ranchers went to town for supplies and social life on Saturdays, and merchants in the scattered small towns like Riley and Leonardville focused on Saturday trade for profit, probably more so than the county seat of Manhattan.

Kirsten, attired in her boots and denim britches, sat on a bench on the wide and spacious front porch of Cameron Locke's home, gazing off into the horizon, hypnotized by the waving stalks of the tallgrass prairie and the puffy white clouds breaking up the azure sky. Such scenes had enraptured her when she first came to the Flint Hills and hooked her like a catfish on a line. They just wouldn't let her go.

It had been a week since what she had taken to calling the 'incident' had occurred. Her wounds were healing nicely, and Doc had promised to stop by today or tomorrow to remove stitches. He had been a regular visitor at the ranch, ostensibly to check up on her physical condition, but they had spent some time firming up their business arrangements for the land purchase he had finalized with Clem Rickers. The deal was scheduled to close at the bank in ten days. She had been surprised to find that the good doctor was actually a very organized and methodical businessman. She liked that he listened to what she had to say and that he was neither insistent on his own view nor intimidated by hers. They had worked the details out quite nicely. Cam Locke still did not like the arrangement and was concerned that rumors would get out, but his younger brother, while respectful, would not be bullied by Cam, either.

She had cabin fever and planned to get in the saddle today and ride up to her place. On the way she thought she might swing by Thad Locke's, and if he was home, see if he might take care of the stitches. Now she waited for Pilar to join her, since at breakfast she had asked if they might talk a spell before Kirsten left the ranch. She had come to like and admire Pilar immensely and she trusted her totally. She could not recall ever having a woman friend before, and she did not know quite what to make of the alliance they had formed, but it gave her great comfort.

Kirsten had not told Pilar much about herself. She had always been guarded about her personal life and uneasy about letting anyone get too near, but she knew she could confide in Pilar if she chose. The house door opened and Pilar came out, wearing baggy denims and her artist's smock—and still looking beautiful and elegant, Kirsten thought.

Pilar sat down beside her, and followed her gaze. "You see something," she commented.

"That far ridge, north of the big tree."

"I see something. I can't say what it is . . . a horse, perhaps?"

"A horse and rider. He's been there ever since I came out. Hasn't moved. Like a statue. So he's not likely a cowboy."

"You think he's watching the place?"

"I do."

"I wonder why?"

"I'd guess the reason's sitting on this bench. And it's not you."

"A sheriff's deputy?"

"Could be. Keeping an eye on me, maybe."

"Bastardo." Pilar swore on occasion, but she invariably used the Spanish version of the expletive.

"Could I borrow a Winchester when I take my ride?"

Pilar hesitated. "Yes."

"I'm not planning to kill anyone."

"I know. You're not a killer."

"But I killed."

"You're not supposed to admit that to me."

"Any fool can see I shot Max between the eyes. Who else could have done it? Henry? This pretense seems to be so damn silly."

"It's not like you planned it. If any man did what he did to you to me, he wouldn't live to brag about it."

"I loved him once . . . or thought I did. I didn't have much experience with men before I met Max . . . actually none at all in a romantic way. He was my first and only, if you know what I mean."

"I understand."

"I was raised the youngest of seven kids. My mother died when I was three. I had six older brothers, whose devilment assured Paps couldn't hold on to a housekeeper more than a year. I didn't have any lasting female influence when I was growing up. I suppose that's why I probably seem a little rough-cut sometimes, lacking in the social graces so to speak."

"You're being too hard on yourself."

"Paps was a big cattleman in southwest Missouri, and he dabbled in a lot of businesses . . . banking, grain brokerage, you name it. If there was a dollar to be made, Ben Cavelle wanted in on it, and he taught me a lot about managing money. I tagged along with him everyplace he went, and he spoiled me rotten. Some of my brothers resented it, and that may be one reason we're not close."

"But you must have liked the cattle business best."

"Oh, yes. Paps sold me my first heifer when I was six. I actually had to sign a note and pay him back when I sold calves over the years. I didn't understand at first, but then I came to realize he was teaching me the ways of business and the pride of doing for myself. He saw that all the kids got a good education. When I said I wanted to go to college and study agriculture, he never hesitated. He told me to find the best school and he'd help me all he was able. I picked the Kansas State Agricultural College, which was just starting to get some attention at the time."

"So that's how you ended up in the Flint Hills?"

"Yes. Paps came out to check the school, and all this prime grass made him drool. He said he wished he was starting over. While I was going to the college, he'd search out land bargains while he was here. He ended up with a section of land, and when I got out of school, I told him I wanted to stay in the Flint Hills, so he sold me a quarter section for the home place. I'd studied about the different cattle breeds in husbandry classes at the college and got interested in Red Angus. I sold my mixed cow herd in Missouri to my oldest brother, Arnold, and started building a new herd."

"It seems you've done very well with it."

"I won't pretend to have done it all on my own. Paps died two years ago and left me all his Kansas land and a small amount of cash. My brothers got good inheritances, too, but some thought Paps had favored me and they aren't speaking to me these days."

"The Judge . . . Cam's father . . . always says inheritance is not a right; it's a bonus some folks get in life, and the receivers have a responsibility to be good custodians of it. I think your father would be very proud of what you've done with your inheritance."

"I hope so. That's when things really went south for Max and me, though . . . when I got the land from Paps. He started fussing about changing title to the quarter section a month after we were married, and then when I got the rest of the land, he really went loco . . . harped on it day and night. I knew Paps wouldn't have wanted me to make the change, because he expressed concern about Max's drinking soon after we married. We weren't a family of drinkers, but I thought I could change him. I wonder how many foolish women think they can do that . . . change a man? Any problems always get worse after the knot's tied."

"I gather you met Max at the ag college?"

"Yes. He wasn't much of a student and a little lazy, but, as I said, I'd never had much to do with romance, and he courted with determination. It didn't take all that much frankly. He was the class stallion, and he turned me into a filly in heat. I started thinking with my muffin, I'm afraid. Looking back, I can see that Pap's money didn't hurt Max's enthusiasm. He started pushing for marriage right away."

She turned to Pilar and smiled wryly. "Hell, he didn't have to marry me. By that time I'd have spread my legs without a ring."

Pilar smiled back and leaned over and gave Kirsten a hug. "I do understand. I felt that way about a man. I just got lucky and it all worked out."

Kirsten suddenly knew with certainty she could speak honestly to this new friend. "I'm frightened," she said. "It took several days for me to see the reality of where the incident has left me. It really struck last night when Cam said the county attorney is going to announce his decision Monday. He will file charges. There's nothing vindictive about it. He just has to do it."

"Even if Frank Fuller files, it doesn't mean you'll be convicted. Let me tell you a few things about the Cameron Locke I married. Under his rather brusque façade is a kind man who cares deeply about his clients. He is persistent above all else . . . it's a Locke family trait. These people never quit. He will fight like a wildcat for you. Trust him. Put your fate in his hands. And . . . Kirsten?"

Kirsten began to sob uncontrollably. "Yes?"

Pilar again wrapped her arms about Kirsten's shoulders. "Count on me, too. I will be with you every step of this journey."

20

THAD HAD RETURNED home after a long morning of dehorning Hereford yearlings at Karl Schenk's farm. Karl was primarily a crop farmer with a fair amount of bottomland, but like most farmers he carried a small cowherd to diversify his income. This was always nasty work, because the cattle had to be roped and snubbed to a fence post, and they fought like blazes as the vet sawed off the horn at the scalp. A major artery under the base of each horn spewed blood which showered the vet until he pinched off the flow with a forceps.

They had worked fifteen head, and Thad was tuckered out. Quincy was trying to fashion a powerful clipper that would hasten the dehorning process, and he was anxious to try it. Many of the ranchers did their own dehorning work, and they were welcome to it.

He washed off at the pump but decided more drastic action was called for, so he pulled out the big wash tub and put it in the office room, while Henry watched with casual interest. He heated several buckets of water and poured them in the tub and then lugged more water in from the pump. He grabbed a bar of lye soap and a towel, stripped off his blood-caked clothing and slipped into the tub, where he encountered heaven. He washed off the blood and morning's scum and leaned back to enjoy the soothing warmth of the water. He had dozed off for a few moments, when the office door cracked open.

"Doc?"

"Wait," he yelled. "I'm in the tub."

She was undeterred by his plea and entered the office and closed the door, standing not more than ten feet from the tub. He covered his private parts with cupped hands. "Kirsten, I told you I was in the tub."

She cast a disgusted look at the pile of blood-saturated clothes on the floor. "And a good idea I might say."

Henry, from his perch on the desk, meowed in recognition of his former servant. Kirsten moved to him and began rubbing his ears. "Henry, how's my baby? Is Doc taking good care of you?"

"Kirsten," Thad said, interrupting the family reunion, "I'd like to get out of the tub."

"Oh, that's fine, Doc. Go right ahead. Henry and I don't mind."

"Would you be so kind as to hand me that towel?" He pointed to the towel that was hanging over the back of the desk chair.

She plucked the towel off the chair and walked it over to the tub, standing above Thad as she placed it in his hand, which had to vacate its shield function. "You're welcome, Doc," she said.

"Sorry. Thank you. Now, perhaps you can continue your conversation with Henry and turn your back while I get out of the tub. I'll change into some clean clothes in my living quarters and return in a few minutes."

He climbed out of the tub, dried off quickly and darted for the door that connected the office to the living area. He tossed a quick look over his shoulder and saw that she was watching with her lips formed into a small smile. She lifted a finger in greeting.

After he had dressed and returned to the office, he found her perusing the tintypes that nearly covered one wall. There were dozens of them he had taken of interesting inhabitants and special places in the Flint Hills. The wall was the nearest thing he had to a gallery.

"She is beautiful . . . absolutely stunning."

"Who?" Thad moved next to her.

"The Indian girl."

"She's colored." It disturbed him for some reason to apply a racial label to Serena.

Kirsten pointed to a tintype of Serena standing near what to Kirsten would have been a pile of rocks, a portion of a stone circle in the background and the landscape of the Big Blue River Valley beyond. "That's one of the buttes." It was not a question.

She turned and looked at him, studying Thad with her greenish-brown eyes. He thought she was preparing to interrogate him about Serena, but she evidently found her answers in his face and decided to drop the subject. He was grateful and a bit touched by her sensitivity to his privacy. This woman was a growing enigma.

She turned away and returned to Henry, stroking his back as she spoke. "I stopped by to see about having my stitches removed. I was going to ride over to the C Bar C to see how Chet's getting along with the place, but I changed my mind."

"Why?"

"I'm being followed. It gives me a creepy feeling. When I'm done here, I'm heading back to Cam's. I don't want to chance being in the saddle after dark."

"Any idea who's following you?"

"It could be a deputy. Maybe the law's watching to be sure I don't slip out of the county. And maybe it's somebody else. The same rider was spying on your brother's place this morning."

"I'll ride back with you when we're done here."

"No, Thad, that's alright. I've got a Winchester in my saddle holster."

"The last thing you need is to shoot somebody else right now. I'll ride back with you. I'll try to wrangle an invitation to supper from Pilar. Now let's see to your stitches."

Thad motioned for her to sit on the desk. "I don't have a proper examination table," he explained. "I generally only see emergency human patients, usually at their homes."

Kirsten had healed remarkably well, making removal of the stitches a bit more uncomfortable for her. She flinched once in a while when he removed the stitches from her face but did not complain. He noted that the swelling in her nose had pretty much disappeared, leaving only a residue of raw flesh and tenderness. The black and blue blotches on her face were starting to fade to pink and yellow, and the swelling was nearly gone.

He hesitated noticeably, he guessed, when it came time to deal with the wounded breast. She simply unbuttoned her shirt and exposed the injured nipple and her unencumbered breast. "What do you think, Doc?"

He examined his handiwork and proceeded to extract the sutures. "A masterpiece. You were fortunate to have a skilled surgeon."

"Yes," she agreed, "one who cares for udders."

SUMMER 1874

21

THE TWENTY-MINUTE climb to the top of the mesa had not been unduly arduous. It had been a steep, rugged hike, following a winding, well-worn deer path, but there was nothing particularly treacherous or dangerous about the trail. Thad often marveled at the instinctive engineering prowess of nature's creatures, as they carved out their private roads and crossings.

Serena was a bit gimpy on her ankle, he noted, obviously hurting some, but she had not complained and had spurned any assistance when encountering a few rough spots on the trail. She stood beside him, looking at him expectantly as he took in the scene. The mesa was roughly fifty yards in diameter at the widest point running east to west, he figured, and possibly twice that long going north from where they stood on the south end. The ground lay almost perfectly flat like someone had sliced off the top with a knife —not all that unusual in the Flint Hills. The theories of some geologists suggested this was a product of a great glacier carving its way through eastern Kansas eons ago. Lush prairie grass cloaked the surface, no doubt the draw for the deer that had blazed the trail. A few old cottonwoods had somehow dug their way into the surface and held fast near the east edge of the bluff. He could see for what seemed like miles, and the view of the Big Blue River and its surrounding valley floor was breathtaking.

The stillness reminded him of an empty chapel. Whoever or whatever God is, this is His real temple, Thad thought. This is where you have your best chance of finding Him.

"This is beautiful," he said. "If this is what you wanted me to see, I'm not disappointed."

"But do you see the stones?"

"What stones?"

Serena pointed toward the center of the bluff top where he spotted an array of white limestone rocks barely sticking out above the tall grass.

"Yes," he said, "I see. Is there something special about them?"

"That's why I brought you here. Leave the canteens and lunch fixings by the trees and come look." She took off, limping slightly, toward the strangely arranged rocks.

When he joined her, she was sitting on the edge of what seemed to be a circular stone cairn or altar that rose about three feet above the ground. The cairn sat in the center of a near-perfect ring of stones, perhaps fifty or sixty feet in diameter. Four larger stones broke up the ring with arrowhead-like ends pointing outward, and lines or spokes of small stones extended from the cairn to the four points.

"What is this?" he asked.

"It's my medicine wheel."

"Your medicine wheel? You made this? And what's a medicine wheel?" He began walking the perimeter of the circle, studying the limestone components.

"Don't be ridiculous. Of course, I didn't make it. But I found it, and I've made it mine. I came across it last summer when I visited, and now I come here every chance I get. I read about the formations when I went back to school. There are as many as a hundred of these, maybe many more as yet undiscovered in the northern United States and Canada. I didn't read of any this far south."

"I'm guessing they're made by Indians."

"You are a master of deduction. Of course they're made by Indians. It's kind of a mystery what they're all about, but it's a fair guess they have something to do with ceremonies or religion. There are all different kinds. They don't all have a cairn in the center, but they all have a hub of some type. Some may have fire pits or what appear to be sacrificial altars. Others may have more spokes."

"Hence, 'medicine wheel.'"

"Yes, and many have the four stones placed at the four points of the compass—north, south, east and west. Do you have your compass?"

"In my saddle bags."

"These stones will line up precisely with the directions on your compass."

"I'll take your word for it. This is quite a finding. Have you reported this to anyone?"

"Only you." She came up to him now and took his hand. "I'll share it with you but nobody else. Do you promise?"

She behaved like a little girl when it came to her medicine wheel, he thought. Keenly aware of her hand in his, he would have promised her anything at this moment. "I promise. It must have been Kansa."

"That's what I wondered. I couldn't find any other tribes that were ever settled near here. Pawnee and Osage seemed to pass through but weren't permanent to the area, and you wouldn't make something like this for an overnight stay."

"No, and the Kansa . . . some call them the Kaw . . . lived in this part of the Flint Hills for a long time before the 1850s. Manhattan's located on an old Kansa village, my uncle El says. It was called Blue Earth Village . . . had over a hundred lodges. Some of them were still up when my family came here in the late 1850s, after most of the Kansa had been moved to Council Grove or further south in Oklahoma Territory."

"I don't think anybody else has stumbled on to this place, or if they did, they weren't curious enough to report it to anybody who cared."

"I doubt if there have been many pass this way. It would take some effort to get up here, and there wouldn't be much point in it. For that matter, what pulled you here?"

"I don't know, really. I was taking a run down in the valley, and I caught sight of this lonely bluff and was just drawn to it. I knew you would have to be able to see forever from it, so I turned this way, found the trail and climbed it. I've claimed it as mine ever since."

Thad smiled and squeezed her hand gently. "Well, I don't see anyone fighting you for it yet. By the way, do you ever get hungry?"

22

THAD UNROLLED THE oil cloth poncho he had removed from his saddle bags before their climb up the bluff's wall and spread it in the soft grass at the base of one of the cottonwoods. Shade was sparse, but the mesa caught a generous breeze, and it seemed to him an idyllic spot for a picnic with a fetching young woman. Of course, he admitted to himself, any spot and any weather might have suited him for a few moments alone with Serena.

They leaned back against the tree trunk, Thad facing south and Serena facing east overlooking the Big Blue River Valley, munching on their sandwiches with a canteen between them. They had two canteens of water, but somehow the sharing of the single water container had become sort of an intimate act between them.

"I'm curious," she said. "You're nineteen years old. You live with your aunt and uncle, I gather. Are you planning to be a rancher?"

"I'd like to. I have a few cows of my own now that I run with Uncle El's herd in exchange for ranch work and vet services. But I hope to be a veterinary surgeon, too. The Judge isn't real keen on the idea, but he's sort of given in to it with some conditions."

"You said the Judge is your father?"

"Yes. He's not really a judge . . . not now. He was a judge back in Illinois, but most folks call him 'Judge' and his kids refer to him that way. But we usually call him 'Dad' when we're talking to him. He had hopes I would be a lawyer like most of the family, but it's never interested me. I want to do something that keeps me outdoors. The idea of living out my life in a cramped, musty law office doesn't appeal to me much. I told you I'm kind of a vet now, and I could just declare myself one and keep on learning by doing and make a living at it. The Judge wants me to go to school, though, and since there aren't any veterinary schools in the country, he insists I attend medical school, and says that will help me tend to animals."

"That's strange, but I can see the argument."

"I can't dispute it that much. He's probably right, but I'm sure he expects that after I finish school I'll decide to be a medical doctor, which he sees as the next best thing to being a lawyer. That won't happen, though. I'm going to set up a vet practice here in the Flint Hills and have my ranching dream at the same time."

"Well, your brother's a lawyer: that should please your father."

"It does, but it's a family disease. Cam's twin, Ian, is a lawyer north of here in Nebraska. My twin sister, Hannah, is in law school . . . plans to go to Wyoming or Colorado when she's finished. I've got cousins and uncles and whatever all over the country who are members of the bar. My brother, Franklin, escaped the plague; he's a Methodist preacher . . . rides a circuit in Nebraska. Think I'd rather be a lawyer."

"Well, I'm going to be a lawyer, too," Serena announced confidently. "I've known for a long time."

"Oh no," he said. "Anything but that."

"Like Charlotte Ray. She's the first colored woman admitted to the bar in Washington, D.C. She went to my school and then graduated from Howard University School of Law a few years ago . . . Phi Beta Kappa, no less."

Thad replied teasingly, "Seems I can't get away from the

varmints."

Serena abruptly changed the subject again. "Your family's like mine, a lot of difference in the kids' ages."

"Different mothers. Cam, Ian and Franklin were born to the Judge's first wife, Sarah. She died back in Illinois where the Judge served on a court of appeals of some kind. Later he married my mother, Deborah . . . she was twenty or so years younger than the Judge . . . and they came to Kansas with my Aunt Nancy and her husband, El . . . Eldridge . . . Clay, along with other Free Staters when my mother was with child . . . or children, I guess I should say. She died after they arrived here, giving birth to Hannah and me. Aunt Nancy and Uncle El didn't have children of their own, so they took the babies in to care for and we just pretty much stayed. The older brothers remained with the Judge and a housekeeper he took on."

Serena reached back and took his hand. "How sad."

"I guess it would seem so. I just never thought about it that much. I never knew my mother and it's hard to miss someone you never knew. She was only nineteen, and I do wonder sometimes what she would be like now or what life would have been like. But I couldn't have had better parents than Aunt Nancy and Uncle El, and the Judge always kept me in his life, made sure I got to know my brothers. He never let me forget we were family and demanded that I spend time in town. I still can't miss Sunday dinner at the Judge's without accounting for it."

"So you come from a line of abolitionists?"

"Oh yes, and I'm kind of proud of that. And Republicans . . . except Cam. He's a Democrat, which makes for some interesting Sunday dinners. I don't have much interest in politics."

Serena inched nearer to him and rested her head on his

shoulder, still clinging to his hand. Thad tried to pretend this was the most natural thing in the world, while his heart hammered in his chest.

"Do you have a girlfriend?" Serena asked.

"Not really. You have a boyfriend?"

"Not really."

"Ever had a girlfriend?"

It embarrassed him to admit it, but he replied, "Not really. I've taken a few girls to barn dances and the like, but I've always had so much work with the animal care and helping Uncle El, I haven't had much social life."

"How'd you get time to meet me today?"

He grinned sheepishly and blushed noticeably. "Uh, I'm fixing fence . . . in the north pasture."

Serena laughed and looked up at him and, her eyes twinkling mischievously, said, "And I decided I liked you because you were the least devious person I'd ever met. I sure had you wrong. You're as bad as I am. Maybe you'd better rethink this business of not being a lawyer."

He shrugged. "Sorry to disappoint you. I just couldn't stand the idea of not seeing you again. Besides, I did fix a little fence before I rode off to meet you."

She put her hand behind his head and gently pulled it toward her. Their lips met, and she kissed him softly. "A secret? I've never had a boyfriend. Ever."

"I'd like to make an application." This time his head moved toward hers, and he kissed her with fervor.

"Application accepted."

She lay back on the poncho, and he leaned over her and they kissed and caressed and touched tentatively, but although Thad was keenly aware of the coals smoldering in his loins now, he did not explore her most private places. He would never offend or disrespect her.

Abruptly, Serena slipped from his embrace and got up. Obviously flustered and breathing heavily, she said, "I have to go. Papa will wonder what's taken me so long in town."

At this moment she looked like a frightened deer. He rose and took her in his arms. "But when will I see you again?"

"I . . . I don't know. It's so complicated and I'm confused."

"But it's simple. We want to see each other, spend time together. You said I'm your boyfriend. Remember?"

"I don't know . . . I wasn't thinking."

"When?"

"When?"

"When will I see you? We have to talk about things, and we have so much to learn about each other. I want to know everything about you."

She hesitated. "Tuesday. It will be a little later. About two o'clock. There will be too many questions if I miss dinner."

23

THAD SAT ON the hub of the medicine wheel, what he now thought of as the altar. He had become convinced that the focal point of the circle held religious significance for the Kansa. He supposed there could have been animal sacrifices made there—or even human in ancient times—but he preferred to think not.

Serena should be here soon. It was mid-morning, and he was an hour early. This was their fifth meeting—yes, he kept count—and he always arrived ahead of the scheduled rendezvous. He loved the calm and serenity of the place and was lulled by the whisper of the tall grasses waving in the ever present breeze and had come to understand the spell that the medicine wheel had cast upon Serena. But, most of all, he did not want to miss a moment's time with his special 'girlfriend' as he teasingly called her. He was 'boyfriend' to her.

Today, they would have most of the day together. The entire Belmont family sans Serena was attending a festival sponsored by the Riley County United Church Council in Manhattan, and Serena had generously offered to handle evening chores by herself. Her father had objected only mildly because he had been invited to give the featured sermon at the post-supper tent meeting. Thad had taken the day off from ranch work to tend to vague vet calls.

"Hello, boyfriend," came a soft, seductive voice from behind him.

Thad nearly fell off the hub. He turned to see Serena smiling broadly, almost within reach, her arms loaded with a blanket and basket of breads and fruits, and no doubt some ham. "You scared me half to death," he scolded.

She moved in beside him and kissed his cheek as he got up from his stone perch. "Poor boyfriend," she said. "I didn't mean to frighten you."

"I guess I was day dreaming. And you move so quietly . . . like a damned Indian."

"I am that. Among other things," she laughed, as she moved toward their shady oasis beneath the cottonwood. "You hungry?"

"Not yet. It's an hour yet before noon. I brought a bottle of wine and some cheeses, so with the feast you have stashed in your basket, we should have plenty to eat. But I want to try out my new ferrotype camera."

Serena put her basket down and spread out the soft cotton blanket. "Your what?"

"My camera." He picked up a burlap sack and began to unpack the contents. Holding up a black metal box with short tubes extending like elongated eyes, he said, "This is what some call a tintype camera." He pulled it apart revealing an accordion-looking fabric. "This is the bellows. It's not as complicated as it looks. The plate will take four photographs, and then I take them to my emulsion laboratory . . . my closet actually," he smiled, "and I can produce four tintypes of the same picture."

He plucked out what appeared to be a jumble of sticks and began assembling them. "My tripod to rest the camera on. The legs are hinged, so I can fold them up and carry them with me."

"So, Mr. Photographer, just what are you going to take pictures of?"

"As if you didn't know. My favorite subject. Why don't you go over and sit on the hub. I've just got six plates, so we'll have to pick our scenes carefully."

For the next hour they set up poses, laughing until they were breathless as Serena made faces and clowned in front of the camera. He remarked that she would make a fine actress, which should serve her well as a trial lawyer. He was confident these would be among the best photographs he had taken. The sun was perfect, and the subject glowed with her flawless beauty.

Before they finished, he had collected three plates of Serena tintypes, including one with her posed near the hub of the medicine wheel, another of her standing winsomely in the cottonwood grove and a final pose with a backdrop overlooking the Big Blue River Valley. At Serena's insistence, she had, following his precise instructions, taken one of him.

Thad carefully wrapped each of the plates in soft cotton cloths and placed them in a compact wooden box he had purchased for that purpose, and put away the equipment. Then he joined Serena on the blanket and emancipated the bottle of red wine from the saddle bags he had carried with him up the trail. He dug deeper and plucked out two small tin cups. "Not fancy," he said, "but they work. I don't know anything about wine. This comes from the Flint Hills Winery. Aunt Nancy says their wines are kind of bitter but as good as you'll find in Kansas probably."

"Papa doesn't believe in imbibing in the spirits," she said, her face turning serious.

"Oh, God. I hadn't thought about that. I'm sorry. I guess I just assumed—"

She suddenly grinned brightly. "I said Papa doesn't believe in imbibing. We have wine at my aunt's on occasion. I enjoy it."

He shook his head. "Got me again."

They sat down on the blanket, and Thad poured a bit of wine into a cup and handed it to Serena. Then he poured some into his own cup.

Serena lifted her cup. "A toast to the medicine wheel."

Thad clanked his cup to Serena's, and they both sipped at their wine. Thad grimaced at the bitter taste, but Serena seemed to savor it, smiling benignly. She raised her cup again. "To boyfriends and girlfriends."

Thad found that the second drink was not quite so repelling. Serena scooted closer, and he wrapped his arm around her. She lifted her face and they kissed, lingeringly and deeply. He tossed his half-filled cup in the grass, and hers followed.

Serena lay back and pulled him gently with her, their bodies pressed tightly and their lips and hands roaming into territory neither had explored before. Her hips thrust against his, and he feared he might explode.

Serena pulled back slightly and their eyes met, sharing something just short of desperation. "Yes," she said simply and moved away and began slipping out of her riding britches.

Silently, he disrobed and soon they were both naked on the blanket, their clothes scattered helter-skelter at the edges. Serena's body was even more incredible than his imagination had conjured, lithe and smooth and dusky with small, tapered breasts and dark nipples. Somehow he did not feel shy as her eyes studied him with interest and, hopefully, approval. They lingered a moment on his swollen member, and then she said, "This is my first time."

"Mine, too," he replied as he moved on top of her.

Their coupling was clumsy and urgent, and after she helped him enter, she winced and emitted a soft groan, but there was no stopping him now and he drove hard and deep, suddenly erupting his seed.

Afterward, they lay naked and silent on the blanket, staring skyward for some minutes.

"I hurt you," he said, reaching for her hand. "I'm sorry."

She turned her head toward him. "Don't be silly. That is the way of things. Other girls have told me. It will be okay next time."

"Next time?"

She laughed and moved to him and tentatively danced her fingertips along his phallus which responded instantly. "I have heard of this," she purred, as she mounted him. "Don't move."

He did not argue and let her ride. Soon she shuddered and sighed and took him with her.

After that they agreed it was time for lunch, and, leaving their clothes strewn on the ground, ate heartily and made more progress toward emptying the wine bottle. They discovered they were both drowsy, and they napped in each other's arms for a spell before resuming their lovemaking.

Spring 1885

24

THE NEMESIS ARRIVED home after attending services at the First Methodist Church and dining at a luncheon served by the church ladies afterward. He always felt Father's quiet presence as he sat among a congregation of the righteous and joined in the singing of the hymns and the recitation of the prayers. And while he was not by instinct a social creature, he enjoyed the fellowship with the church members and circulated congenially before and after lunch.

But later the vulture carrying the black mood would descend upon him, and he would become anxious and agitated, especially when he was embarked on an important mission of vengeance.

Upon entering the house he headed directly for the rocking chair and was soon lost in his obsessive, rhythmic rocking, his mind wandering and finally finding its way to the day Father had returned and ultimately led him to his first rendering of vengeance and the beginning of a purposeful life. Yes, he remembered it clearly now, as events unfolded before his eyes.

It was the third anniversary of Father's death, and the boy, at age seventeen and on the verge of manhood, had entered the barn, as he always did on that date. He had no special objective there beyond revisiting the worst moment of his young life. He had no desire to forget, and the moments that preceded Father's death and the instant his mother rammed the fork into Father's back replayed again and again in his mind. He would inevitably become excited and be driven to relieve his urgent need as he had that fateful day.

This day, though, Father visited for the first time. It happened midway in the crescendo of his frenzy. The mixed tobacco-sweat smell crept into his nostrils, and his eyes commenced searching the seeming vastness of the old barn. He felt no fear, only curiosity and a sense that something very significant was about to happen. He waited for some moments, watching and listening, savoring Father's smell. Father was very near when he spoke, as he would be in all of their future meetings.

"It is time, my son, to take vengeance on the disobedient slut who does not deserve to be your mother," Father proclaimed.

This was the moment the boy had been waiting for. He understood Father's message. "I am ready," he replied.

"Can you do it? Can you kill her?"

"Yes, I can. I have thought about it for many months."

"How will you do this?"

"I will get her into the barn, and then I will take the bullwhip to her. I have practiced for many hours here at this very spot."

"I have watched. You are very skilled."

"After she has taken her whipping, I will mount her, and then she will die with the tines of the pitchfork buried in her soft belly, and she will not die quickly."

"You will have to leave this place."

"I have thought about this. I have completed high school, and my teachers praise my work and ability. There is a business school in St. Louis, and I will attempt to enroll there for its two-year program."

"What will you do with the body?"

"I will bury it in the woods near the river. I have searched out a spot where she will never be found. The house and land will have to be

abandoned. I will just disappear and take the two horses with me for sale in St. Louis. I am not afraid to work, and I am smarter than most."

"You will do well, and I will be near when you need me."

He spoke with Father many times over the next month, and when it was time he crept to his mother's bedside one morning after her debaucher of the night before had departed. She slept soundly while he slipped the noose over her head, and she awakened groggily when she felt it tighten about her neck. He dragged her to the barn, where she writhed and choked and screamed as he administered the whipping. Afterward, he tossed her on the barn floor, dropped his trousers and coupled with her, finishing quickly. He got up and pulled up his trousers and buckled his belt, giving his mother a hard kick in the ribs for good measure. There was little reaction, and she had no strength remaining to resist and helplessly watched in horror as he towered above her and the tines of the pitchfork arced downward.

Father had arrived, as he knew he would, claiming his spot on the settee. The Nemesis brought the rocking to a gradual stop, waiting some moments for Father to speak.

"You are very tired, my son."

Father always sensed the way he felt. He alone understood the burdens the Nemesis carried, the intense pressure of his responsibilities and the tribulations incident to his mission. What would have become of him without Father's wise counsel? "Yes, Father," he said in a near whisper. "The bitch remains free and flaunts her sins before me."

"You have been watching then?"

"Yes, she stays at her lawyer's home, but she is never alone there. However, she cannot resist the call to her slutty ways for long. I followed her yesterday to the veterinary surgeon's home . . . he is the brother of the lawyer. The itch in her crotch must have cried for relief, for she was with him several hours. She must have humped him dry. She was doubtless off fornicating with this man while Maxwell worked himself to the bone, all the while suffering silently from her defiance."

"She is, indeed, an evil woman."

"I had decided yesterday I could wait no longer for the law to carry out its duty. The rage overwhelmed me, and I was prepared to take her when she left the doctor's home. But he joined her and escorted the slut back to his brother's home. I then decided to abandon the plan."

"It is just as well. You should not make the kill in rage. It carries greater risk of mistakes. You must be calm if you have to do this. And you must let the law run its course. Patience. Above all else, patience. God will tell you when it is time, and I will be His messenger. A question: did she see you? Did she know she was being watched?"

"No, I'm certain she did not."

"Good. Then just wait a few days more. It is not likely the prosecutor will dally much longer. Promise me you will be patient."

"I promise, Father. I will be patient."

The sweet smell had dissipated. Father was gone.

25

AFTER HIS MEETING with Frank Fuller, Cam stopped by the Locke & Locke offices on Poyntz Street. The law firm's offices were located in a narrow brick building sandwiched between an imposing mercantile store and Longtree Furniture and Funerals, lying two blocks east of the county courthouse. He was greeted with a perfunctory wave by Reva Duncan, who was engaged in an argument with one of the two Remington typewriters owned by the firm. Reva, an attractive woman in her mid-forties, pretty much ran the office. The copper-haired dynamo filled all the cracks in the office operation and still managed a household with five children and a husband whose bad back tended to flare up at the mention of work. She had been with Myles Locke since her youthful marriage before the war and protected him with fierce loyalty.

Cam and Reva got along fine, but when he joined the practice a few years after the war, he felt something like an intruder, and some days she made him wonder if he was still just visiting. "Is the Judge busy?" Cam asked.

"He's always busy. But nobody's with him."

On his way down the hall, he called back. "Do I have any messages?"

"A stack of them on your desk. You might take a look while you're here. I'm done making excuses to these people."

Duly chastised, he did not reply and tapped softly on his father's door.

"Come on in," came the reply.

Cam entered his father's office and slipped into one of the oak captain's chairs that sat in front of the desk. Myles Locke's eyes were fastened on some papers spread out on the top of his cluttered desk. His was a working office. The Judge handled no trial matters—that was Cam's forte. The Judge's office was his fortress and his first home, and the seeming disarray contrasted sharply with his fastidious dress and otherwise orderly habits.

Studying his father's intent face, Cam found it hard to believe the Judge had reached his seventieth birthday. His head of thick, short-cropped, white hair suggested he carried some years on his shoulders, but his face was shallowly lined and the lean body was still good for a serious walk or horseback ride. Moreover, he could work any lawyer, including Cam, under the table.

Myles looked up from his papers. "Sorry. I'm rather absorbed in this one."

"That's alright," Cam said, thinking that his father was absorbed in something most of the time.

"A man made a will ten or so years ago that left his entire estate to his wife. Then five years later he moved in with his mistress, and a few years after that he made a holographic will leaving everything to the mistress. No witnesses, but that's not a problem if he wrote it all in his own hand . . . which can probably be established with some certainty. The mistress wants me to handle the probate of the holographic will. I told our prospective client that, since her lover was still married, the wife can probably claim a statutory share of half or so, but, otherwise her will revokes the earlier. She's fine with half, since her paramour owned a section of land. She and the wife will be unlikely partners, so it will probably end up in partition . . . more work for lawyers. Fascinating case."

"It sure is," Cam lied.

Myles rolled his steel-gray eyes. "I know my cases don't excite you much, Cameron. What's on your mind?"

"I want to pick your brain."

"You can pick what's left of it."

"I haven't had a chance to talk with you. I'm representing a client in a murder case. You've probably heard about it."

"Our client is Kirsten Cavelle. She's been staying at your place pending charges. The county attorney's going to file charges at ten o'clock tomorrow morning."

"How'd you know that? I just came from Frank Fuller's office."

"Reva told me."

"How'd she know?"

"She was at the probate judge's office this morning, and the clerk said she'd heard the rumor. Gossip runs through the courthouse like small pox, and the people there tell Reva everything."

"Shit. I haven't even talked to Kirsten yet. I need to get out to the house and talk with her."

"No need. She'll be here in an hour or so. Pilar sent a rider in to make an appointment. It seems your client wants to make some financial arrangements."

"And she wants to meet with you?"

Myles shrugged, "I guess she wants the best. Come on, Cameron; that's not your cup of tea."

"No, but she might have asked me. Then I could have referred her to you."

"I suspect Pilar gave the referral. She generally cuts right to the chase."

"Yeah. Well, anyway, I wanted to get your thoughts about this."

"I know next to nothing about criminal law."

"I just want your gut reaction."

"Fire away."

"I'll have to explain the options to Kirsten, but Frank's offered a deal."

"What kind of deal?"

"If she'll enter a guilty plea, Frank will charge her with second degree. Otherwise, he goes for first."

"She hangs for first. What happens with second?"

"Not less than ten years."

"What're your chances of a 'not guilty' verdict?"

"Hard to tell. She put a bullet between her husband's eyes while he was sleeping. Of course, he beat the hell out of her earlier, tried to chew off her breast like a damned beaver and raped her."

"Rape won't fly. A man's wife and a jury of twelve men."

"Probably not. But we have tintypes and witnesses to testify to the beating. I'm a little concerned that we had too much family on the scene. Thad was the first doctor to see her, and Pilar was there. It could hurt my credibility examining them on the witness stand. Thad took the tintypes, too. I didn't have any choice under the circumstances."

"Do you have anything to gain by accepting the deal? First degree murder . . . doesn't there have to be premeditation?"

"Yes, that's some of what bothers me. Frank claims to have evidence of premeditation. He doesn't say what it is, and he doesn't have to."

"What do you think your client is going to say about the proposed deal?"

"After you meet her, you'll see for yourself. She's going to say something like 'shit no.'"

Myles lowered his head and rubbed his brow. Then he leaned back in his chair. "Have you thought about associating with another lawyer on the case . . . someone who could handle examination of family witnesses?" He added quickly, "You'd still run the case, but two heads are good . . . and you'd remove some awkward moments that might have a negative impact on the jury."

"And you've got someone in mind, of course."

Myles shuffled through the desk clutter and plucked out an envelope. He slipped out a letter and passed it to Cam, who began perusing the neatly typed pages. "A woman. Interesting," Cam remarked.

"Her family lives in Riley County. Her father's Quincy Belmont. We've done some legal work for him. A good man."

"I know him. We buy some pork from him. She has quite a distinguished background. General Counsel for the Bill of Rights Society. First in her class at Howard University."

"She's represented mostly women in Bill of Rights cases . . . several of those were accused of murder. She wants to move here to be nearer to her family and wants to talk with us about employment prospects. The young woman's speaking in Topeka next week and offers to catch a train to Manhattan to meet with us. I'd need to reply by telegram. No chance the mail would get to Washington before she left."

"With her background we couldn't afford her. You're always saying we have enough work for three or four lawyers but enough money for two."

"Maybe she'd work for what she bills less an allowance for expense share."

"She's colored."

"I can't believe that would be a problem with you."

"Of course not. I was thinking we might get a colored man or two on the jury. Her color might not hurt. Perhaps, we could persuade her to stay over . . . sort of an audition, you might say. The trial won't take more than four or five days. The evidence is pretty damn short on both sides. I could push for a speedy trial. I think Frank is anxious to get this behind him. He's not that fond of high profile cases. I do think associate counsel could be helpful."

"I'm glad you thought of it," his father said sardonically. "I'll have Reva get off a telegram to Serena Belmont."

26

REVA LED KIRSTEN to Cam's office following her meeting with Myles Locke. After she was seated across from Cam's desk, Cam asked, "Did you and the Judge hit it off all right?"

"I love him," she replied. "He doesn't just hear you . . . he listens. He actually listens. And you may call him 'Judge' but he doesn't judge. He's kind and has a sense of humor and knows exactly what needs to be done."

"You're talking about my father?"

"Who else? He really put me at peace, and he'll have my legal paperwork ready for me to sign tomorrow."

"May I ask what paperwork?"

"A will and power of attorney. When we were riding back from his place Saturday afternoon, I asked Doc if he would look after my ranching business during any period I might be in jail. I know he didn't want to, but he doesn't say 'no' very easily if you haven't noticed. He told me he would if you and your father had no objection. Your father had none."

"You hadn't asked me yet. You should have talked to me before telling the Judge to go ahead with preparing a power of attorney."

She lifted her eyebrows and looked at him quizzically. "You have an objection?"

"I'm not fond of the idea. He's a key witness in your case. It might encourage the notion he's a biased witness if the jury is made aware Thad's handling your business. We already have a situation with the land purchase I'm not comfortable with."

"I want him to do it. He knows something about the cattle business. We're different. Sometimes he's kind of an innocent, expecting the best of people . . . I tend to expect the worst. But I trust him and I'll rest easy if he's looking after my business."

Cam shrugged. "Have it your way. We've got more serious things to talk about."

"The charges."

"Yes, Frank Fuller's filing tomorrow, but he's made an offer you have to consider carefully."

"Somehow that doesn't reassure me."

Cam explained the county attorney's proposal in detail and then asked if Kirsten had questions.

"I do have some questions. As I understand it, murder in the first degree says the killing had to be willful, deliberate and premeditated. I don't understand much of the legal shit, but I don't see how Fuller can prove I planned to kill Max. So if he charges me with first degree, what if he can't convince the jury . . . am I free?"

"Not necessarily. The jury can still find you guilty of murder in the second degree. Premeditation isn't required for second degree. The killing just has to be purposely and maliciously. Manslaughter of some degree is also an option for the jury, but I don't think that's likely at all. Your facts just don't fit manslaughter as defined by the Compiled Statutes of Kansas. You're looking at first or second degree murder."

"Why do you think he's considering the first degree murder charges?"

"Two possibilities. One, he's using that as a hammer to get you to enter a guilty plea, so he won't have to try the case. Or two, he knows something I don't know that would give a jury cause to believe you intended to kill Maxwell all the time and that, perhaps, you provoked the beatings as a cover."

"That's total bullshit."

"Did you ever tell anyone, even in jest, you were going to kill Maxwell?"

She did not reply for a time, obviously tracking through her memory. "Chet. I probably told Chet a dozen times I was going to kill the son of a bitch someday. But I never meant it. Chet knew I was just blowing off steam. He wouldn't go to the law with that."

"But the law might have gone to him. Have you talked to Chet lately?"

"Not for three or four days. He's been busy looking after things at the ranch, and I haven't been out to the place."

"I'll talk to him and find out if the sheriff has been poking around. Can you think of anything you've said or done that might lead someone to think you had reason to kill your husband?"

This time she did not hesitate. "Nigel Baker at the bank. I talked with him several times about a loan for Clem's half section. He said that even if I took title to the land in my own name, Max would have to sign the mortgage for me to get the loan. It was my debt, and I couldn't understand that. I was totally pissed about it. I think I said something once to the effect it would be a hell of a lot easier if I didn't have a husband."

This was not a pleasant development. There was no way at this moment of knowing if Fuller or Sheriff Mallery had spoken with the banker, but Cam suspected Baker had been interviewed. If not, Kirsten's statement would likely come to light sooner or later, or he would learn she had made similar statements to someone else. She was a stubborn, opinionated woman who was not inclined to keep her opinions to herself. She was an intelligent woman, but her quick temper could leave an unfortunate trail of unhelpful words.

"Kirsten, I don't think Fuller's bluffing. If you don't agree to his proposal, he'll file the first degree charges."

"Can he convict me?"

"There's a definite risk. But we do have a defensive theory provided by Section 11 of Chapter 32 of the Compiled Statutes. It says that if the alleged homicide was committed under circumstances where it was justifiable or excusable, the jury is to return a verdict of not guilty. Lawyers will fight over just what that means, but the statute gives a jury a lot of wiggle room. And remember, you must be found guilty beyond a reasonable doubt. That gives the defense attorney something else to work with . . . planting seeds of reasonable doubt."

"Can you win?"

"Yes, of course. But there are no guarantees. Juries are unpredictable. That's one reason my father abhors the courtroom . . . says he'd as soon toss a silver dollar. Keep in mind, though, that the uncertainty cuts both ways. Fuller can't be assured of a prosecutor's verdict, either. That's why he's made the offer."

"So, if I'm found guilty, I'll either hang if it's first degree or do at least ten years . . . maybe more . . . in prison if it's second."

"You understand correctly."

She suddenly looked very glum and took on a whipped puppy look. "I'd as soon hang as do that time in prison. Shit no. Tell Fuller to stick the deal up his skinny ass."

"I'll tell him you turned down the offer. He'll be formally filing the charges tomorrow morning. I told him you'd surrender at the courthouse . . . I'll be with you, of course. No reason to have the sheriff bring you in and cause a public spectacle. I'll try to get the district judge to set bond, but most judges don't in capital cases, or the bond's so high you can't raise it. In other words you'll probably sit in the county jail for a while." He could see that the reality of her situation was sinking in. The future must seem terrifying to her, Cam thought.

"I'll need to stop here and sign my will and the power of attorney in the morning. Can we take time to handle the signings?"

"Of course. I have one other item to put on the table . . . and we can talk about it more at the house tonight, if you like. With your permission I'm considering associating with another lawyer to act as co-counsel for your case."

"You're scaring me. You really are concerned."

"I have family members who are going to be witnesses in this case. It would be better to have another lawyer dealing with their examination in the courtroom."

"I guess that makes some sense."

"We expect her in town late next week. She's very experienced in representing women. I haven't met her yet, so I reserve the right to change my mind after I've talked to her. I'd want you to meet her, too. You have the last word."

"She? A lady law wrangler? I thought you guys were a boys' club." Kirsten shrugged. "Hell, why not?"

27

THAD SAT IN the waiting area of his father's office waiting for Cam and Kirsten to show up. He knew that Reva could see that he was nervous, because she kept making small talk. She was a totally sweet woman, unless somebody was making life difficult for the Judge, and then she could be tougher than a boot. She had covered his father's backside since Thad was a small child.

Thad had spoken briefly with his father when he arrived, but the Judge had an appointment with a farmer client, and he barely had time to elicit Thad's promise to show up for Sunday dinner before disappearing into his office. He would welcome more time with his father, but they both led busy lives and would often go weeks without seeing each other for anything but several Sunday dinners a month. Someday, he knew he would look back and wish they had made more time. But the Lockes had the comfort many families didn't have. They were all there for each other when the going got rough. They had never been split by petty feuds or envy. The Judge had seen enough of that in his probate practice over the years and instilled in his progeny the foolishness of quarrels over money and sibling bickering.

Thad was unclear as to his purpose here this morning. Young Chuck James, Cam's only full-time hand, other than Cookie, who was not much of a cowhand, had shown up at his place last night and informed him that Cam needed his help in town with Kirsten this morning, and he wanted him to be at the law offices before ten o'clock. Thad had beaten the deadline by a half hour.

Fortunately, Thad had an open day other than emergencies that might come up, not that it would have mattered to Cam. He was, though, getting a little annoyed with his summonses, and whenever he heard from Cam these days, he seemed to get drug deeper and deeper into the Kirsten Cavelle mess. Indeed, it appeared to have a life of its own and Thad had a sense it was beginning to take over his.

He gave a start when the door opened and Kirsten entered the office, trailed by Cam with a carpet bag in each hand. Thad hardly recognized Kirsten in her black, high-necked dress. He guessed Cam had costumed her as a widow in mourning for her public appearance today. He'd never seen her gussied up like this, and he thought she looked quite striking in black. Her grim face, however, betrayed her anxiety. Thad stood and nodded, at a loss for words for the occasion. She returned a small nervous smile.

Reva was on her feet, taking command of the gathering. "Kirsten, why don't you join me in the library? I'll go over the documents with you. I can notarize the power of attorney, and I'll ask Myles to step out and answer any questions. Myles didn't think he should act as a witness, and I have Mabel from next door in the spare office, waiting to act as a second witness if you're ready to sign the will." She turned to Cam. "You might want to check your messages while you're here."

Cam shrugged and grinned. "Yes, ma'am." He headed for his office, but returned as soon as Reva disappeared with Kirsten.

"You're probably wondering why I asked you to come in?"

"Yeah, I'm a little confused about what I'm doing here."

"Kirsten seems more at ease when you're around, and I'd like you to accompany her to the jail after she's arrested. You can explain you are her doctor and that she's still gravely ill and you want to check out her accommodations."

"She's not gravely ill. That's obvious to anybody."

"Well, make it clear she needs to be checked periodically for follow-up. She's going to be facing hell in there, and for some reason she trusts you more than anybody. She's going to need support, and you're in the best position to see how she's doing emotionally and physically. I've got to work on her case, and that's where my focus will be every waking moment."

"I'll see what I can do. It will give me opportunities to check with her about C Bar C business, I guess."

Cam slapped him on the back. "Thanks. I'm counting on you."

When Kirsten and Reva returned, Reva handed Thad an envelope bulging with papers. "Your power of attorney is in here. The will goes in our safe. You'll need this at the bank to access Kirsten's accounts. You have general power to handle any business that comes up."

"Thanks, Doc," Kirsten said, "I really appreciate your doing this. Tell Henry you're in charge of him, too."

"He won't believe it. Besides, I don't think I'm even in charge of me."

28

THE RILEY COUNTY jail amounted to little more than a decrepit barn, which was, in fact, its former use. Construction of a new jail was in progress, but in the meantime the crudely-built, limestone structure housed the sheriff's office and his prisoners.

Cam and Thad accompanied Kirsten to the sheriff's office, and Sam Mallery was there to greet them. No sooner had they walked through the door than the sheriff stepped forward and announced formally, "Mrs. Brannon, it is my duty to inform you that you are under arrest for the murder of Maxwell Brannon, and it is now my responsibility to take you into custody. My deputy, Gid Dagenhart, will escort you to your cell, where you will change into the clothing provided prisoners of this county."

"I generally go by 'Miss Cavelle' if you don't mind," Kirsten replied.

"Sorry, ma'am. The complaint says 'Brannon' and that's what it will be. Now if you will go with Deputy Dagenhart—"

A dark, cadaverous man with aquiline features emerged from the shadows behind the sheriff. "Follow me," he snapped.

Cam interceded. "Sam, I've asked my brother to take a look at the facilities and help my client get settled. As you know, she suffered severe injuries little more than a week ago, and she's far from recovered. Thad has been her physician, and I expect him to have ready access to Miss . . . Mrs. Brannon to look after her continuing care."

Dagenhart snorted. "A goddamned horse doctor. Well, she'll be boarded in a horse stall. Maybe they're a good fit."

The sheriff turned and glared at the deputy. "Shut up, Gid." He sighed and spoke to Cam. "You've never given us any trouble, Cam. I don't see why Thad can't help get your client moved in, and as long he stays out of the way of our work, he can visit no more than once a day for a reasonable time . . . and we'll decide what's reasonable."

"Thanks, Sam. We won't abuse your courtesy."

Cam assured Kirsten he would return the next morning to discuss her case and then departed.

"Follow me," Dagenhart ordered.

Kirsten and Thad walked side by side down the wide hallway, which he suddenly realized was the now plank-floored walkway between two rows of horse stalls that had been converted to jail cells, with the space between the wood partitions and ceiling filled in with stout steel bars that matched those of the front wall and cell doors. It appeared there were five cells lined along each side of the hallway and the three nearest the office area were occupied.

Kirsten had been assigned the last cell at the dead-end of the hall. Dagenhart pulled the barred door open. "This is your room in our hotel. Your jail garb's on the bed. Get out of your things and into your new outfit. Your doctor friend can take your clothes with the bags." He nodded at the carpet bags Thad had taken from Cam.

Kirsten's eyes sparked. "My underthings are in one bag. If I cannot have that one, I insist on speaking with the sheriff."

She had wasted no time initiating combat with one of her keepers. Thad feared this was not a good start. "Surely one of the bags can do no harm," he said. "I understand you'll need to check the contents. I'd appreciate your consideration." Kirsten looked at Thad with disgust.

The deputy scowled and opened his mouth to retort before evidently thinking better of it. "You can keep one. Get in there and get changed while I go through the bags."

He made no move to leave while Kirsten changed, so Thad stepped between the deputy and the cell bars in an effort to partially block his view. Dagenhart got down on one knee and began rummaging through the bags, holding up her undergarments and studying them lasciviously and then tossing them haphazardly on the floor.

Shortly, Kirsten tapped Thad on the shoulder, and he turned to see her standing in the doorway, dressed in what looked like wool pajamas, drab gray in color. The outfit draped on her slender form like a scarecrow's costume, and the pant legs fell just short of her ankles, but he had seen the woman at her worst, and it seemed nothing could make her ugly. She handed him the dress and petticoat with some long stockings. "These go back to Pilar."

He noticed she was barefoot. "Do you have anything to cover your feet?"

"No. I hadn't thought about it."

"I'll bring some moccasins tomorrow. Maybe the sheriff has some socks. I'll ask on my way out."

"We've got socks," Dagenhart said. "And I'm the head jailer. You ask me if you want something." The deputy dropped the allowed carpet bag at Kirsten's feet. "Pick up what you want and put it in your goddamn bag. Then be in your cage when I come back." Then he shot Thad a disdainful look. "You got five minutes, Doc."

Kirsten sorted through the scattered clothes, and Thad helped her separate them into the two bags. She kept mostly undergarments, and he stuffed everything else in the bag he would leave with Pilar. When they finished, they stood there silently perusing her new residence. It was worse than bleak, he thought. There was a narrow window opening in the rough limestone exterior wall, perhaps 18 inches wide, divided by a single bar. The room included a sagging cot with a straw mattress covered by a ragged, wool blanket decorated with streaks and spots of brown and yellow stains from sources he preferred not to know. A rickety table about three feet square and a spindle-legged chair sat in the far corner of the room, and on the floor nearby was a lidded crock, which would obviously serve as Kirsten's latrine. The reality of her incarceration here suddenly struck his stomach, and it made him queasy.

Kirsten broke the silence. "I've dealt with worse. I'll just pretend I'm camping out on the range." Her voice cracked with the last words and betrayed her tough façade.

Thad heard the door to the sheriff's office open, signaling Dagenhart's return. He turned to Kirsten. "I will check in on you tomorrow. You can count on it."

She nodded her head and gave him a tight-lipped smile. Thad impulsively wrapped his arms around her and gave her a gentle and lingering hug. She did not protest.

He released her as Dagenhart approached and brushed past him without a word. As he walked down the hall, he was overwhelmed by a feeling of great sadness. He could not unscramble what he felt about Kirsten Cavelle. Before the night of Max Brannon's death, he had known her only as an occasional client, who was married to a faceless man who never seemed to be around when they were working cattle. Then, that fateful night she had launched herself uninvited into his life, and somehow he had ended up as her physician, photographer, business partner, agent and friend. Yes, he had become Kirsten's friend, he admitted. She may have killed a man—technically murdered her husband, he supposed—but he was determined to wear all the hats she'd dropped on him and take this journey to the unknown destination with her.

29

THE NEMESIS HAD decided to rendezvous with Father at the saloon late afternoon. Knowing the bitch was locked up within a few blocks of his workplace was almost more than he could bear. During his workday he had been distracted and unfocused, and a torturous headache had descended, almost sending him home sick when Father threatened to visit him at work. That could not be allowed to happen.

He had somehow fought his way through the assigned tasks, even forcing a smile when a customer's telling of a feeble joke called for it. He was not a serious drinker, but this afternoon he had already downed a second whiskey. He would probably drink Father's before he departed the place, since Father never touched spirits, and the Nemesis only ordered him one as a courtesy.

The odor of stale sweat and tobacco began to drift into the corner where his table sat, and he waited patiently for Father to make himself known. Father had visited often of late it occurred to him. On the other hand, Father usually made more frequent appearances during the days before the kill and the triumph of justice.

"You seem agitated, my son." The sound of Father's voice came from behind him.

The Nemesis turned to the sound and spoke. "I was afraid you were not coming, and I am desperate for your counsel."

He was aware of Father taking the chair next to him where the barmaid had deposited the extra glass of whiskey. "What troubles you, son?"

"The woman. She has been charged with murder, and she is being held at the jail."

"Then, she will die if convicted."

"But she may not be convicted. As I have told you, she has a lawyer of substantial reputation. He is wily and will stop at nothing in defense of his client."

"You have nothing to lose by waiting. If she is not convicted, you will take her when she is released, and then you can do all of the things you want to do before you kill her."

"But if she is sent to prison, she will live, and I may not have the opportunity to kill her. I am so afraid she will escape her punishment."

"Do you know where she is kept?"

"Yes, I easily drew that information from a deputy caught up in his own self-importance."

"Is there a window in the room?"

"Yes."

"Do you still keep the serpents?"

"Of course, I have always had my snakes." And then he understood. And Father was gone, leaving the whiskey behind for his son.

30

KIRSTEN LAY ON her back staring at the warped ceiling boards. Moonlight sifted through the narrow window, lighting the cell enough to allow her eyes to make out the blurred lines of the bars and outlines of the sparse furnishings. No oil lamps were allowed in the cells, of course, so her hours of light followed nature's clock.

This was her fourth night in the "county hotel," as some locals called it. The days passed quickly enough. Thad Locke had brought a stack of books from her home library. Her friends, Alcott, Twain, Thoreau and several others had kept her entertained between visits from Thad, Cam and Pilar. Yesterday, she had asked Thad to bring Alexis de Touqueville's *Democracy in America* for some more serious reading. Between running the ranch and the ongoing battle with her late husband, she had neglected her reading passion, another legacy of her father's, for too many months. This was a hell of a way to find the time, she thought. Nonetheless, she treasured her library, which had been stocked largely by Ben Cavelle before his death.

Thad had not stopped by today. He and Chet were going to inspect fence on the Rickers place, even though they couldn't start repairs until after closing. He was also busy with calving, and he had warned that he would not be able to get back in for a few days. They had agreed the line between their quarter sections would remain unfenced for now, since C Bar C cattle would be running on both quarters for the foreseeable future. The barbed wire fence separating the pasture from the bottomland was pretty much broken down and would take some days to put in shape. Thad, with her approval, had taken on a new hand, a young eighteen-year-old, not dry behind the ears, but eager to learn the cow business. Thad thought Asa Morgan might be foreman or manager material someday. They would split the cost for now and lodge him at Kirsten's, since Thad didn't have a bunkhouse yet.

Kirsten's senses suddenly leaped to the alert. Someone was outside the window again. She heard the footsteps crunching softly on the crushed limestone covering the path that ran between the jail and the adjacent court building. Then it was quiet for some moments before she heard the raspy breathing, like someone catching breath after a long run or under serious stress. Tall as she was, the window was a good foot above her eye level, so she could not get even a glimpse of the visitor who had been there for an hour or more every night since her arrival. She had mentioned it to Dagenhart the morning following the first visit, and he had simply laughed at her. She had said nothing about the subsequent visitations.

This time she heard the visitor mumbling softly, almost like cooing to a baby. Then, suddenly she sensed, more than heard, motion at the window, which was three or four feet from her bedside. After the first visit from the eavesdropper, she had moved the bed from under the window, concerned that some unpleasant object might drop through the window.

She looked over her shoulder when she heard the plop on the planked floor. She noticed a pile of something on the floor, lifted her body up on one elbow, and then froze. The heap began to unravel and elongate. Shit. A snake. She remained still as a statue as her uninvited guest began to writhe across the floor. It had to be a timber rattler. She could make out the dark, irregular bands on its back, and it was a good three and a half feet long, too big for a copperhead, and she thought she could discern rattles on the tail-end, which a copperhead would lack. The more common Flint Hills rattlesnake was the massasauga, which might average no more than two feet or so in length, but they were mean, feisty devils, Kirsten remembered. The timber rattler, on the other hand, shied away from people and wouldn't strike unless surprised or cornered. She decided to give him all the space she could in her cramped quarters and hoped the snake would find its way to the front of the cell and exit between the bars.

The rattlesnake started to head toward the front as Kirsten had silently suggested but abruptly made a sharp turn, slithered over to the crock and appeared to be examining it before slipping into a comfortable coil and taking up a station adjacent to Kirsten's chamber pot. And, of course, she had to pee.

Kirsten remained motionless, her eyes fastened on the snake. She didn't know anything about a rattlesnake's eyesight, but she had the sensation he was staring back. She couldn't wait out the night with this guy. For one thing, the more she thought about it, the worse she had to pee.

She became aware of the breathing of the man outside—she assumed the night visitor was male, but you never knew. Maybe Max had a girlfriend who was seeking revenge for her lost lover, but she strongly doubted it. It occurred to her that the rattler might have some friends being readied to join the party. A man crazy enough to cart around a poisonous snake might own a herd of them. She wondered if you could have a "herd" of snakes—certainly not a flock. What would you call a collection of snakes? Why was she even thinking about this?

She decided she was not going to wait for another snake to catapult through the window, and, furthermore, she was not going to wet her pants—that bastard Dagenhart would never let her forget about it. The snake was not going to attack her, as long as she left the big guy alone. She knew from catching rattlers with her brothers that the snakes were not especially muscular and strong as snakes went. Paps had told her they were kind of lazy and caught their meals by poisoning their victims and didn't have to work their bodies like some snakes did. They could not strike effectively suspended in the air and were pretty much helpless if you got them off the ground. As a twelve- and thirteen year-old, she'd grab small rattlers slithering out of her way by the tail and then swing them over her head like a lasso and see how far she could throw them. But Paps had caught her doing that once when they were out on round-up and told her in no uncertain terms how stupid that trick was. She lived for Paps' approval and gave up snake throwing then and there.

This reptile was larger than any she'd ever handled, and she sure couldn't whip him head-on, but right now he wasn't within striking distance. She slowly lifted her feet off the bed and planted them on the floor, ready to move in an instant. Then she stood and inched along the bedside, moving a bit further away from the snake. She stopped when she reached the wall, a few feet from the window, leaning against the rough limestone and keeping her eyes locked on the rattlesnake. The man was still outside the window, his breathing rapid and heavy.

"I hear you out there, you son of a bitch," she said softly and deliberately, "and if you're still here by the time I count to three, I'm going to scream so loud I'll wake the whole goddamned county. One, two—" She heard the crunch of feet on loose rock and decided she had quickly cut her adversaries in half.

Now she stepped toward the snake which uncoiled and started slithering across the room and nearly made it under the bed before Kirsten raced after it and snatched the tail. She yanked it back and held the rattlesnake suspended in the air, twitching and jerking helplessly, before starting to swing it back and forth, raising her arm gradually until momentum carried the snake above her. She moved closer to the barred entrance, swinging the snake faster and faster before she slammed its head against the bars; then she swung it around a second time, striking the bars again and splattering blood on her face and prison clothes.

"Hey, what the hell's goin' on down there?" It was the voice of a drunk who had been tossed in for a night's lodging in one of the front cells.

"I'm killing snakes," she replied, as she gripped the still writhing rattler by its tail-end, recognizing that its muscular length had not yet caught up with its dead brain.

"Well, be quiet about it."

She heard the man stumble back to his bed. Kirsten then pressed the snake's spasmodic body between the bars and let it drop on the hallway floor, where it twitched for a few more minutes before its body became still. She stared at the dead reptile for a few minutes, collecting her thoughts about what had just happened. Abruptly, her body took control. *Damn, I've got to pee—bad.* She turned and rushed to the crock, removed the lid and pulled down her britches. After relieving herself, she crawled into bed and fell instantly into deep sleep.

31

KIRSTEN WAS AWAKENED by a blood curdling scream. "A snake. A fucking rattlesnake!" Deputy Dagenhart yelled.

Another voice said, "Shit, I thought I was dreaming. She *said* she was killing snakes."

"Don't go anyplace," Dagenhart ordered. "I've got to find the sheriff."

"Now, where in the hell might I be going?" the prisoner called after the retreating deputy.

Kirsten pulled her blanket over her head and went back to sleep. An hour later she was awakened again by the sheriff's voice. "Mrs. Brannon? Are you alright?"

She tossed back the blanket and sat up. "Yeah, I'm fine, Sheriff. I'd just like to get some sleep."

The sheriff stepped over the dead snake and unlocked her cell door. "What in the hell happened here?"

"Some bastard dumped a rattler through the window. Big son of a bitch."

"He was dead?"

"He is now. I killed him. Am I going to be charged with murder?"

The sheriff failed to catch her attempted humor.

"*You* killed it?"

"It sure as hell wasn't that dumb deputy of yours. He about scared the shit out of me with his screaming this morning."

"He's scared to death of snakes."

"Even dead ones?"

"He wasn't sure it was dead . . . and wasn't about to get close enough to find out."

"It gives me a lot of comfort having that cowardly bastard guarding the place at night." She hesitated. "I want to talk to my lawyer."

"I sent Deputy Stewart over to the Locke offices to tell Cam there was an incident here. I'm sure he'll be here soon. In the meantime, why don't you come up front and have some breakfast. Saturday's flapjack day at Charlie's Chuck Wagon, and somebody should be over with the jail meals soon. While we're up front, I'll have Deputy Stewart get rid of the snake and clean up your cell. Do you want a new cell?"

"No, it's more or less home now, and I like the privacy back here."

Nodding at her blood-spattered clothes, he said, "And you'll need a change of garb."

"I think I'm due a bath, Sheriff."

"No argument. I'll have the deputy get the tub out and heat up some water. You'll have your bath after breakfast and after we talk to Cam."

Sheriff Mallery escorted her down the hallway and past the two occupants of the front cells, one of whom clung to the bars and seemed to look on her with awe. He raised his hand and made a circle with his thumb and forefinger. "Snake killer," he said. She guessed the whiskery, bleary-eyed man could hardly wait to race to the nearest tavern to tell his wild tale of the incident.

The sheriff pulled out an old library table for Kirsten and slid a straight-back chair up to it, motioning her to be seated. She noted that Dagenhart stood sullenly and silently in the corner of the office.

The door opened, and a parade of people marched in. George Stewart, the fuzzy-cheeked deputy with the cherubic face entered first. George was probably twenty-five, but he looked sixteen, Kirsten thought. She liked him. He was consistently kind and respectful—the opposite of Dagenhart. He was followed closely by Myles Locke, who stood nearly a half foot taller than the young deputy and, as she would have expected, was dressed impeccably in a dark pin-striped suit.

Bringing up the rear was Charlie Archer with a big basket containing the prisoners' breakfasts. Charlie evidently had some kind of contract with the county for jail meals, and she had to admit the occupants were well fed.

"Leave Mrs. Brannon's plate on the table here, Charlie," the sheriff said.

"Yes, sir." The lean, middle-aged man with the shiny scalp was a former army cook. He was businesslike and efficient, and in a few moments Kirsten looked upon a plate of huge pancakes with several small sausages and a steaming cup of coffee. "And here's a pitcher of hot maple syrup, ma'am," he said, setting the little glass container on the table. "Now, I expect you to clean your plate." He smiled broadly.

She returned the smile, thinking she must look like she'd been working in a slaughter house during the night. But the old soldier seemed unfazed.

"George will help you feed the others," the sheriff said. Then, turning to the young deputy, he directed, "After he's had breakfast, you can let Higgins out. He was just sleeping off a drunken night. There won't be any charges."

The deputy and Archer disappeared into the jail complex. Myles Locke pulled up a chair across the table from Kirsten who was attacking the hotcakes like she was devouring her last meal. The sheriff took a seat at his desk about five paces away from the table, and Dagenhart remained standing in the corner of the office, glaring angrily at her, but she was undisturbed and just ignored him.

"I should explain," Myles said, "Cam caught a train to Topeka last night. He's going to attend a lecture by the young lawyer we spoke about."

"Is he going to speak to her about my case?"

"Possibly. Mostly he would just like to hear her speak and evaluate the lady's skills and demeanor when she speaks in front of an audience." He hesitated. "Do you wish to speak with me alone?"

She pondered the question. "No, I think not. I just want somebody who's on my side to hear about what happened here last night." She finished her breakfast, pushing the empty plate aside, and picked up the coffee cup.

Myles wrinkled his brow and his intent gray eyes met hers, telling her she had his attention. "You've obviously experienced something unusual, but you appear unharmed."

"I murdered a rattlesnake."

Myles gave her a small smile, but otherwise displayed no surprise. "And have you been formally charged with the serpent's murder?"

Sheriff Mallery interrupted. "Enough of this 'murder' talk. It's not funny. Mrs. Brannon, you wanted to see your lawyer. He's here, and we're not giving you the whole morning to have your conversation."

Kirsten shrugged, and the jail complex door opened. Charlie Archer appeared and quickly cleared her plate and empty cup and was on his way. Kirsten proceeded to tell Myles Locke her story. His face was impassive as she spoke, as if he had heard the story many times. Unflappable, Kirsten thought. Yes, that was the word— unflappable. His presence immediately calmed any anxiety or nervousness. He reminded her of someone. Of course, it was Thad, who had not yet attained this level of self-possession, but in thirty years he would likely be his father.

"You say a person, presumably a man, had been outside your cell window before?"

"Yes. Every night since I got here."

"And did you say anything to the sheriff about this?"

"No, but the first night I told the deputy."

"And what did he say?"

"He laughed and said I was imagining things. I didn't bother complaining after that."

The sheriff interrupted and, glaring at Dagenhart, asked, "Is that true . . . she told you somebody was outside her window?"

The deputy cast his eyes from side to side, as if seeking an escape. "Uh, yeah. Like I said, I thought she was just hearing stuff . . . it being her first night and all."

"Why didn't you say something to me?"

"Just didn't think it was important, and she never said anything after that."

Kirsten enjoyed watching the deputy squirm but didn't think the matter was worth more fuss.

"Sam," Myles said, "may I make a suggestion? You obviously can do what you want, but Cam told me someone had been following my client for several days before she was taken into custody. As I understand it, he asked you if a deputy had been assigned to do this and you assured him that was not the case. It seems to me that if it's the same man, he is being quite persistent, and he's a definite threat to Miss Cavelle's life. My first concern is for the safety of my client, but it seems to me it wouldn't reflect well on the sheriff's office for a prisoner to be harmed while in your custody. I think it would be prudent to have a second man on duty at night and to post him at the back of the building within sight of Miss Cavelle's window."

They would not dare decline Myles Locke's "suggestion," she thought. He was not technically making a demand, she gathered, but the deal was good as sealed. Cam would have accomplished the same goal, but he would have bruised some feelings, probably ripped Dagenhart's ass to verbal shreds. She noticed the sheriff hadn't corrected him, either, on his references to "Miss Cavelle." She appreciated what she considered a show of respect for her, and the gentle rubbing of the sheriff's nose in a cow pie.

"She'll have two guards," the sheriff said.

Myles turned back to Kirsten. "Is there anything else we need to discuss?"

"No, thanks so much for coming over."

"My pleasure. Cam will return on tomorrow afternoon's train, but if you need to talk me in the meantime, I'm sure the sheriff will send somebody to fetch me."

"What I'd really like right now is a bath and a change of clothes and a long nap."

The sheriff stood up. "George should about have things cleaned up back there. We'll take care of the bath shortly." He tossed a glance at Dagenhart. "Gid, get the hell out of here, and be back after supper."

32

THE NEMESIS ROCKED in his chair, sweating profusely and breathing heavily as a result of his nearly mile race from the county jail. The bitch had totally unnerved him when she spoke so calmly and deliberately to him through her cell window. She was far different from any woman he had ever encountered, frighteningly so. No wonder Max had been unable to manage her. His fate had been settled the moment he met the she-devil.

And Aldo. What had she done to Aldo? He knew the rattlesnake's life was ultimately at risk when he released it through the barred window, and that after the snake had accomplished its mission, it would likely be captured and killed. But he had not known he was sending his old friend into the devil's den.

He smelled the stale sweat and tobacco and began to regroup and recover his composure as he sensed that Father had taken his place on the settee. "I lost Aldo tonight, Father, and I learned that the woman is someone to be feared. She will never submit quietly to her end."

"She is only a woman. She is no one for you to fear. Where did you lose Aldo?"

"At the jail. I dropped him in her cell. And then it was quiet for a long time before she came to the window and spoke and threatened to scream if I did not leave. I was a coward. I did not want to be found there, so I ran until I nearly collapsed."

"There is no shame in running. Only a fool would wait to be caught."

Father's reassurance calmed the Nemesis. "Somehow she escaped the snake. I will learn what happened tomorrow. But what do I do now? She will be waiting for me, and she may alert others to watch for me. I thought of myself as the hunter, but I am wondering now if I am becoming the hunted."

"You are making too much of this woman. She is not a witch or a goddess or some supernatural being. She is a woman . . . a stronger adversary than most, perhaps, but still just a woman. But now is a time for calm. You must not panic. No matter how much the force calls you to take action, you must wait. Let the law run its course. If she hangs, justice will be done even if it is not at your hands. Patience."

Of course, Father was right. It was too risky for the Nemesis to try again just now. He must subdue the inner demons who called him to do his work. He must wait.

SUMMER 1874

33

SERENA LAY ON her bed, staring at the rough, plastered ceiling of the second floor bedroom of the recently constructed Belmont home. School would be starting at the institution in two weeks. She would need to depart in a few days if she was going to get settled in for the next school session. But what about Thad?

She had another assignation planned with him tomorrow afternoon. Decisions had to be made—and soon. And their clandestine trysts were coming to an end no matter what choices were made. Her father was more than suspicious. He had become more confrontational and often angry about her rides or runs into the Flint Hills. "You're not carrying your share of the load around here," he had declared more than once. And she supposed he was right.

She sat up and reached over and opened the drawer of the small clothes chest next to the bed. She rummaged beneath her underthings and withdrew the tintypes. She had eight of them, two of each of the poses photographed at the medicine wheel. Serena studied them thoughtfully. She did not know much about such things, and she carried a strong bias in her heart, but she suspected these met high artistic standards. The tintypes flattered her greatly, she thought, but she could not object to that. Thad, of course, his sandy hair even lighter in the photograph, was his handsome, robust self, and it seemed his eyes were reaching into the depths of her soul. His lips were closed in a small bemused smile.

She couldn't help but smile back at the face. His image made her hunger for him. Their appetites for each other had been insatiable these past weeks, and whenever they met now, they had to make love almost before they said "hello."

There was a soft tapping at her door. "Who is it?"

"Mama."

Serena hesitated, glanced again at the tintypes. It was time.

"Come in, Mama."

Rachael Belmont entered the room, glanced at the tintypes spread out on the bed next to her daughter, but said nothing.

"Would you close the door, Mama? I would like to talk."

Rachael closed the door and took a seat near the bedside in the room's only chair. She still said nothing.

Serena handed her a set of tintypes, and Rachael shuffled through them slowly and then repeated her perusal, evidently studying the images more seriously. She looked at her daughter quizzically. "They are extraordinary. The photographs of you are breathtaking. May I be so bold as to ask for one?"

Serena smiled sadly. "You may have one of each, Mama. I have another set."

Rachael held up the tintype of Thad. "I gather this is the young man you've been meeting?"

Of course, she knew, probably had been aware very early on. "Yes. He's the one who took the tintypes."

"That's obvious. The photographer is in love with his subject . . . and she with him."

"You can really see that?"

"Yes."

"I don't know what to do, Mama."

"About what?"

"School starts soon. I should leave within a week at the latest for the new term."

"But?"

"I don't want to leave him. I love him, and he loves me. He's already hinted at a life together. He'll ask me to marry him if I mention leaving for school. I've been avoiding the topic. Tell me what to do, Mama."

"I would never tell you what to do about something like this," Rachael said sternly. "But I will be on your side no matter what decision you make. You just have to ask yourself what you really want to do with your life. You also have a right not to make a decision just yet. Many times we force decisions upon ourselves before we are prepared to make them. Are you prepared to make this one? I know you have other dreams. How important are they now? We can change our dreams."

"I want to go to school. I want to be a lawyer. But I want to be with Thad, too."

"What does he want to do?"

"He wants to be a veterinary surgeon and a rancher."

"Would he be willing to do something else? Would he be happy living in Washington?"

"He would not be happy in Washington."

"Would you be happy living here?"

She hesitated. "I love the Flint Hills. But could I do the things here I want to do with my life? And, Mama, I can't forget, in the eyes of society, I'm a Negro. You and Papa have made lives here, and I guess most white folks have treated you alright. But you have your own community. What about a Negro woman married to a white man? And would folks come to a lawyer who's both colored and a woman? I want to be somebody, Mama . . . somebody folks respect and look up to. I don't know. Right now I'm confused. I'm not even sure what I want to do with my life."

Rachael said, "Our lives are one choice after another. You come to one fork in the road and you pick a path, and your entire life story will be different. It will happen again and again, and after each of those forks we never get to know where the other path might have led us. We just have to use our best judgments and make the most of our choices. And don't ever look back."

Serena's tears began to trickle down her cheeks, and Rachael rose and sat down on the bed, took her in her arms and held her close while she sobbed.

34

SERENA'S BUCKSKIN MARE was already tethered at the base of the bluff when Thad arrived. He tied Cato and snatched a poncho from his saddle bags and headed up the trail. A deep rumbling came from the southwest, and flashes of lightening lit up an ominous darkening sky in that direction. An hour from now, it would be pouring buckets, a welcome reprieve from a nasty dry spell but a hostile intruder on his afternoon rendezvous with Serena.

As Thad came over the lip of the mesa, he spotted Serena pacing nervously at the hub. He raced over, took her in his arms, and instantly noted her unresponsiveness. He stepped back. "Are you okay?"

"I have to spit it out now, Thad. I'm leaving in two days. I'm going back to school . . . to Washington."

Her words struck him like a horse's kick in the gut, and he was hit by a wave of panic. "But you can't. What about us? Serena, marry me. Tomorrow if you want. Just stay. I love you. I want to make a life with you. You've said you love me. You still do, don't you?"

She turned away from him. "I want to go to school. I want an education. I cannot . . . will not . . . make a commitment now. You go ahead with medical school. I'll come back next summer. We can talk then . . . see how things are between us. We don't have to make decisions now."

He thought her words sounded rehearsed, and he moved to her and turned her toward him, and with the palm of his hand gently lifted her face, so she had to meet his eyes. He saw something akin to fear in her tear-filled eyes. "Tell me you don't love me," he said. "Just tell me that, if you can."

She kissed him softly on the lips and pulled away. She took a lingering look at the medicine wheel and then darted like a frightened doe for the trail.

Thad started after her. "Serena. Wait. We need to talk." Then he thought better of it.

He sat in a daze on the hub, watching the storm move in. The thunder and lightning roared and cracked above the bluff, and soon the rain came in torrents, mingling with the tears on his cheeks. But he barely noticed and didn't care.

SPRING 1885

35

CAMERON LOCKE STEPPED quietly into the vestibule of the small Methodist Church that was nestled in the tidy, middle-class neighborhood crowding the western boundary of the Kansas capital city. He peered through the open doorway and surveyed the sanctuary before entering. The pews were perhaps one-fourth filled, he guessed—twenty-five or thirty people, more women than men. Seated near the pulpit were an older man with a clerical collar and a petite, young woman with skin tinged the color of burnt sienna. He assumed this was Serena Belmont.

Cam slipped into the sanctuary and claimed a seat in an otherwise unoccupied back row pew. It seemed strange to be in church for something other than a funeral. Most of the Lockes took after the Judge, somewhat neutral in their approach to things religious, respectful but not dedicated church-goers. The sole exception was his brother, Franklin, an ordained Methodist minister who would have been very much at home in this edifice.

This afternoon, though, he was not in church for a religious service. The congregation apparently made its facilities available for other respectable events, and today's was a lecture sponsored by the Topeka branch of the Bill of Rights Society. The speaker was Serena Belmont, who was also general counsel for the national organization, and, from what Cam had learned, the most sought after speaker in its lecture bureau. The title of today's lecture was "Equal in Slavery?"

The elderly gentleman rose and stepped up to the pulpit, introducing himself as Reverend John Miller, the pastor of the host church, who also happened to be vice-chairman of the Topeka chapter of the Bill of Rights Society. He presented a brief summary of the organization's purpose, which Cam gathered was two-fold: to increase public awareness of the importance of the Bill of Rights and to provide legal counsel in selected cases where an individual had been denied one of those rights.

The Reverend Miller moved smoothly to his introduction of the speaker, reciting an impressive list of court victories in defense of the Bill of Rights, including three successful arguments before the United States Supreme Court, a court before which a country lawyer like Cam would never even dream to appear. Why, in God's name, would this woman want to relocate her practice from Washington, D.C. to Manhattan, Kansas?

The audience clapped politely as Serena Belmont stepped to the pulpit. She was breathtakingly beautiful, Cam noted, attired modestly in a crisp, pale-green dress. She wouldn't be more than an inch or two over five feet in her stockinged feet, he thought, but she had a natural poise and presence that filled the room. Her dark eyes surveyed the sanctuary, pausing occasionally, evidently making eye contact with an audience member and smiling an acknowledgement before moving on. Then her eyes fastened on Cam, and he met her gaze evenly. She seemed bewildered for an instant before she looked away. That was odd he thought; she acted as if she might have recognized him. But his decision to attend the lecture had been impulsive, and he had not told her of his plans. Besides, she had never seen him before, as far as he knew.

After acknowledging her sponsors and thanking the audience for attending, Serena launched her speech. "Sometimes Americans worship at the altar of equality. Yes, the ideal is equality before the law, but beware of this beast. Alexis de Tocqueville wrote almost fifty years ago that 'Americans are so enamored of equality, they would rather be equal in slavery than unequal in freedom.' The Frenchman searched the American soul during his travels here, and what he wrote does not bode well for the future of freedom, and I will be alluding to this man and his words again as I share my thoughts this afternoon."

"Our constitution was designed to provide the framework for a free country in the context of its time, but as most of you know, guarantee of personal liberties came a few years later with the ratification of the first ten amendments, which were midwifed by James Madison and came to be known as the Bill of Rights."

"These are the gatekeepers of individual liberty, and I repeat— individual liberty. These are all that stand between one person and the mindless mob. The thirteenth, fourteenth and fifteenth amendments were adopted to assure expansion of these liberties, particularly with regard to the former slaves, but these amendments were never intended to be used as a sword to slice away the sanctity of the first ten. Most women await the adoption of another amendment that will guarantee their rights to cast the ballot, and this will happen, but in the meantime the Bill of Rights stands as the guardian of our other liberties."

Cam found himself mesmerized by Serena Belmont's voice and the clarity of her thinking and her manner of expression. There was no shrillness in her speech, and the words flowed like honey off her tongue. Sitting in the furthest pew from the pulpit, he could clearly hear every word. His eyes wandered over the audience and observed that the other attendees were equally hypnotized. It occurred to him there had been no applause, and he realized the listeners were so caught up in her words they had not thought to applaud. Also, she did not utilize the techniques of many other speakers of delivering so called "applause lines" or inserting the poignant pause signaling for audience response.

He checked his pocket watch. She had been speaking for nearly forty-five minutes but it seemed half of that, and he wanted to hear more—but of course that was how an effective speaker wanted to leave the audience.

"The Bill of Rights is not, as de Tocqueville said, an endlessly expanding list of rights: the 'right' to education, the 'right' to medical care, the 'right' to food and housing. That's not freedom; that's dependency. Those aren't rights; those are the rations of slavery . . . hay and a barn for human cattle. Democracy is not freedom. As I remarked earlier, the mob is the purest form of democracy: a majority of the moment deciding, for whatever reason, who will die and why. The Bill of Rights is the last line of defense from the tyranny of kings and other ruling despots, and, yes, in America, sometimes from an irrational and unthinking majority. Thank you."

Serena stepped down from the pulpit and returned to her seat, as the small audience stood in unison and applauded. She rose from her chair and waved and smiled and the applause continued.

As he joined the standing ovation, the thought passed through Cam's mind that he had just heard and watched someone who could quickly take command of a stage shared with any speaker in America. She was indeed a force to be reckoned with.

Cam waited in the rear of the sanctuary while audience members slowly filed out. Serena remained on the stage, surrounded by half a dozen women who were engaged in animated dialogue with her. He wished they would get the hell on their ways. Waiting was not his forte.

Finally, the group of admirers dissipated, and Serena gathered up her things and prepared to depart. She looked up when Cam had nearly reached the stage. She smiled brightly and stepped down with hand outstretched to greet him. "Cameron Locke, I presume." Her statement was not a question.

He accepted her hand, and was mildly surprised by her firm grip. Somewhat taken aback by her instant recognition of him, he replied, "How did you know who I am?"

She stepped back and seemed to be appraising him. "It took me a moment when I first caught sight of you at the back of the church, but I was quite certain you were a Locke. Then when you came down the aisle, and I saw the eyes, that confirmed it."

"My eyes?"

"Yes, I've seen them before. Steel gray, always searching and not missing a thing."

"I don't recall we've met."

"We haven't. But I encountered your brother some years ago."

"Ian?"

"Thaddeus. But enough of that. I'm hungry and I'm tired. It's nearly six o'clock. Would you be my guest for dinner . . . or is it supper here?"

A woman buying him dinner? This was too strange. "It's usually supper if we're eating at home but dinner if we're eating out. Don't ask me to explain the logic. And, yes, I'd be pleased to join you."

"I suggest the Worthington Inn. It's near my hotel. I have a rented horse and buggy in front of the church. If you're on horseback, perhaps, you can tie your horse behind and join me in the buggy."

36

THE WORTHINGTON INN was an elegant, and Cam surmised, expensive, dining establishment. The maître d' had instantly recognized Serena and escorted them to a corner table that afforded considerable privacy. It was ironic, Cam thought, that there were eating places in Topeka that would have denied service to a colored woman, and here she was treated as royalty. Casting his eyes about the dining area, he observed several Negro couples eating at another table. Serena obviously staked out her eating places carefully, with an eye toward avoiding incidents.

He dined on a huge steak and fried potatoes, but despite the fact Serena had earlier claimed to be hungry, she picked at the half-serving she had ordered, and in the glow of the new electric lighting —that had not yet arrived Manhattan—she looked a bit drawn and gaunt. Traveling across the country by rail and sleeping in a different bed every night would be wearing, he guessed.

"How long have you been with the Society?" Cam asked, deciding it was time to abandon the small talk.

"A little over six years. Immediately after being admitted to the bar I learned there was a vacancy in the general counsel's position, and a law professor of mine at Howard lobbied very hard for me to get the position. I had been enraptured by Bill of Rights cases during law school, and my writings on the subject intrigued several members of the board. The Society has several wealthy benefactors, and, fortunately, the position pays well . . . and I am permitted to take private cases from time to time as long as they are not inconsistent with the Society's purposes."

"You have very impressive credentials. And when I watched you this afternoon, I concluded you could choose to do anything that suited you and you would be successful at it."

"Thank you." She hesitated, and her dark eyes bore in on his. "Was I auditioning this afternoon? Is that why you were there?"

Cam smiled. "Not exactly. I am interested in the work of your organization. But I was curious. I admit I would not have made the trip if you had not written to my father about a position. And I think he has notified you that we have a case where you might be of some help to us."

"Yes. But I'm not sure I can be away from my Washington office that long. Tell me about the case."

Cam gave Serena a nutshell version of the case, carefully explaining his family dilemma with some of the key witnesses. When he was finished, Serena looked thoughtful.

"It sounds to me like you've got a guilty client, but it is second degree, not first."

"She's charged with first degree, and there is at least one witness to establish motive. And in hindsight she made some very foolish statements."

"So what would you expect of me?"

"You would be my co-counsel. With my sponsorship the district judge will allow your appearance in the Kansas courts. This is quite common. We'll agree on strategy together. You would definitely need to handle the testimony of my wife and brother . . . perhaps another witness or two, if we agree your examination would be more effective. You will be paid your usual hourly rate for the case."

"No," she replied, "your client can't afford my usual rate. I'll be satisfied with your rate . . . if I decide to get involved."

"And when can we expect a decision?"

"After I meet with the accused. I plan to take the train to Manhattan the day after tomorrow . . . I have a meeting tomorrow afternoon with some Society donors. I should arrive in Manhattan before noon and will dine with my family. After that I will go to your office and meet with you and your father about the possibility of a position."

"You can meet with the Judge. You and I have already talked, and I can assure you that it's just a matter of coming to terms. You will have the Judge eating out of the palm of your hand."

"The Judge. That's the term the children use to reference your father, but you don't really call him that in direct conversation with him, do you?"

"You seem to know more about the Lockes than we know about you."

"It depends on the Locke." She smiled wistfully.

"You said you met my brother, Thad. When did you do that, may I ask?"

"A long time ago, more than ten years. I injured my ankle, and he patched it up and gave me a ride home."

"That's Thad alright. Always looking after injured strays." He had a feeling there was more to this story, but it wasn't his business.

"Anyway, after I meet with your father, I would like to confer with the client. I will inform you of my decision after I have met with her. When do you expect the trial to commence?"

"Monday, the week after next. The evidence is pretty straightforward. I'd say a day to empanel a jury. Two or three days trial . . . and then the wait for a verdict."

"This is Saturday. That would allow almost two weeks to prepare . . . if I take this on. Not much time, but it would allow me to get back to Washington sooner, and I assume you've laid most of the groundwork."

37

MYLES LOCKE HAD been forewarned by Cam that Serena Belmont would quickly overpower him with her forthrightness, charm and verbal skills. He knew that Serena had leaped over any barriers when Reva nodded approvingly as she showed the young woman into Myles's private office.

The young lady sitting across the desk from him was self-assured and confident and did not seem the least nervous. On the other hand, why should someone who had argued cases before the highest court in the land be intimidated by an old, worn-out country lawyer?

"Well, Miss Belmont," Myles said, "your reputation precedes you. I must tell you that you made quite an impression on Cam."

"Thank you, and, please, call me 'Serena.'"

"Very well. And I'm 'Myles'"

"That doesn't seem right somehow."

"Why? Because I'm an old codger?" He chuckled.

"No, no. It just seems disrespectful. You're not old . . . you're distinguished."

"Distinguished? Now I like that. Try to convince Cam . . . especially about the respect part. Call me what you are comfortable with. Anyway, let's talk about the position. Why you wish to associate with our firm ordinarily would not be my concern, but given your credentials and current position, your interest baffles me."

"Your office is highly respected by other lawyers and judges in the state. I've made inquiries."

"That's nice to hear, but you obviously thrive in the courtroom. I have an office practice . . . business, real estate, wills, estate settlements and that sort of thing. Cam has an active trial practice, but the consistent bread and butter is on my side of the practice, and given my age, we are probably under more pressure to find a potential successor for me."

"Cam says you'll be here at your desk when you're ninety, and that you still work him into the ground."

Myles shook his head from side to side. "Cam refuses to accept my mortality, because his greatest fear is that if I drop dead he'll be stuck behind a desk . . . and there's not much of an audience there. But seriously, Serena, we'd love to have you join us if we can reach financial terms."

"I would like to be paid fifty percent of my gross collected billings. The rest goes to overhead you and your partner split . . . I wouldn't share in that, of course. I'll have to give up my full-time position with the Bill of Rights Society, but I think they would keep me on their speakers' bureau and would refer selected cases. Any fees from these sources would be shared with the firm the same way."

"You're more than fair. The way you present it, we have absolutely nothing to lose by taking you on, and, if it works out for all of us, we can look at partnership later. Of course, we'd be honored to have you associate with our firm. When do you think you would be able to start?"

"Six to eight months. I have to wind down my affairs and pending cases with the Society. Of course, I may help Cam with one case immediately, depending on the outcome of my meeting with his client. I'm not committed yet."

"That's what Cam told me. It's your decision, and it has no bearing on the agreement we just made."

"Thank you. But we have not reached a final agreement yet. There is more you are entitled to know, before you make a final decision ... and, if you are willing, I need your help as an attorney."

"This is growing very mysterious."

"I will solve the mystery for you quickly. First, I must inform you that I have an illness."

He noticed that her composure was crumbling a bit, and tears glistened in her eyes. "Tell me what you wish. I'm listening."

"For nearly two years now, have been having what I call 'spells' where I will have a week, sometimes two, of nausea, occasionally followed by vomiting. I have a raging fever during these spells and have lost consciousness a few times. Severe headaches are often a warning of a forthcoming siege. I pretty much force myself to eat most of the time, but I will feel quite well for several months following a spell ... until it strikes again."

"And you've seen a physician?"

"Four of them now. They can't tell me anything. Several have diagnosed it as consumption and told me there is no cure. One told me I could live many years with this and that it might just suddenly go away one day. That's what I would like to believe, of course."

"Understandably."

"I am often tired, but I can usually put in a good day's work. I have to manage my time carefully, though, and allocate my energy where it's most needed. This is why I wouldn't commit to Cam's client. I have to decide if this is a person I am willing to devote my time and energy to."

"None of this makes any difference to your position here. You would control your own workload, and the firm is not affected financially if you choose to work less. I fully understand now why you need to give up your current position. We can hope that a more manageable work schedule would speed up your recovery. Regardless, it would be good for you to be near your family."

He could see the tension rising in her as they spoke. Her hands were trembling now. His heart went out to the young woman.

"There is something else," she said. "And I am afraid you are going to hate me for this. I am taking a terrible risk in telling you, and I can only beg you not to repeat it until you have helped me work out a way to deal with my dilemma."

She was falling apart in front of him. "Trust me," he said.

She bit her lip and then suddenly blurted, "I have a son. His name is Edward Thaddeus Locke. Thad is his father, but Thad doesn't know about him."

Serena had certainly captured his undivided attention. It took him several moments to sort out her words. Serena Belmont was the mother of his grandson. "Okay, that was quite a mouthful of information, and I must confess I'm having a little trouble carrying my part of our conversation. Let's just unwind this slowly. Thad is the father of your child. How old is the boy . . . Edward?"

"Ned, I call him 'Ned,'" she replied, her lips quivering. "He's almost ten. He was born April 20, 1875, a few weeks early, I think, but he's big for his age now." She looked up and met his eyes, showing faint traces of a smile. "And he's smart as a whip."

"That doesn't surprise me somehow. So, if my math skills serve me correctly, you . . . uh, encountered Thad in the summer of 1874."

"I was visiting my parents for the summer. I let it slip to Cam that I had known Thad. I told Cam I had injured my ankle when I was running, and Thad came along and rescued me, so to speak. That much is true. That's all Cam knows. But after that Thad and I became friends and fell in love . . . or thought we did. Thad wanted me to marry him, but I decided I wanted more than that. I wanted my education, and more than anything else, I dreamed of being a lawyer. I know I hurt him deeply when I left. I didn't know about the baby at that time, of course."

"And Thad never had a clue?"

"No, I planned to tell him after the baby was born, but I lived with my aunt, and she helped me care for him. The way I looked at it, Thad would just complicate things. I knew what I wanted. He'd insist on getting married, and if I wouldn't, he would have moved to Washington so he could be a part of Ned's life. Am I wrong?"

"No, it sounds like you did know Thad. His middle name should have been 'Responsible.' Still, don't you think he was entitled to know . . . to make his own decision?"

"Yes, I was wrong. I always knew that. My mother told me I was wrong and once threatened to tell Thad, before she decided it wasn't her place. I kept telling myself I would tell him next year, and next year would arrive, and I'd say next year. Well, I guess next year is here."

"It appears so."

"My health problems made me realize that Ned needs to know his father, and that I need to be near my family for his sake. My aunt's health is frail, and if something happens to me, she won't be able to care for Ned. It's time for him to see another way of life."

"So when do you plan to tell Thad?"

"Before I return to Washington, but if I choose to help Cam with the trial, I'll wait till that's over. Neither Thad nor I need the additional turmoil the news would bring in the middle of a trial."

"I cannot argue with that."

"Can you help me with legal arrangements for Ned, just in case —" He could see she was struggling with her composure, and he got out of his chair and walked around to the other side of the desk. She looked up at him, and he stretched out his arms. She rose and buried her head in his chest as his arms folded about her and held her close until her tears stopped flowing. Finally, she stepped back, but his hands still gently clasped her shoulders. "Where are you staying?" he asked.

"My bags are in your reception area. I have to find a hotel yet. Papa gave me the name of one that welcomes colored folks. My parents wanted me to go out to their place, but I want to meet with Cam's client early in the morning, and I thought it would be easier if I stayed in town. I promised I would visit at the farm Sunday and decide on accommodations then. If I'm working on the case, though, I won't stay there. I will need to be near the office and the client."

"Forget the hotel. You'll stay at my home while you're here. We have several spare bedrooms. I have a . . . uh, housekeeper, Vedette Joliet, and the two of you will get along famously, I promise. She's very wise, and I hope you will let me share the story of our little dilemma with her. We all need to talk this out together. We can discuss your legal concerns after you've settled in."

38

SERENA FELT BETTER this morning than she had for weeks. Maybe there was something in the clean Kansas air that would heal her ailing body. It was a nice thought, although she did not believe it for a moment. But she had found some peace last night, gathered into the bosom of Myles Locke's modest home, and it felt right. She had loved Vedette instantly and had been surprised to find she was a colored woman like herself. Vedette's skin might have been a shade darker than her own, but they shared the sense of dislocation that went with being not quite light-skinned enough for those whites who cared and not black enough to avoid suspicion by some darker skinned persons with whom they shared the arbitrary designation of "colored" or "Negro."

The easy rapport between Vedette and Myles Locke quickly made it clear they were not employer and employee. It was very unlikely an ordinary housekeeper would share her boss's bed with a guest settled in the house. It was obvious these two were friends and lovers, and, as Vedette told Serena, they had shared the home for some twenty-five years. Was this why Myles seemed so unfazed by the information his son had fathered a child with a colored woman? She decided it had more to do with the fact that Myles Locke always expected the unexpected. And the Judge was not a judgmental man. It didn't matter to her. She was totally comfortable staying with Myles and Vedette. Myles had even told her she was family now, since she was the mother of his grandson. That had brought her nearly to tears again.

It was Tuesday, and Myles was already at work. Vedette was acquainted with Serena's mother, Rachael, and had offered to take Serena out to her parents' farm in the buggy this afternoon and support her in explaining the need to stay in town during the course of the trial—if Serena decided to participate. That would be known before they left Manhattan.

Vedette had shopping to attend to this morning and had dropped Serena off at the office, where she had agreed to meet Cam. While she waited, Myles led her to a vacant office furnished only with a small oak desk and a straight-backed chair. "We'll have more suitable furnishings in place when you return from Washington," he assured her.

"I just need a place to work. Truly, I don't require anything fancy."

"Fancy won't happen, but Reva will delight in digging up functional."

He also showed her the small, narrow library, its walls lined from floor to ceiling with law books. A rectangular table surrounded by half a dozen chairs stood in the room's center. "This room doubles as a conference or meeting area," he explained.

Cam arrived and she joined him on a brisk walk to the jail. She found her breathing a bit labored and remembered those days when she raced through the Flint Hills without so much as a pause to catch her breath.

As they arrived at the jailhouse, Cam said, "I'm going to introduce you to Kirsten . . . she's expecting you . . . and then I'm going to get the hell out. You need to talk woman to woman."

"I would like that."

"I'm going to go back to the office and look at the jury pool list. Reva sneaked one from the court clerk yesterday afternoon."

"Is that ethical?"

"You can bet the county attorney's got his greasy paws on it already. Anyway, I want the Judge to take a gander at it. He knows everybody in Riley County. We'll all talk about the prospective jurors the first of the week . . . assuming you're with us on this."

Serena noted that Cam had not answered her question. She decided she would avoid asking Cam too many questions about his information sources. She would likely be well-advised not to know the answers.

They entered the sheriff's office. A friendly young man was on duty and escorted them down the walkway between the cells to the end of the long hall. Serena didn't notice any other occupants, so they should enjoy some privacy. Kirsten Cavelle was standing at the cell door, clothed in something that looked like baggy pajamas. Serena was struck by her unusual height, and it made her aware of her own diminutive stature. The woman's pallid face was marred by a few scars and bruises, but she would "clean up good," as her father used to say. Most men would find her quite attractive, but short of stunning, she thought.

The deputy unlocked the door. "I'll get another chair from the next cell," he said. "You need one, Cam?"

"No, I won't be sticking around, but thanks." He spoke to Kirsten. "This is the lawyer I was telling you about, Kirsten. I'm going to leave the two of you to talk. It's kind of a mutual interview. When you're done, Kirsten can let me know if she wants to bring on Serena as a lawyer, and Serena will decide if she wants to be involved in the case."

Serena took a pace forward and offered her hand to Kirsten who clasped it so firmly, it stung. A cowgirl thing, she supposed. Cam and the deputy disappeared, leaving the cell door wide open. Evidently, Kirsten was not considered much of a flight risk.

Kirsten stepped aside and gestured for Serena to be seated at the table. "Welcome to my humble abode," she said, her face expressionless.

They each slipped into a chair and faced each other across the table. Serena noticed that Kirsten's eyes were studying her face intently. "What is it?" Serena asked.

"I've seen you before."

"Perhaps a newspaper photograph?"

"That's it . . . a photograph. It was a tintype on Doc's wall."

"I'm afraid I'm not following you."

"I'm sorry. I was in Thad Locke's office and looked at a collection of tintypes on his wall. You were the subject of several, and I might add that the tintypes . . . and the subject . . . were stunningly beautiful. The subject and the photographer obviously had a special relationship. I'm sorry. I just had no idea the lawyer I would be meeting was the girl in the tintype. I'll shut my mouth now."

Serena returned a wistful smile, appreciating that Kirsten had quickly closed the subject. "We need to discuss your case. Together we should decide if I can be helpful. If you are not comfortable with my participation, then I board the train and return to Washington. If I conclude I cannot make a contribution, I take the same train. Let me say this: you are represented by a very fine lawyer, and he will fight for you with every tool at his disposal. He is not too proud to accept help if he thinks it might be useful in winning your case. I like him and respect him."

"So, what do you need to know from me?"

To the point. Serena liked that. "Cam has told me about the facts of your case in some detail. I've viewed the tintypes Dr. Locke produced. You were brutalized by your husband. I failed to ask, though, were the beatings frequent occurrences?"

"No, he had only beaten me one other time . . . about two months earlier. That's when I decided to see Cam Locke about a divorce. He threatened many other times over the past year, and after the beating, I told him to leave."

"And what was his reaction?"

"He laughed and said I could leave. I reminded him I owned the place, which only made things worse, because this was always a point of contention between us. I do understand that to a man like Max this was a bitter pill. To him, a woman had her place, and it wasn't running a ranch."

"So it would be fair to say you didn't love him?"

"Not since our first year. I can talk to you more easily about this than I can with Cam, I guess. Our attraction was pretty much all physical, and early on we about humped each other's brains out. Then he seemed to tire of me and would be gone without explanation for several nights at a time and come home drunk. The drinking worsened, and I wasn't naïve enough to think that a young male who was gone a few days and didn't come home horny wasn't fence jumping to other pastures. It stung, and I wouldn't let myself believe it for a while. I had been thinking divorce for more than a year, but I couldn't prove grounds until he beat me."

The women spoke about the couple's marital history at length, and Serena found herself feeling a kind of sadness for both of them. They were a mismatch for an enduring life together, having little in common beyond the initial passion of young love. "I want to talk about the night Maxwell died." Serena said.

"Certainly, that's why I'm sitting here."

"I've been told about the beatings and how he drug you into the bedroom and savagely attacked you there. I've seen the tintypes, and it will be difficult for anyone to deny the harm he did to you. Cam was very wise to arrange for the photographs so quickly, and they are very persuasive."

Kirsten replied, "Good photographer, don't you think?"

Serena looked at her. Kirsten had a straight face, but her eyes were teasing Serena a bit. She ignored the question. "There are several things I want to explore with you. First, there is a little segment of time no one has been able to fill me in on that seems very important to me. But before we talk about it, can we agree that I am one of your attorneys for the duration of our meeting? This is necessary to ensure confidentiality of our conversation."

"You're on the payroll. Dun me for your time."

"The segment of time I'm interested in is the period between the assault in your bed and the time you sent your dog for your hired man."

"Chet."

"Yes, Chet. I believe Chet will testify that you told him Max had 'died.' That seems a strange way to state it. 'He died.' It sounds like he died of a disease or a heart attack or some natural cause."

"Well, I knew he was dead."

"How did you know?"

"I just knew."

"Did you know he had been shot?"

"Not at that time."

"You're confusing me. Are you saying you didn't kill your husband?"

"I'm saying I don't remember it. I assume I did. I was the only one there. Who else could have done it? I remember wanting to kill him."

"You don't recall pulling a gun from a holster and taking it into the bedroom and pulling the trigger and shooting your husband?"

"I'm sure I did it. I just don't remember it."

"I'll have to think about that. There is another item I want to discuss with you. Cam has explained that you cannot be forced to testify at the trial?"

"Yes. I've left that decision to him. He hasn't said what he's going to do."

"Are you afraid to testify?"

"No. I'd just tell the truth, but Cam says it's very risky."

"It can also be risky not to in a case like yours. You are the only witness who was there when it all happened. If you don't testify, you allow everybody to use their imaginations. Much of the jury's decision depends upon how believable you would be . . . frankly, how much the jury would like you. I'll be blunt, Cam says you can talk somewhat on the rough side on occasion, that you show some temper."

"He's worried I'll cuss up a storm."

"He'd like to see you appear less independent, more conciliatory."

"More like a helpless woman?"

Serena smiled. "Stinks, doesn't it?"

"Have you heard me cuss today?"

"No."

"I was raised with six brothers. Talk was on the profane side sometimes when we worked cattle. But my dad saw that I was taught appropriateness . . . not to swear in front of children or in social situations. My instincts guide me pretty well. You may assure Cam I won't embarrass him in the courtroom. I'll behave like a lady . . . I'll even dress like one if they'll let me."

"They'll let you. Cam will see to that. Kirsten . . . it's okay if I call you 'Kirsten'?"

"Of course."

"And I'm Serena. I'm going to inform Cam that I'm willing to assist with your case. You can think about it and let Cam know if you want me to help defend you."

"No need to wait. I want you to represent me. I very much want you to."

Serena reached her hand across the table. Kirsten extended hers and they sealed the deal with a handshake.

"One final thing," Kirsten said. "I'm trying to be brave about this . . . stiff upper lip and that sort of thing. But I'm absolutely scared shitless."

39

VEDETTE JOLIET HANDLED the reins as the one-horse buggy bounced over the rocky road that carved its way north through the Flint Hills. Serena relaxed beside her, savoring the soft breeze that caressed her face and taking in the limestone-sprinkled hills that were cloaked with tallgrass prairie just starting to awaken from a winter's slumber.

After visiting with Kirsten, Serena had stopped at the Locke office to inform Cam she was on the defense team. She had been mildly surprised to find his reaction ecstatic. She had wondered earlier if his seeking her out had been born more from a sense of client obligation than a desire to share the stage. He did not seem like a man who easily surrendered the leading role. On the other hand, she admitted, she did not so easily reject public attention herself. There might be some friendly competition between them, but that could be fun, and, channeled properly, it could work to their client's advantage.

Cam had chided himself for not having previously uncovered Kirsten's possible absence of memory regarding Max's actual killing. He was skeptical of their client's claim. Serena was inclined to believe her. Regardless, Serena had pointed out Kirsten's testimony was the only way to raise the issue. And would Kirsten's story make a difference in the outcome, especially when weighed against the risk of putting her on the witness stand? And was the story just a bit too convenient? They had agreed they would meet Sunday afternoon to review the jury pool list with Myles and to further discuss strategy.

She turned to Vedette, "I'm sorry, I haven't been very good company . . . lost in thought, I guess."

"That's quite alright, dear," Vedette replied. "Myles and I are quiet people. Sometimes we're in the sitting room for several hours at a time reading or visiting someplace in our minds before one of us breaks the silence. I just draw on the comfort of his nearness."

"You really love him, don't you?"

"More than life."

"How long have you been together?"

"Nearly twenty-three years now. I was almost thirty years old when I arrived in Kansas. It was in the middle of the War of Rebellion. I was raised in Louisiana. My father was a former slave who had purchased his freedom . . . you could do that near New Orleans. My mother's family were free Negroes who had owned land for several generations and were quite well to do by standards of the colored community." She smiled and shook her head from side to side. "There was some debate in the family about whether we were really white folks, since under the old French law, if you were an octoroon . . . only one-eighth Negro . . . you were really white. Our blood was so mixed up with Indians and French and Spaniards and English, we didn't know what we were. It was very complicated."

"You were purebred mongrels. That's what someone told me once about mixed blooded people."

Vedette laughed. "That sounds like something Myles would say. I suppose we were that. But enough of the Negro showed through on my skin, I had to be careful because I'd be a suspected slave. There were some who were known to capture free Negroes and take them to slave auctions in other parts of the state or Mississippi or Alabama. Anyway, my father died a half dozen years before the war, and my mother sold their small land holdings for gold coin. I lived with her, teaching at free Negro schools ... it was against the law to teach slaves to read, of course . . . and was well on my way to becoming a spinster school teacher when the war came along. My mother was always a frail woman, and she suffered from some kind of breathing ailment that finally took her after the war started. In the days before she died she insisted that when she was gone, I should find my way to a free state. She said it was too dangerous for me to stay there without the protection of family ... and she was the last of mine. So when she passed, I decided Kansas was the safest, shortest journey to safety for me."

"And how did you meet Myles Locke?"

"Well, when I arrived in Kansas, I didn't have any teaching credentials or anything to prove I could read or write. It likely wouldn't have mattered much. While the Free Staters were anti-slavery, many had their notions of where colored folks belonged in society ... maids, tenant farmers, laborers and the like. I didn't take it as a malicious thing ... mostly ignorance. I'm sure you've had to deal with that."

"Yes, and I usually just shrug it off to that ... ignorance. That allows me to laugh about it on occasion, but not always."

"Anyway, I bought the town paper and saw an advertisement for a live-in housekeeper. I thought, well now, that would solve two of my problems ... a job and a roof over my head. I went to Myles's office and presented myself. He was instantly easy to talk to. I learned he was a widower whose two small children were being primarily raised by his late wife's sister, but they were also frequently a part of his household. Since I had been a schoolteacher, I didn't find that too intimidating. He struck me as a kind man. I was a little wary about living in a house with a single man . . . maybe I was just wary of me. He had grown sons who were off to war . . . one on each side, strangely . . . so he was some years older than I, but he was not quite fifty, and I thought him very vital and handsome."

"And he offered you the job on the spot?"

"Yes. And our relationship was very chaste and proper for over a year . . . or on the surface it was. But I was in love with him most of that year, crying myself to sleep some nights, thinking this was a man I could never have, whose life I could never share. Evenings, when he came home from work, he made me feel welcome in the sitting room . . . the house didn't have a housekeeper's quarters other than my separate bedroom. We sat and read like we do now, but sometimes we talked and gradually shared our histories and began telling each other things we'd never told anyone else. You understand what I'm saying?"

"Certainly. You became friends."

"Yes, and one night it suddenly became more, and after that I only returned to my room when his young children were staying in the house. Now I never leave his side."

"You obviously love each other. Did you ever want more?"

"You mean marriage? He asks me at least twice a year, but I have always resisted. It's probably assumed in his social circles that I'm his mistress, but it's not too scandalous to have a colored lover. A Negro wife, however, is quite a different matter."

"But Kansas hasn't had anti-miscegenation laws since before statehood. It is perfectly legal for you to marry."

"There are still unwritten laws in polite society. The Free Staters opposed slavery, but that didn't mean they all condoned marriage between the races. I just have never seen any reason to make Myles the subject of scurrilous gossip and, perhaps, malicious acts. But who knows? Times change, and I might change my mind, too."

"You're devoting your life to someone, but when he dies, you'll have none of the property rights of a spouse."

"I'll be fine. I don't need much. I still have my mother's gold coins. Myles has made me the beneficiary of his will, so I'd have the house and what other meager assets he's accumulated . . . country lawyers don't get rich. Myles works not only because he loves to, but because he needs to earn a living."

"But you really have everything, don't you?"

"We do."

"I've made money in my short career, and I already have a nice nest egg set aside, largely because a certain man convinced me to invest my earnings in railroad stocks and Thomas Edison's company." She shrugged. "But my son is my real treasure. And I wonder sometimes what life would have been like if I had married his father and tried to build a life in the Flint Hills . . . wondered, mind you, because I have had an unbelievable life. I am what I had to be."

"And no time for love?"

"There has been one man since Thad. I loved him, and I would have married him."

"But?"

"He was a dynamic business man . . . a speculator or entrepreneur, depending on your perspective. Ezekiel brokered cotton and corn for hundreds of Negro tenant farmers and took his commissions and invested in real estate and other businesses. This incredibly handsome man with flawless ebony skin contacted me because he wanted to hire a colored lawyer, and one of the professors from the law school referred him to me. I helped him set up a few business partnership arrangements, but in a matter of a few weeks he swept me off my feet. He traveled a lot and so did I, of course, so we could only get together when we were both in Washington . . . but when we did . . . need I say more?"

The women looked at each other, and both broke into naughty smiles and rolled their eyes.

"It's none of my business, but I've got to ask . . . what happened?"

"This went on for almost two years, and I had evolved to the point where I thought I would be willing to marry this man, until I received a visit at my office."

"A visit?"

"His wife. A very pretty young woman my age. It seems they had a home in northern Virginia not far from Washington. Some of his so-called business trips were to visit his wife and two children. She was pregnant with a third. She had a cousin who worked as a maid at the hotel where we often rendezvoused. Ezekiel had no idea she worked there. Anyway, the cousin wrote to the wife, and I endured a very unpleasant confrontation. I never saw him again."

"I'm sorry."

"Don't be. It wouldn't have happened if I had known about the wife, but I wouldn't erase those two years from my mind if I could." She paused. "Sometimes we can't scrub the bad out of our heads without washing away the good. I choose to remember fondly the wonderful times we shared and just consider his treachery another lesson learned. I've never had time to hold onto anger long enough for it to eat me up."

40

IT WAS LATE afternoon, and Vedette, Rachael and Serena relaxed in the kitchen, taking coffee and enjoying a small platter of ginger cookies with apple slices that Rachael had placed on the table. Their conversation was superficially relaxed and casual, but Serena noted the worry creases on her mother's forehead and in the soft flesh at the corners of her eyes.

"What is it, Mama?" she asked.

"I'm fine. It's nothing."

"You've never fibbed well, Mama. Say what you've got to say. Vedette knows everything."

"Everything?"

"Yes, she knows about Ned and my illness . . . everything."

Rachael sighed. "Very well, I might as well say it: I wish you weren't taking on this case. I'm afraid it's too much, and you should get home to Ned."

"Mama, I'm feeling fine right now, and this is my first opportunity with my new firm. Aren't you glad I'm coming home? And as for Ned, this means I won't have to travel all the time. I'll have more time with him . . . and he'll have you and the whole family."

Rachael reached across the table and clutched her daughter's hand. "I'm thrilled you're coming home. I just wish you were coming because you truly wanted to be here, not because you feel you have to."

Serena had no answer.

"And," Rachael continued, "you haven't told Thad about Ned, have you?"

"No, he's an important witness at the trial. I will be handling his examination. That may frustrate him enough when he finds out. I can't risk telling him about Ned until the trial's over. But he will know before I return to Washington."

"I'm afraid of what he'll say," Rachael said. "He asks about you, and I just tell him you're doing fine and that I can't say more. But I feel like I've been a part of a terrible plot to deceive him."

"I know, Mama. I've been wrong. I've known that for a long time. And I've lied to my son. This is a terrible burden I've placed on too many people. And I've got to make this right before—"

Serena felt Vedette's arm wrap around her shoulders. "Don't worry too much about Thad's reaction. I think you're right not to upset him now. But he is his father's son in temperament, more than any of the other boys. He'll be hurt and angry, but he won't go into a rage. He'll more likely go quiet and brood some and then think about it for a spell. After that he'll want to help do what's best for the boy."

"He is a good man, Serena," Rachael said.

"I never doubted that."

She turned to Vedette. "We need to be heading back to town if we want to get back before dark."

"I won't argue with that," Rachael said, "I worry about the two of you being out there on the road. The races get along pretty well here, but there are still a few I wouldn't trust if they came across a couple of unescorted colored women."

Serena reached into her bag which sat on the floor next to her chair. She smiled when she saw the astonished look on her mother's face when she displayed the pistol she had plucked out. "You have nothing to worry about, Mama. This is our escort."

"A pistol? Since when did you start carrying a gun?"

"Since I finished law school. Washington is not the safest place for a young woman and I travel to cities where I might not be welcomed. This is a Smith & Wesson Second Model .38, sometimes called a 'Baby Russian' and I know how to use it. I target practice quite regularly, and I'm quite competent with the weapon, if I say so myself."

"You left me speechless."

"Just know that I can take care of myself if the need arises."

"I pray to God it doesn't."

The kitchen door opened, and Quincy Belmont barged in from the mud porch. His eyes fastened on the gun and then he looked at Serena who met his astonished stare evenly. He turned toward Rachael. "I've got a serious problem. That pen of new Duroc gilts . . . I've got some sick ones. I'd say one's near dead. I've saddled up Rusty and sent Elizabeth over to Dr. Locke's to fetch him over. I thought I should tell you."

Quincy made a hasty retreat out the door. Serena put her gun away, and pushed her chair away from the table. "We'd better be on our way, Mama. I prefer not to meet up with Thad here. I'll be working on trial preparation this next week, but if you come to town stop by the offices and we can talk some more."

41

THAD WAS DEEPLY concerned when, during their ride to the Belmont farm, Elizabeth, who clearly was committed to becoming a veterinary surgeon, told him about the crisis, precisely describing the symptoms shown by the ailing porkers—skin lesions, insatiable thirst, diarrhea. The dying gilt was convulsing. Elizabeth had explained that her father hauled ten Duroc gilts with his team and paneled freighter from the Manhattan railroad depot several days earlier. They were to be seed stock for a purebred herd he wanted to establish to sell breeding animals in addition to the market hogs he sold and slaughtered. He had acquired a prime Duroc boar a few weeks earlier that would service the virginal Duroc females in addition to selected market sows and gilts. A tough life, Thad thought.

Duroc boars sired long, heavily muscled progeny, and were favored by many hog producers for cross-breeding. According to Elizabeth, the always savvy Quincy Belmont figured to cash in on the new demand for the red boars as more land became cultivated in the river and valley bottomlands, and farmers started small swine herds as "mortgage lifters" to provide a steady income when crops burned up or grain prices faltered. Quincy's monopoly in butcher hogs would be fading over the next few years, and he planned to increasingly shift to selling breeding stock, keeping only enough market animals to supply his own meat processing operation.

Dusk was coming on when they arrived at the Belmont farm, and Thad could see Quincy's shadowy profile standing next to a board fence some distance north of the outbuilding site, a flickering kerosene lantern at his feet. Thad removed his saddlebags and tossed them over his shoulder, and Elizabeth took charge of Cato. Such a special young woman, he thought, beautiful and intelligent like her sister and not the least full of herself. Like Serena, she knew what she wanted and she'd be off to Iowa State Agricultural College for a real veterinary education in a few years. He'd bet on it. He hoped the Kansas State Agricultural College in Manhattan, like Iowa State, a land grant institution, would establish a veterinary program soon.

As he approached Quincy, Thad thought he had never seen the taciturn man so outright grim. "Good evening, Reverend. Elizabeth says you have some sick gilts."

"Yes, Doctor. One's died since Elizabeth left for your place. At least two others are coming down with the sickness."

Thad leaned on the fence, his eyes studying the young hogs that moved listlessly in the close confines. Elizabeth's description had been flawless. Some of the animals competing aggressively at the water trough indicated that at least a few were suffering high fevers. Another pig in a corner of the pen was in agony with convulsions. Then he noticed the dead pig had been dragged from the pen and lay just outside of it on the other side of Quincy.

"I can't keep them in water," Quincy said.

"Reverend, I need to post the dead one. That may answer some questions. It'll be dark before I'm done. Can we get some more lanterns down here?"

"I'll tell the girls to gather whatever we can spare. I've got chores to do soon."

"You've been in this pen, I assume."

"Yes, to drag out the dead pig."

"Has anyone else?"

He thought a moment. "No. These are special. I've been looking after these pigs myself."

"I'd like Elizabeth to help us here. Can Rachael and the other girls do chores?"

"Of course. Everybody knows chores around this place."

"Turn the job over to the rest of the family and ask them to stay away from here. Also, would you see if Elizabeth can boil a bucket of water and bring it with her? I'm going to need a few tarps of some kind . . . canvas would be ideal."

Quincy hurried away to issue orders. Thad could tell Quincy was scared. He had never seen the man so obedient and unquestioning. He feared the Reverend had good reason to be frightened. He turned toward the dead gilt and knelt down beside her, running his fingers over the animal's bristly hair, feeling the lesions that marred the tough skin.

Thad got up and looked around, taking note of the location of the other hog pens. He guessed there were at least five large pens dotted with small A-frame hog houses spread over the ground that sloped away from the out buildings—probably about ten sows with litters in each pen. The nearest pen was likely a good 100 feet distant from the one that enclosed the sick hogs. That was positive. Quincy at least had the good sense to keep new stock separate from the old stock until he was ready to introduce them to the herds. Of course, the new gilts were to be the foundation of a purebred herd and likely would not have been commingled with the others in any event. Thad searched his mind. There were no handbooks for something like this. If he was dealing with what he suspected, he was facing a lot of ignorance and would have to rely upon instinct.

Soon Elizabeth appeared with a bucket of water and two more lanterns, and a few minutes later Quincy followed with an armful of canvas tarps. "I use these on the kill floor of the slaughter house," he remarked matter-of-factly.

"Perfect," Thad replied. "Spread one out next to the gilt, and then we'll roll her on top."

In a matter of a few minutes, the two hundred fifty-pound pig was stretched out on the tarp and the lanterns were lighted up to maximum illumination. Thad retrieved his leather packet of surgical knives from the saddle bags and then knelt down again next to the dead gilt. He removed a scalpel that was about half the size of a butcher knife. Darkness was closing in now. "Elizabeth, I want you to hold a lantern over my shoulder, and move it to give me all the light you can while I'm cutting." He looked up at her to see she was staring with wide eyes at the knife in his hand. "Can you do this?" he asked.

"Yes, sir," she replied in a near whisper.

"Good girl." Thad took the knife and sliced open the pig's belly, opening a cavern that framed the animal's internal organs. "What we're doing here is called a post mortem," he explained to Elizabeth, "but vets often call it 'posting.' You can often tell what killed a dead animal by examining the internal organs. This might help us know what to do for the others."

He reached into the mass of organs and clutched the bulging, snake-like intestine, slit it open and spilled the contents of that portion onto the tarp, slopping some of the waste on his trousers in the process. "More light," he mumbled, and the lantern moved closer to his hands, lighting up his workplace considerably. He put down the knife and manipulated the gut between his fingers. "This should be smooth. See all the sores? Some are full of pus."

"What are they called?" Elizabeth asked.

"Ulcerations. Look carefully. They tend to be in clusters." He dropped the intestine on the gilt's sliced belly and looked over his shoulder at Quincy who stood behind him, sober and silent. "It's swine fever," Thad said. "It's also known as hog cholera."

"Oh, no," Quincy moaned. "What can we do?"

"They're likely all going to die. Even if one or two survived, you wouldn't want to mix them with the rest of the herd. Your biggest risk is having the disease spread to your other hogs. That has to be your priority."

"And how do we do that?"

Thad spoke as he got up and washed his scalpel in the bucket and then plucked a bar of lye soap from his saddle bags and scrubbed his hands. "You've heard of it, I know, Quincy. Swine fever's been a scourge for hundreds of years. We're just starting to learn something about the disease . . . but not enough. It's very contagious and can become an epidemic when it strikes a farming community. We need to try to stop it here . . . at this pen. The first thing we do is kill all of these Durocs, sick or not. Tonight. Then we scoop out the manure from the pen and throw it in the pit with the dead animals, before we bury everything. Our shoes and boots should be burned. There's strong evidence the disease gets spread by farmers tracking the manure from a diseased pen to another. I don't have any medications for this. We just have to anticipate anything that might carry the contamination from the sick animals to the others."

"Does this disease live in the soil?"

"I don't know, but I would tear down this pen and never use it again. I'll do some research and see if one of the new chemicals might be applied to the ground. The important thing is that this gets immediate attention."

Quincy said, "I've got a pit down the hill where I've been mining limestone rock for building. It won't hold all of the hogs, but it's a good start. I can widen and deepen it, but it will take time."

"I'll help." Thad turned to Elizabeth. "We'll need shovels and at least one pickaxe . . . a wheel barrow would be useful. Could you scout those up while your father and I do what has to be done?"

"I'll have to get my Winchester," Quincy said.

"I've got an old Army Colt in my saddle bags and enough bullets. I'll do this. Why don't you go on down the hill and see if you can start clearing loose rock out of the pit?"

"But—"

"We don't need two for this. Go ahead."

Thad watched the big man plod away from the pigpen, his shoulders slumped dejectedly, and waited until he disappeared into the darkness before, one by one, he carried out the executions with a single bullet in each brain.

Afterward, he joined Quincy and Elizabeth at the burial pit, and they labored until after sunrise readying the pit, dragging the dead animals to their burial place and covering them. When they were finished, Elizabeth recovered Cato from the horse's guest stall in the barn and led him to his owner. "Saddled and ready to ride," she said.

"Thank you, Elizabeth. You are a remarkable young woman. You'll make a fine veterinary surgeon someday. The work is not always as unhappy as this."

He could see the exhaustion in her face, but she beamed at his words. He turned to Quincy, who had said little the entire night.

"Reverend, I'm sorry. Get ahold of me immediately if you see signs of sickness in any of the other pens. I understand incubation on the disease is about two weeks. If none of the others come down with swine fever in that time, you can rest a bit easier."

Quincy stepped forward and offered his hand. "Please call me 'Quincy.' You're a true friend, Thad, and I will never forget that you fought through this night with us. You may not visit the Lord's house often, but you carry on His work in your own way. Count on me if you ever need a friend." Their eyes met, and Thad nodded. It had not gone unnoticed by him that he had been addressed by his given name, and that Quincy's wariness of him had melted away.

42

CAMERON LOCKE SAT at the library table, studying the thirty-member jury pool list. He expected his father and Serena Belmont to arrive together, since she was staying at his father's house while she was in town. The Judge had obviously taken a liking to the young woman, and Serena was safely nestled under Vedette's protective wing for the duration. That was fine. Vedette would relieve Serena of any responsibilities beyond the trial.

He had spoken only briefly about the case with Serena after her visit with Kirsten Cavelle, but she had shocked him with the suggestion that Kirsten might testify at her trial. This was a rare occurrence and a decision not to be made lightly. He had opened his mind to the idea, though, and was interested to hear Serena's reasoning on that point. He wondered what his father might have to say about it.

He heard a key rattling in the office outer door and the door closing and then footsteps moving his way. Serena appeared in the doorway, and the Judge followed. Serena was attired casually in denim britches—not often worn by city women—and a long-sleeved, turquoise blouse, which he bet had cost a pretty penny. He knew because Pilar did not have cheap tastes, either—nor, he admitted to himself, did he. His father, on this Sunday afternoon, had abandoned his tie, but otherwise casual was absent from his wardrobe.

When they were all seated at the table, Cam said, "I've been going over the jury list and your notes, Dad, but I'd like to talk about something that might have a bearing on our jury preferences." He nodded toward Serena. "You spoke about the possibility of Kirsten testifying at her own trial. I, frankly, had considered this but tossed the idea aside. Convince me."

"First, what evidence can the state put forth? The sheriff and the county attorney arrived at the Cavelle-Brannon home in the midst of a Locke family reunion."

Cam smiled. "Clever. Continue."

"They entered the bedroom and found Max Brannon dead with a bullet hole between his eyes. The prosecutor cannot be sworn as a witness, so that leaves the sheriff to testify that Max was dead. Thad will testify that Max was dead with a wound between his eyes. The county coroner will testify Max was dead and will produce a bullet that is of the same caliber as a pistol in the house and that there was an empty chamber in the revolver. Pilar and Thad and, I guess, the ranch hand will testify that Kirsten admitted Max had died. She did not say she killed him . . . never, as near as I know, did she even state he had been shot. There are zero witnesses other than possibly . . . and I say, *possibly*, the defendant."

"That's true, but the jury can convict without a witness, if the circumstantial evidence weighs heavily enough . . . and there is motive or prior incriminating statements made by the defendant."

Serena replied, "I know how it looks, but I think Kirsten would be a compelling witness, and if she testifies she remembers nothing of any killing, you plant a seed of doubt . . . was someone else there who did the shooting and then escaped? How can you have intent if you don't even remember doing something? There are other places we can take this to chip away at the prosecution's case."

"Frank Fuller is smart as hell. When you put Kirsten on the stand he could twist and turn her testimony to get everything but a confession . . . and maybe even that. And what if she loses her temper? That could kill any sympathy she might garner from the jury."

"I admit there's risk, but this woman is smart and much more in control than you might think. I don't mean this in an evil sense. She's just very thoughtful and capable of doing what she has to do. She can play a role if called upon to do it. I think we risk more by not having her testify."

"You're not suggesting she didn't kill Max?"

"Oh, she probably killed him. It sounds to me like the son of a bitch needed killing."

Cam was taken aback for a moment. "Do you think she's telling the truth . . . that she doesn't remember killing Max?"

"She might be. I don't know. Anyway, I favor Kirsten testifying, but you're in charge; it's your decision. Kirsten will follow our advice."

Cam looked at his father, who had been silent throughout the exchange. As usual, he wore his poker face. "What do you think, Dad? You've met the woman."

"I'm not going to try the case."

"But?"

"I'd have her testify."

Serena had already nearly persuaded Cam that downside risk was minimal. "I'm uneasy about this, but I'm convinced. I'll tell her tomorrow morning to keep thinking about what happened that night. Now let's talk about the jury. Do you know most of the jury pool, Dad?"

Myles nodded, "I don't know them all personally, but most of those I haven't met, I know by reputation."

"Are there some you definitely would not want to see on the jury from Kirsten's standpoint?"

"Gilbert Slade is a violent man . . . he drinks a lot and is a tavern brawler. No proof, but I've heard he's a chronic wife beater."

Cam looked at Serena. "We can strike three without cause. I don't think he'd admit to beating his wife in *voir dire*. Strike?"

Serena nodded in agreement. "Strike."

Myles continued. "There are two known Klan members . . . Jake Coble and Emil Jensik. That doesn't mean there aren't other unknowns, but I don't think it's too likely. There are three colored people in the pool, and a lot of the other names have Free State roots."

"Klan members would likely resent Serena as a defense attorney. Would they admit to Klan membership in open court?"

"No," Myles replied emphatically.

"Regardless," Cam said, "Klan or no Klan, you wouldn't expect these assholes to be open-minded jurors. Are there others we should be particularly wary of?"

"I wrote up a summary on each prospective juror. I had Reva type it up. It's in my office. Approximate age, marital status, education, religion that sort of thing. I've noted those with possible troubled marriages and alcohol problems . . . interestingly, most of the noted persons score on both counts. Now, if you're finished with me, I've got other work on my desk, and I'll take my leave and fetch the list for you."

Myles got up and went down the hall to his office, returning with the summaries. He put it on the table between Cam and Serena and, without a word, departed again.

Serena picked up the notes and began perusing them, as Cam watched silently, his mind racing ahead to the trial. They needed to decide today how the responsibilities are going to be divided, he thought.

His mental strategizing was quickly halted by Serena's voice. "Your father's very thorough. This will be a huge help when we question the potential jurors during *voir dire*. I see several we can probably get dismissed for cause . . . others we'll have to question thoroughly, for instance, one Milton Haldeman. He's a Quaker, so you would assume he would not think kindly of violence . . . but that cuts both ways with victim and accused. And how would he feel about putting a young woman to death?"

Cam shrugged. He didn't want to talk about jurors anymore. "I don't know. We'll have to talk about that. What I'd really like to go over is how we're going to divide up the trial work."

"This is still your case. What do you want me to handle? I'll tell you if I have any reservations about it."

"Okay. I'll do the opening statement and do cross-examination of any of the state's witnesses who aren't my family members. The sheriff and the coroner come immediately to mind . . . perhaps the undertaker. I suppose Kirsten's hired hand, Chet, will be a witness, and, possibly, the bank officer on the question of motive. I don't think they'll call Pilar or Thad. From the prosecution's standpoint Fuller will want to talk as little as possible about Kirsten's beating. I don't see the county attorney's case taking more than a day, if that."

"So I shouldn't be involved until after the state rests?"

"No. I thought I would handle the *voir dire* examination of the jurors. You can observe their reactions, and we can consult on any motions to strike. You're going to carry the burden of the defense case. I assume you will be responsible for Kirsten's testimony . . . you seem to have established a rapport with her, and, obviously, you have confidence in her. I want you free to prepare the defense witnesses. I'll leave it to you whether you want to do the closing argument or not. I can do it if you prefer."

"I think I'd like to. And if I'm examining the defense witnesses, there would be some continuity in my doing this."

"If you change your mind, let me know. We have a week to get ready. You need to talk to Thad and Pilar soon. I'll ask Pilar to come in to the office tomorrow afternoon. I'll track Thad down and see if we can work out something for Tuesday. You'll need at least a half day with him." For the first time he caught some uneasiness in her eyes.

"There's something you should know about Thad and me."

"I know you've met Thad."

"It's more than that. It's very complicated, and I don't want to get into any details. But we thought we were in love once . . . it's been over ten years."

"Ten years. You were kids."

"Yes, we were. But our parting wasn't a happy one, and I haven't seen him since."

"Is this going to be a problem?"

"No. But as far as I know he isn't aware I'm participating in the case. I think he should be forewarned before he meets with me."

"I'll ride out and make the meeting arrangements. I'll warn him that his old girlfriend is back in town. The rest is up to you."

"Thank you. Thad and I have issues to deal with while I'm in Riley County, but they'll hold till after the trial. Nothing will get in the way of that."

The woman was staying at his father's home, she was his brother's former lover and now she was a soon-to-be member of the

Locke & Locke firm. She had very quickly entrenched herself in their lives. Cam hoped this was the end of Serena Belmont surprises.

43

THE NEMESIS UNTIED the end of the burlap sack, pulled it apart and dumped the two small copperheads at his feet, knowing they would have no interest in biting him. He watched them slither away in opposite directions along the creek bank. He felt morose and depressed at the departure of his young reptilian friends. He had reared them since they were mere babies, having plucked them from the same nest several years earlier. Since Aldo's murder by the bitch woman in the county jail, he had feared the discovery of his fondness for snakes, venomous ones in particular. It would not do for his friends to be discovered at his home in the event of suspicion of his involvement in the incident. So farewell, Caesar and Anthony. He knew there would be others, but it was still difficult to release them.

"Don't be sad, my son," came the raspy voice from behind him.

He did a quick about face. "Father, what are you doing here?" His father's presence startled him, because it was not preceded with the usual warning odor of smoke and stale sweat. He found himself troubled and confused by this development.

"Son, I sensed you needed me, and I came quickly. You are feeling great stress, and the pressure builds."

"Yes, the slut has another lawyer, a nigger woman who has a reputation for great skill and cunning. It is a bad sign."

"You're afraid of a nigger wench?"

"Afraid? No. If she wins her case, she will die along with Max's assassin. She may anyway. They both may die before the trial. I am not certain I can wait. I am called to render justice. Soon."

"Don't be a fool. Yes, you must kill them, if necessary. But the trial must happen. There will be others for you to avenge in the years ahead. You must not take unnecessary risks. If the law puts the Brannon bitch to death, you can still kill the nigger woman . . . but you can choose the time and place. Do you understand? Wait for the right time and place."

"I feel the need. It is tearing at me." The Nemesis began to sob.

"Listen to me," Father said. "Be a man. The time is near. One way or another, it will all be over soon."

44

THAD LEFT CATO at Cantwell's Livery and walked the three blocks to the Locke offices. He felt a little foolish, but he was attired for a social occasion, wearing his brushed leather jacket and pale blue shirt sans tie and freshly polished dress boots. He had trimmed the ragged hair that was hanging over his ears a bit the previous night and taken extra care with his morning shave.

His mind still reeled. Serena Belmont had reappeared as suddenly and unexpectedly in his life as she had left it. He found himself conflicted. On the one hand he was excited at the prospect of seeing her, but on the other he was a little annoyed at the disruption she brought with her. And according to Cam, she was returning permanently to Riley County, to join the Locke law firm of all things. He was incredulous that this could be happening. He certainly had no notion they would take up where they left off ten years ago. They were mere children then, he realized, and they had followed very different paths. He was prepared for the likelihood that the Serena of his nostalgic fantasy was not the Serena of today's reality. Certainly, he was not the boy of those idyllic weeks of their romance. They had both taken roads they had planned before their meeting that summer ten years previous, although when Cam related the level of Serena's success, he found himself somewhat in awe.

As he reached the law office door, he wondered how one greeted a former lover—a polite handshake, a quick nod of the head? A wave of queasiness gnawed at his stomach, as he entered the office.

Reva smiled warmly when she saw him and got up from her chair and hurried over to give him a warm hug. "Thad," she said, stepping back. "You never stop by anymore. I've missed you."

He returned her smile. He loved Reva—almost everyone did unless they tried to cross his father. "Busy. Between the vet work and the ranching, I only get to town for quick supply runs. I'll try to do better."

"See that you do. I know you've got business here today. Let me see if Serena's ready to see you." She turned and headed down the hall.

Momentarily, Reva returned with Serena close behind. The coffee-brown eyes met his, and she moved briskly past Reva to give Thad his second hug of the early afternoon. Only this one was brief and perfunctory. At least he didn't have to worry about whether to shake her hand.

"It's good to see you, Thad. It's been a long time."

Thad caught a glimpse of Reva watching them with interested and inquisitive eyes and a mischievous, tight-lipped smile on her face. He'd have to slip out quickly or face an interrogation when he left the office.

"It has been a long time," he agreed. A brilliant turn of phrase, he thought, feeling like a tongue-tied fool.

"Come back to my office," Serena said. "Such as it is." She led him back to the spartanly furnished office.

He noted that the desk and her chair comprised an island surrounded by a sea of law books and scattered papers. The books on top of the desk were stacked with some semblance of order.

"Sit down," Serena invited, gesturing toward the single chair across the desk from hers.

She pulled her own chair up to the desk, and they faced each other across a barrier that separated them by little more than three feet. This felt beyond strange, and he waited for her to initiate the conversation. Her dusky beauty hadn't waned, he observed, although she looked a bit tired and gaunt. She wore a charcoal-gray dress to enhance her professional demeanor, he supposed, and her thick, black hair was pulled back and fastened with a silver barrette before dropping to shoulder-top.

"This is a little awkward," Serena said softly. "There are things we must talk about before I leave for Washington, but for now we have to focus on the trial. A woman's life is at stake."

"That's why I'm here," Thad replied, a little more testily than he had intended.

"Very well. I would like to start from the beginning. Cam has given me a summary of your involvement, but you are the one who is going to have to tell the story under oath. I will be asking the questions during the defense presentation. I will not ask a single question I don't know the answer to, so I must know before the trial what your answers will be."

"I understand that."

"Would you tell me in your own words everything you remember about the night Max Brannon . . . died?"

"My first contact was when Myles . . . that's my nephew . . . showed up at my place and told me Cam wanted me to get to the C Bar C as soon as possible. He said I was to bring my medical bag and my photographic gear . . . which I thought very strange. On the other hand, Cam makes a habit of surprises."

"From my brief acquaintance, I can imagine. Go on."

She was like a stranger to him in her demeanor and in this environment, and it somehow made it easier for him to relate his part in the bizarre events of that night. He set forth his narrative of the events as he remembered them without interruption. When he finished, he said, "That's pretty much what I recall."

"Okay, I'd like to get a little more specific now. Did Mrs. Brannon . . . that's how we're going to refer to her. This is the name used in the criminal complaint, and we don't want a fuss with the prosecutor. Besides, there is a possibility some jurors would have an unconscious bias against a woman who declined to use her husband's name. Did Mrs. Brannon say that she killed her husband?"

"Never."

"Did she say he had been shot?"

"No. She said he had died."

"Didn't you find that a strange way to put it?"

"Well, at the time it didn't make much sense in light of her condition, but I hadn't examined Max yet."

"Since you were there in your capacity as a physician, what did you observe when you examined Max Brannon?"

"Only that he had a wound between his eyes, obviously a gunshot. Minimal blood. I have to say my examination was rather cursory. Cam didn't encourage me to spend much time checking out the body. He later mentioned we'd let the coroner worry about Max. He said I didn't need to take any photographs."

"What if I told you that Mrs. Brannon doesn't remember killing Max?"

The question caught him by surprise, and he paused before answering. "Well, I've spoken with her on many occasions since that night. She hasn't told me she didn't remember, but she hasn't said anything to indicate she remembers, either. Frankly, I don't know what to make of the statement."

"Is it possible someone else could have done it?"

"Possible, I suppose, but under the circumstances, it's difficult to imagine. Who's the suspect?"

"Pilar said Mrs. Brannon thought that someone had been following her since the night of Max's death."

"Yes, I accompanied her back to Cam's after she visited my office to have her stitches removed, because she thought someone was following her . . . and someone tried to kill her at the jail with the rattlesnake."

"Could this have been the same person who killed Max?"

"Anything's possible, I guess."

"You sound skeptical."

"I am. I guess you can try to plant a seed of reasonable doubt with that theory, but I can't quite buy in to it."

"Do you think it is possible Mrs. Brannon could have killed Max and not remember it?"

"Yes. There are a number of recorded case studies where people who have suffered horrible, traumatic events can't recall the incident. 'Amnesia' is the medical term being applied to these situations. I think it's a plausible explanation for her lack of recall."

"Let me take it a step further. Is it possible Mrs. Brannon was so traumatized by her beating and mutilation that she could have killed Max Brannon without even realizing she was doing it . . . temporary insanity, so to speak?"

"Possible? Yes, I could testify that it is possible."

"What do you really think?"

"I couldn't . . . and wouldn't . . . testify that I thought Kirsten knowingly and consciously killed her husband. That cannot be objectively proven or disproven. But I think she was aware of what she was doing when she killed Max . . . and that she was the one who pulled the trigger. To me, it is more possible she does not remember doing it, but I truly do not know. I have become acquainted with Kirsten since that night, though, and I don't think anyone other than Kirsten herself will ever know what she remembers. She is a damn smart and shrewd woman . . . and I mean that as a compliment. You and Kirsten should make a dauntless team."

She smiled. "May I take that as a compliment, too?"

Thad returned the smile. "You may."

"Thank you. There is one other matter I would like to discuss. Cam told me about a business arrangement you and Mrs. Brannon have. He's concerned this will come up at trial and could be problematic."

"How could this be?"

"First, it could adversely affect your credibility as a witness. If you are Mrs. Brannon's business partner, how objective is the rest of your testimony? Fortunately, we have the photographs to back up some of your testimony . . . but when we get into the area of less objective opinions, such as her mental state, the prosecutor will try to impeach your analysis as biased."

"I can see that."

"There is also the question of a pre-existing romantic relationship . . . which would raise the issue of motive."

Thad flared, but kept his voice soft and even. "There *was* no romantic relationship and there *is* none. I had done some vet work at the C Bar C on, perhaps, two occasions before the night of Max's death. I hardly knew Kirsten. Since that time, I have been her physician and, more recently, become a business partner."

"If you can be that emphatic in your testimony, we should be able to overcome any romantic innuendo. The business matter is more difficult to explain. My intention would be to disclose this to the jury before the prosecution does. It makes it much more difficult to cast the business arrangement in an unfavorable light. Tell me about it."

"The land deal? There's not much to tell. Kirsten had an opportunity to buy a half section, but she had only enough cash to buy a quarter section. The bank wouldn't loan her the money for the whole thing, and then after her husband's death, it became even more complicated. That would not have been a good time to pursue other financing. She told me about the property, and I was very interested in the north quarter . . . you would be familiar with the land. Anyway, she proposed I buy the entire half section and take title in my name. I would arrange a loan for half and she would advance the other half, with the understanding that when her legal troubles were over, I would transfer the south quarter to her. Her part was handled as a loan. I gave her a note carrying two percent interest for the money she put up. She will have a second mortgage on the whole thing, and we'll have to work out details to release her quarter from the bank's loan sometime."

"This was not a good idea." Thad recognized reprimand in her voice and resented it.

"Cam didn't like the idea, either."

"With good reason. You said I would be familiar with the land. What do you mean?"

"My quarter is where the medicine wheel is located."

For the first time since their reunion, Thad felt he had left her speechless.

After a few moments, Serena said, "I find that very strange."

"Don't make more of it than it is. I obviously was familiar with the land. It will fit nicely with my other holdings, and Kirsten's going to lease it for now. She's a very astute business woman, and by coincidence, she led me to a good investment . . . and I like the idea of owning the tract where the medicine wheel sits. You're not the only one who found magic there." She could damn well think on that—he didn't much care how she took it.

"Well, trying to camouflage the transaction was a totally wasted effort. It only looks worse. The best we can do is make disclosure. There is some logic to a woman facing legal problems working out a temporary arrangement for her business affairs. We can put the best face on it, but it hardly seems that a grieving widow would be worrying about business matters."

"She doesn't pretend to be a grieving widow. She's not good at pretense."

"Oh, I think she can pretend if she has to. I will be speaking with her, and I think you will see in the courtroom a widow who has some sorrow and remorse for the evil and twisted deceased husband. After all, she loved him once, and that counts for something." Serena stood and said, "I think this is enough for today. I will want to speak with you again before the trial. It was nice seeing you, Thad." She reached her hand across the desk and he took it, receiving her firm, businesslike grip.

He had been summarily dismissed.

45

THAD WAS ALLOWED to bring an extra chair into the cell, and he set it down next to the little table where Kirsten was already seated. It was early Friday afternoon of the week before the trial. "I thought I'd stop by for a spell before I talked to your lawyer again. I'm supposed to meet with her for a final 'rehearsal,' so to speak." He sat down. "She doesn't like that word . . . Rehearsal . . . so I find myself using it to annoy her. It seems to me that's what it is."

Kirsten was unresponsive and appeared deeply in thought, so he waited silently, knowing she would speak when she was ready. Odd, he thought, how he was getting so accustomed to her moods and habits.

Suddenly she broke the silence. "They're going to run the railroad north to Randolph."

He was starting to get used to her doing this, popping up with statements that made no sense in the context of their current conversation. "That's nice," he said noncommittally.

"No. Listen. I heard the sheriff talking about it with the deputy. It's going to follow the Big Blue. They didn't say which side, but it will have to be on the west side . . . our side. The west is on higher ground. A big part of the east will flood. Don't you see what this means?"

She looked at him in seeming expectation of the correct answer.

He would have to disappoint her. "Well, it will be nice for the folks in the Randolph area."

"Think, Doc. Who owns land on the west side of the river?"

"Let me guess. Thad Locke and Kirsten Cavelle?"

"You're doing better, Doc," she said. "And the railroad is opportunity knocking. Your north quarter has the perfect level site in the bottomland for a spur. We could put up a livestock yard there where people could bring their hogs and cattle to ship. Better yet, we could build an auction house where buyers come and bid on livestock to ship to the big slaughter houses. We'd take commissions on both selling and shipping. There's space for all kinds of businesses that need railroad access: grain brokers, limestone producers, saw mills . . . the list is endless. We could set up these operations ourselves and hire managers. We'd make jobs for people and have nice profits for ourselves. The railroad is the future and will be for as far as we can see."

"Kirsten, slow down. You're making my head spin. I'm just a simple country vet, and you've got me building a commercial empire."

"Hell, Doc, you could even build an animal hospital at that site. And we could require veterinary livestock inspections before shipping. You could make some extra gold eagles from that, and buyers would have extra protection against buying diseased hogs or cattle."

Remembering Quincy's swine fever tragedy, Thad thought her idea had merit. "I'll see what I can find out about the rail plans. This isn't going to take place overnight." Damn. Her enthusiasm was sucking him into the scheme.

"No, it will take several years to get lines built to Randolph. But we could be ready for it."

"I'd have to think about how involved I'd want to be." She was crazy as a loon to be thinking about these things with the gallows possibly looming in her future, but her vision had him in its clutches.

"You think I'm nuts, don't you?"

"No, you've got some interesting ideas. I'd be lying if I said they didn't intrigue me, but—"

"You're wondering why I'm even thinking about this when I might be dead or in prison in a few weeks."

He shrugged. "Okay, the thought had crossed my mind."

"I would be insane if I didn't plan ahead and put my brain to challenges. Pops taught me that. He was over fifty when I was born and several years past seventy when he died, but he never stopped moving, even when he accepted he was dying. He kept right on buying breeding stock he'd never see a calf from and land he'd never see harvested. He always said he'd never retire and never quit working. The only alternative he said was to sit back and wait for the Grim Reaper to show up. The last day of his life, one of the hands helped him into the saddle, and Pops rode out to check out the home place one more time. The horse came back riderless and they found Pops at the top of a hill overlooking his land, leaning against an old oak tree. It looked like he'd just dozed off and never woke up. Well, they may have me in a cage, but I'm not going to live whatever time I've got like there's no future and nothing that needs doing."

"I'll see what I can find out about the railroad and keep you updated."

She reached across the table and put her hand on top of his. "Thanks, Doc. I knew I could make you understand."

46

CAM LIKED AND respected Judge Cyrus Whitmore, who was anything but the stereotypical stern, cantankerous judge so often created in the public mind. On the contrary, Judge Whitmore's round, fleshy face wore a perpetual smile, like that of a man content and pleased with his lot in life. He was generally casual and relaxed in his courtroom, but he good-naturedly maintained order and carried a Peacemaker in the holster beneath his robe. He was loath to hold tight rein on the lawyer combatants, but was quick to call the advocates up short when one or the other abused his generosity. The rotund jurist with the thatch of red hair topping his otherwise bald scalp might be misjudged as something of a bumpkin by a lawyer making his first appearance in Judge Whitmore's courtroom. Cam knew better. Whitmore was one of only a scattering of Midwestern judges with a law school education—Yale no less—and he was nobody's fool.

After opening statements, the judge had declared a brief recess and now consulted with his bailiff. Cam sat at the defense counsel's table, which was parallel to the prosecution's table so that the adverse parties faced each other. The raised judge's bench and witness stand were positioned a dozen feet from the end of each of the tables, and public seating for thirty to thirty-five people commenced about ten feet from the opposite end of the tables. The jury box was positioned behind the county attorney's table, which left Cam facing the jury and suited him just fine.

Cam sat nearest the judge's bench, and Serena at the other end of the table, with Kirsten, attired in mourning black, in between, which gave them each ample access to their client during the course of the trial. Frank Fuller and his tall, pencil-thin deputy were seated at the prosecutor's table and were engaged in what Cam guessed to be an intense discussion.

The spectator seats had been packed from the moment court convened, and Cam noted that at least three newspaper reporters had captured front row observation posts and were not surrendering them, apparently having made a mutual defense pact of some kind. If one reporter left the room, the other two tenaciously resisted any effort of another citizen to claim the vacant seat.

The jury selection had been accomplished quickly. During the *voir dire* questioning, one elderly self-ordained preacher had gone into a diatribe about wifely obedience and repeated firmly at least three times "an eye for an eye." The judge had granted Cam's motion to remove for cause, and two others showing similar proclivities had been likewise removed. The prosecutor was successful in removing four who opposed the death penalty, interestingly, also on religious grounds. The pool was then reduced to "twelve good men and true" by alternating silent strikes by the lawyers crossing off names on the jury list. Cam had stricken the remaining Klansman and the wife beater, as well as another dubious prospect. Fuller had removed the colored men for whatever reason with his peremptory challenges.

The opening statements had been the briefest Cam could remember. The prosecutor had simply declared the state would prove that Kirsten Brannon had killed her loving husband in cold blood while he slept and that said killing was willful, deliberate and premeditated, requirements of murder in the first degree. Cam had pointed out that the opening statements did not constitute evidence and that the facts had yet to be revealed. He had emphasized several times that guilt must be established "beyond a reasonable doubt." He alluded to the defendant having been beaten nearly senseless by the deceased, carefully planting the seed of her fragile mental state.

Cam noted that the bailiff had departed to retrieve the jury and that the judge was straightening the papers on the bench. In a few moments the bailiff returned, escorting the jurors to their seats. During the *voir dire*, Cam had targeted two jurors for special attention. One, a young bachelor school teacher, had seemed a sensitive, non-judgmental person with an open mind. The other was an elderly farmer, who was the father of five daughters, one of whom —Reva had ferreted out of somewhere—pathetically put up with a wife-beating husband. Serena had singled out another young juror, a young storekeeper who could not take his eyes off of her and gave her shy smiles when they made eye contact.

Judge Whitmore tapped his gavel lightly on the bench. "Okay gentlemen . . . and lady . . . are you prepared to proceed? Mr. Fuller you're up first."

The county attorney got up and walked around to the front of the table. "The state calls Sheriff Sam Mallery."

Mallery ambled up to the witness stand, was sworn in by the judge and sat down. He was an old hand at this, and he seemed confident and at ease. Cam knew him to be an honest man, but he could be a cagey rascal and would have to be questioned cautiously on cross-examination.

Fuller established the sheriff's credentials quickly, rattling off the usual name, residence, occupation and experience inquiries. Then he asked Mallery how he came to be at the Brannon house on the day of Max Brannon's death, and the sheriff explained how Chet Grisham had pounded on his door in the early morning hours and how the circumstances Chet had described convinced him to invite the county attorney along to investigate the scene. The county attorney led him through their arrival at the house and the encountering of Kirsten and members of the Locke clan, carefully avoiding any mention of Kirsten's injuries. "And did you have cause to investigate the bedroom of the Brannon house?" Fuller asked.

"Yes, sir."

"And will you tell me what you saw?"

"I found Max Brannon naked in his bed and stone-cold dead."

"How do you know the man was Max Brannon?"

"I'd known him for several years . . . seen him in town a number of times."

"Was anyone else in the room with you at this time?"

"Yes . . . you were."

"Do you have an opinion as to what caused Mr. Brannon's death?"

"He was shot. There was a hole between the eyes, clean as could be."

"Could this have been self-inflicted?"

"No."

"How do you know this to be the case?"

"No obvious powder burns, so there must have been some distance between the gun barrel and his forehead. Take a pistol . . . unloaded please . . . and see how easy it would be to fire the weapon true holding it a few feet away from your head."

"Do you have any other basis for your conclusion?"

"Yes, sir."

"And what is it?"

"No gun anywhere nearby. None in the room."

"Was there a gun on the premises?"

"Three of them. Two Winchester rifles . . . a Model 1866 and a Model 1876 . . . and an Army Colt revolver hanging in a holster near the door."

"And did you observe anything about the weapons?"

"Well, the rifles weren't loaded, but the Colt was short a cartridge in the cylinder."

"You testified that the only people in the house when you arrived were the defendant and members of the Locke family."

"I did."

"Was there anyone else near the house?"

"Cam Locke's boy was outside . . . he was the only one I seen."

Fuller looked at the judge. "That's all I have for the witness for now, Your Honor."

Judge Whitmore widened his smile a bit and nodded at Cam. "Your turn, counselor."

Cam got up and approached the witness stand, leaving his notes on the table. "Just a few questions, Sheriff."

"Yes, sir."

"You said the pistol was short a cartridge. Is that correct?"

"Yes."

"And from that you concluded what?"

"That the pistol was used to kill Max Brannon."

"What caliber bullet does the Army Colt use?"

"It was a .45."

"And the coroner removed a bullet from Mr. Brannon's skull, is that right?"

"Uh . . . yes."

"And what caliber was that?"

"Well, he thought it was a .45."

"He thought?"

"It was all broke up . . . couldn't say for sure."

"I see. Have you seen a revolver with a bullet or two missing from the cylinder before?"

"Well, yeah."

"Correct me if I'm wrong. But could there not be a lot of reasons for that . . . like firing the weapon to scare off an animal, for instance?"

"Well, sure but—"

"So you can't say with certainty that the missing bullet ended up in Mr. Brannon's head?"

The sheriff tossed a look at Fuller as if expecting silent instructions. "Well, not a hundred percent, but it seems likely."

"Likely. And you'd hang a woman on 'likely'?"

Fuller jumped from his chair. "Objection, Your Honor. Mr. Locke's leading the witness and he's asking the sheriff for an irrelevant opinion."

Judge Whitmore smiled amiably. "Now, Mr. Fuller, the sheriff is *your* witness after all. I think the defense has a little leeway here." Then he turned to Cam. "But that's about as far as I'll let you go, counselor. I'd take it kindly if you'd just withdraw the question."

"Withdrawn, Your Honor. I do have just a few more questions, though."

"Proceed."

"Sheriff, I'm having difficulty here grasping a few things. Perhaps, you can help me out." Cam saw the sheriff eyeing him warily. "Did you see anyone fire the Colt?"

"No."

"Did you talk to a witness who saw Mrs. Brannon fire the Colt or any other weapon at Mr. Brannon?"

"No."

"But you concluded Mrs. Brannon killed Mr. Brannon?"

"Yes."

"Why?"

"Because she was the only one there at the house."

"When Mr. Brannon was shot?"

"Yeah."

"How do you know that?"

"Well, who else could have been?"

"I could list a lot of possibilities, Sheriff. But may I remind you I'm asking the questions?" Cam quickly finished his cross-examination with a few perfunctory questions to nail down his message to the jurors that the evidence against Kirsten was essentially circumstantial.

47

SERENA STUDIED THE jurors while the county attorney called the prosecution's witnesses and laid out his case, followed by Cam's cross-examination, which she observed was what she called a "strike and withdraw" attack—making his point precisely and then walking away from the witness. Were it not for his family entanglements, he would have had no need for her at the counsel table. This man was capable of combating the giants of the profession.

A few of the jurors were unsuccessfully trying to stifle yawns, but most were alert and attentive. Several times her young shopkeeper's eyes met hers and then promptly turned away. She thought rapport with key jurors was potentially helpful, but she did not give the weight to such personal relationships that some lawyers did. There was no substitute for preparation, as far as she was concerned.

Serena glanced at Kirsten who sat to her left. The young rancher had shown amazing calm and poise throughout the trial. Her demeanor was relaxed, yet appropriately serious. Kirsten appeared to be following the proceedings intently, but she spoke little even during the occasional recesses, letting her lawyers do their work. This woman was deceptively shallow to many at first meeting, Serena thought, perhaps intentionally so. During trial prep meetings, she had come to realize that she was dealing with a person of intellectual depth and exceptional survival skills—"tough as a boot," as she'd heard her father say in referring to durable, persistent men he'd encountered.

Dr. Horace Kleeb, the county coroner, had taken the stand for the prosecution, and Serena turned her attention to Cam's cross-examination. Kleeb, a slight, balding man who appeared to be in his late-sixties, would obviously have preferred to be elsewhere. He fidgeted in his chair and mopped the sweat from his brow with a handkerchief as he responded to questions.

"Now, Mr. Kleeb," Cam asked, "you testified you have been practicing medicine for nearly forty years. Tell me, what medical school did you graduate from?"

Kleeb sighed deeply before he replied in a high-pitched voice. "I became a physician by apprenticing with a St. Louis medical doctor many years ago."

Cam had gently hammered a small chink in the witness's credibility. She doubted he would attack aggressively on this front, since the coroner's main function was to testify that Max Brannon had died of a gunshot wound and no one was contesting that.

Cam continued. "You testified that you thought Max Brannon was killed by a .45 bullet. Is that right?"

"Yes."

"But you could not say for certain?"

"No, the bullet was too fragmented."

"Hypothetically, let's say the bullet *was a* .45 caliber. Could you match it to a particular gun?"

"No. I guess there are some gunsmiths and other experts who claim to be able to make a match in some cases, but I wouldn't have that capability."

"How many Colts that fire .45 caliber bullets do you think there might be in Riley County?"

"I have no idea . . . a lot."

"Objection, Your Honor. There is no foundation for this question. It calls for sheer speculation and establishes no basis for the witness's expertise to respond." Fuller was clearly miffed at Cam's quick move.

"Sustained," the judge said. "Jury will disregard."

Fat chance, Serena thought, but this was just a small building block in the defense case on the journey to reasonable doubt. Cam had no further questions of Dr. Kleeb, and the coroner made a quick exit from the courtroom. The county attorney called Chet Grisham as his next witness, and if the coroner was nervous, the lanky old cowboy was on the edge of breakdown. Serena noted his trembling hands before they grasped the arms of the witness chair and a tick in one eye that kept the lids flapping.

Frank Fuller led Grisham through his personal relationship with the defendant and the nature of his responsibilities at the C Bar C, before he got to the purpose of the cowboy's testimony. Finally, he asked, "Mr. Grisham, you acknowledged you were interviewed by the sheriff in the course of his investigation of this case. Did the sheriff ever ask you if Mrs. Brannon ever threatened to kill Max Brannon?"

"Yes. He did."

"And what was your response?"

"Well," Grisham replied, his voice shaky, "I told him that Kirsten said, 'I'm going to kill that son-of-a- bitch' . . . that was when he didn't show up to help round up cattle a few months back, but—"

"And did she repeat this on other occasions?"

"Not in them exact words, but, yeah."

"What were the exact words?"

"Well, once she said she was 'going to kill that asshole' . . . pardon the expression. She might have said that more than once." Grisham's face turned scarlet.

"She and her husband didn't get along, I take it?"

"Not for a long spell. Never spoke much to each other when I was around. Or if they did, they was cussin' each other out about something."

Fuller completed his examination by asking the same questions different ways, Serena observed, and then the witness was turned over to Cam.

Cam stood but kept some distance away from the cowboy and looked up at the ceiling for a few moments, as if seeking divine inspiration there, before commencing his questioning. Then he turned to the old cowhand. "Tell me, Chet, you testified you've worked for Mrs. Brannon for about five years. But you knew her before that, didn't you?"

Grisham appeared more at ease now. "Oh, yes, sir. Knowed her since she was a tadpole in Missouri. Worked for her papa, Ben Cavelle. Come to work for Kirsten when she set up her operation here in the Flint Hills. She asked me to come with her, and Ben gave his blessing to it."

"In all those years, how many times did Mrs. Brannon say she was going to kill somebody?"

"Grisham chuckled. Probably hundreds. She was feisty as a bobcat."

"And did she?"

"Did she what?"

"Kill somebody."

Grisham laughed again. "No, hell no, she wouldn't stomp on a spider. Just has a quick temper, and she'd say things like that lettin' off steam."

"Did you think she intended to kill Max Brannon those times when you heard her say she was going to kill him?"

Grisham looked surprised. "Well, no, never gave it a thought. She just said things like that. I tried to explain that to the sheriff and Mr. Fuller."

Fuller interjected, "Objection, witness isn't being responsive to the question."

"He's your witness, counselor. Defense has got a little slack in the rope," the judge responded.

Cam continued, "Just a few more questions, Chet. Did you ever say you were going to kill somebody?"

"Probably dozens of times."

"Did you?"

"Nope."

"Did you ever say you were going to kill Max Brannon?"

"I don't recall it . . . but I thought it a time or two. Surprised I didn't get branded as a suspect."

Serena thought Cam seemed a bit taken aback by the witness's response, but he recovered quickly.

"Why do you say that?" Cam asked.

"Well, I was sleepin' right there on the place. Who's to say I didn't slip in there and pull the trigger on that pistol . . . or my own. I got a Colt just like it."

"No further questions."

Chet Grisham, wittingly or not, had just furnished an alternate theory that the defense, at Kirsten's insistence, had been unwilling to exploit.

48

JUDGE WHITMORE, AT the county attorney's suggestion, had adjourned the trial after Chet Grisham's testimony. Fuller had promised the judge that the prosecution would rest its case by noon this day, Tuesday. Cam and Serena were discussing trial strategy at the dead end of a hallway outside the courtroom, prior to convening of court.

"You're still planning to call Chet as a defense witness, I assume," Cam said.

"Yes," Serena replied. "For some reason, Fuller didn't bring up Chet's involvement the night of Max Brannon's death. I suppose he's avoiding bringing up the injuries to Kirsten. Of course, after Chet's setting himself up as a suspect, I don't think Frank had any interest in touching him in rebuttal. I see it as a tactical error on his part. It will just hit with greater impact when we introduce our evidence."

"I agree. That's why I stayed away from it on cross. I'm concerned about Fuller's next witness . . . the banker, Nigel Baker. I tried to talk with him, but he clammed up and was downright hostile. All I know is that he's going to say Kirsten had motive to kill her husband."

"Well, good luck."

"Thanks. It's pretty much your show after I'm finished with

Baker."

There was a murmuring of voices and shuffling of feet in the hallway outside the courtroom, signaling that the bailiff must be preparing to announce the judge's entry. They hurried down the hallway and joined Kirsten, who was already seated at the defense table. Momentarily, the bailiff announced, "All rise."

As the judge took his seat, he smiled genially, nodded at each counsel and tapped his gavel, and everybody eased into their own chairs. "Good morning, folks. We'll have this show on the road in a few minutes, but first I'd like to have all counsel approach the bench." Cam and Serena and both prosecutors complied promptly.

"Gentlemen . . . and lady," Judge Whitmore said in a soft voice, "this trial's moving along at a nice pace. Mr. Fuller, do you still expect to finish up this morning?"

"Yes, Judge."

"And what about the defense?"

"We'll be ready to proceed after noon break, Judge," Serena said.

"I won't hold you to it, but how long do you think it will take to lay out your evidence?"

"Two days, Judge. I would expect to finish by Thursday noon, allowing for cross by the state."

"With closing statements, this could go to the jury by mid-afternoon Thursday. I like that, counsel. Let's go."

After the attorneys returned to their respective counsel tables, the county attorney called Nigel Baker to the witness stand. Cam felt unprepared for this witness and tried to appraise the man's demeanor for a clue as to where he might take the case. He had a neatly-trimmed mustache planted on a pallid, washed-out face, which suggested he was a man who saw little of the outdoors—not surprising for a man of his occupation. He was a thin, bony man and would stand an inch or two under six feet, Cam guessed. Although he had a grim look on his face, Baker did not show any signs of unease or nervousness that most witnesses displayed at the prospect of being mauled by two dueling law wranglers.

Fuller quickly ran through the preliminaries, establishing that Baker was forty-eight years old, a loan officer at the Manhattan Bank and that he had been employed by a St. Louis bank before taking a position in Manhattan little more than a year previous. He was single and resided in a rented house within walking distance of his work.

Fuller turned to the serious questioning quickly. "Mr. Baker, are you acquainted with the defendant, Kirsten Brannon?"

"I am."

"Would you describe the nature of your acquaintance?"

"She's a bank customer. I have acted as a loan officer for several of her loans."

"Did you see the defendant in your bank in the period immediately before the death of her husband?"

"I did. About two days prior, as I recall . . . on a Wednesday."

"How do you remember that?"

"Because Mrs. Brannon usually dealt with the bank president, Mr. Dawes, but he was out of the bank Wednesday of that week."

"Since you are a loan officer, I assume she was there to discuss a loan matter?"

"She was. She wanted to purchase 320 acres of grazing land from Clem Rickers, but she required a loan to finance it."

"Did she qualify for a loan?"

"Yes. She had considerable equity . . . parcels of land free of debt, unencumbered cattle. She, like most expanding farm and ranch operators are sometimes land poor, and she didn't have the cash to buy that much land."

"So you granted the loan?"

"Yes and no."

"What does that mean?"

"I told her she could have the loan, but she would have to give the bank a mortgage to secure it. She had about half the cash available, so it was a sound loan, and she had an excellent payment history with the bank."

"But there was a problem?"

"Her husband . . . under Kansas law the spouse is required to sign the mortgage."

Cam knew what was coming next, since Kirsten had explained the bank loan problem and her reaction to it. But Baker was a good witness—matter of fact and calm. He decided to let the testimony play out—not that he had any real choice.

Fuller continued. "Why was this requirement that the husband sign the mortgage a problem?"

"Because she planned to take title to the land in her sole name. She did not seem entirely surprised by the necessity of her husband signing the mortgage, but she expected the bank to make an exception. According to bank records his name wasn't on the deeds to any of the C Bar C land holdings. She had taken out loans without his signature in the past, but they did not involve real estate mortgages."

"And you explained to Mrs. Brannon the necessity of her husband's signature on the mortgage?"

"Yes, I did . . . very precisely. No signature, no loan."

"And how did she take this?"

"She was angry . . . rather profane."

"What did she say?"

"She said the law was 'nothing but bullshit.' And that I should tell the bank president to 'shove the mortgage up his ass.'"

A few members of the jury chuckled noticeably. Cam figured they'd probably had a bank loan turned down sometime.

Fuller was nonplussed. "Was that the end of your conversation?"

"No. After she calmed down, she asked if I could suggest any other option for obtaining the loan. I told her there was nothing else I could suggest, and I urged her to reconsider her insistence that her husband's name not be on the title. She was adamant that this would never happen. That's when she made the comment."

This was well rehearsed, Cam thought, giving Fuller a bit of grudging respect.

The county attorney asked on cue, "What comment?"

"She said, 'you mean if I killed the son of bitch, you'd make a loan to his widow?' She left me speechless with those words. And then she got up and stomped out of the bank."

"Did you take her words seriously?"

Cam almost rose to object to the question but decided to save his words for cross.

"Very seriously," Baker said solemnly. "Very seriously."

Cam looked at Serena, who had evidently been watching him for a reaction. She rolled her eyes and had faint traces of a smile on her lips. She appeared to agree that Baker had overacted a bit.

"The prosecution has no further questions of this witness," Fuller said, moving to his seat.

"Mr. Locke," the Judge said, "the witness is yours."

"Thank you, Judge," Cam said, rising from his chair and approaching the witness. "Mr. Baker, from your testimony I gather you've been in the banking business over twenty years, is that correct?"

"Yes, that's true."

"Have you ever had borrowers upset before because they couldn't obtain loans?"

"Of course, it's a common occurrence."

"Then why did you seem to find Mrs. Brannon's anger so unusual?"

"Well, it wasn't the anger; it was what she said about killing her husband."

"Did you think she was going to kill her husband?"

"I thought she might."

Baker stepped nicely into the trap. "Did you alert the sheriff that you thought Mrs. Brannon might kill her husband?"

"Well, no."

"If you thought Max Brannon's life was truly in danger, why not?"

Baker was silent for some moments. For the first time, Cam thought, the man's veil of confidence seemed to have been pierced. "I guess I didn't really think there was an imminent threat to Mr. Brannon."

"So you didn't really take Mrs. Brannon 'very seriously' as you stated earlier?"

"Perhaps that was an overstatement," Baker conceded.

"Just a few more questions, Mr. Baker. Do you have an opinion regarding Mrs. Brannon's competence as a businesswoman?"

"Yes."

"And what would that be?"

"Very competent. An excellent manager. She makes a very good loan. It was just this matter of her husband's signature."

"Then tell me, Mr. Baker, do you honestly think if Mrs. Brannon intended to kill her husband, she was stupid enough to have made that statement in your bank?"

Fuller flew out of his chair. "Objection, Your Honor. Leading the witness. Insufficient foundation."

"Withdraw the question," Cam said. "No further questions."

49

THE PROSECUTION HAD rested its case, and it was only mid-morning. Serena and Cam had another brief debate over the wisdom of calling Kirsten Cavelle Brannon as a witness. Cam told Serena he felt that the prosecution case was leaky and that Kirsten's testimony carried too much risk, but he emphasized it was her decision—and Kirsten's. When she spoke to Kirsten, the client affirmed her readiness to testify but deferred to Serena's judgment. It was an awesome responsibility, but Serena quickly made up her mind.

Kirsten was called first to give the only eyewitness account of the events that unfolded on the night of Max Brannon's death. Serena determined she should lay out the story to the jury and then call her other witnesses and set out the other evidence to shore up Kirsten's narrative.

Kirsten had told the jury of the night's events in some detail, reciting her beating and rape with flawless words and a voice devoid of emotion. She had required minimal prompting, but, perhaps, a little more emotion would have been helpful, Serena thought. She was appreciative, though, of her witness's poise and calm demeanor. She did not act like a person who was guilty of murder. Now Serena had to caulk the cracks in the story.

"Mrs. Brannon, you've related the events that took place the night of your husband's death as best as you recall them, is that correct?"

"Yes."

"You must understand, though, that the jury must wonder why there is no mention of your husband's death. You were aware of it, weren't you?"

"Yes, I knew he was dead."

"Did you know how he died?"

"I just knew he died. I remember nothing of how it happened. The sheriff told me he was shot."

"Did you kill your husband?"

"I don't know."

Knowing that Fuller would press in cross examination, Serena pursued. "But you were there, how can you not know?"

"I know this sounds convenient. But I don't remember anything about my husband's death, only that I saw him dead on the bed."

"Could someone else have killed him?"

"It's possible, but I understand why the sheriff and Mr. Fuller wouldn't think so. I was the only one there when Chet came to the house. And I didn't see someone else enter the house."

"After you were beaten—"

"Objection," Fuller yelled. "Assumes the truth of the defendant's testimony."

Judge Whitmore said, "Could you restate your question, counselor?"

"Certainly. Mrs. Brannon, was there any time during this period that you were not awake?"

"Yes, I passed out at least three times following the beating. I don't know for how long."

"Thank you. Now I'd like to turn to something else for a few moments. You heard the testimony of Nigel Baker about statements you allegedly made at the bank?"

"Yes, I did."

"Do you have any comments about those statements?"

"Yes, Mr. Baker told the absolute truth . . . including his remarks about my unladylike language, I'm embarrassed to say. It's no excuse, but I was angry about the situation. It seemed to me like any woman . . . or man, for that matter . . . should have a right to own and dispose of separate property without restriction. But I assure you I would not have made those statements if I had any intention of killing my husband. I'm not that stupid. I did take some steps to eliminate the problem, however."

"And what steps did you take?"

"I met with Cameron Locke the next day about getting a divorce from my husband."

"Because of the banking problem?"

"No. Because our relationship had deteriorated terribly over the past year and a half, and we were no longer living in our home as husband and wife, you might say. I had been beaten on another occasion and there were other differences I'd rather not discuss out of respect to my late husband. I had already decided the marriage was going to end. The banking problem spurred me to action."

Serena determined she should beat the prosecutor to one more issue he was likely to bring up. "Mrs. Brannon, did you buy the Rickers land?"

"No, but I have a verbal agreement that I can purchase a quarter section of it someday, if I wish."

"Would you explain?"

She outlined her arrangement with Thad.

"So you loaned Dr. Locke half the money to purchase the entire tract with the understanding he would give you an option to buy the quarter nearest your land in the future?" Serena summarized.

"Yes."

"No further questions."

Judge Whitmore asked, "Would you like a break before Mr. Fuller begins his examination, Mrs. Brannon?."

"No, thank you, Judge. I'm glad to continue."

Kirsten's response pleased Serena. Fuller would have less time to prepare. She noted that Kirsten seemed strangely energized by the process, certainly not intimidated. As she sat down, she saw that Fuller's eyes were studiously focused on a note pad as he slowly moved toward the witness. The deep-in-thought act.

"Mrs. Brannon, something you said about your relationship with your husband troubles me. You indicated you had differences you'd rather not discuss. I'm sorry, but I think Judge Whitmore will confirm you don't have the option of not discussing matters that might be relevant to the evidence in this case. I am going to have to ask you about this. What kind of differences were you referring to?"

He bit. Serena knew he would.

"I just didn't see any reason to sully Max's reputation. It had to do with his whoring."

Fuller took a step back. "I don't think I heard you correctly."

"Whoring, as in bawdy houses, Mr. Fuller," Kirsten said, her voice remaining soft and calm. "I had suspected for months that my husband was visiting prostitutes. Several months before his death, when he was angry about something . . . he was always angry . . . he threw it in my face that he was seeing these women. I refused to share our bed after that, not just because of his adulterous acts, but also because I feared catching diseases."

Serena watched the reaction of the jury. Some were unaffected by the disclosure, but others had become quite attentive, especially her key jurors. Fuller didn't seem to know what to do with the subject of prostitutes and made a quick retreat.

"You spoke about an arrangement with Dr. Thaddeus Locke regarding purchase of the Rickers land. Would you describe the nature of your relationship with Dr. Locke?"

Serena's first instinct was to object to the relevancy of the question, but then she thought better of it. It might appear there was something to hide. She would take her chances with Kirsten's instincts.

Kirsten said, not the least defensively, Serena observed, "Before the night of my husband's death, he did vet work at the C Bar C on two occasions, and I had never encountered him elsewhere. As I have already testified, he acted as my physician in treating the injuries I incurred. I became acquainted with him during my recovery . . . on a strictly professional basis, and since parcels of the Rickers place fit nicely with each of our operations, I asked him to enter into a joint venture on the purchase. He was reluctant because of appearances, but I convinced him most Flint Hills people aren't prone to gossip, and those with dirty minds don't matter. He finally agreed."

"Why didn't you just divide the land up at the beginning?"

"My life was obviously becoming very complicated. It's rather difficult to conduct business when you're incarcerated in the county jail. I doubt that the death of my husband under the circumstances would have made Mr. Baker more inclined to make a loan. We have a note and other papers to support what I'm saying and I'm certain that can be produced if the partnership becomes an issue. Some lawyers might find this irrelevant, I surmise."

Fuller interrupted, "Objection, Your Honor, the witness is not being responsive to the question."

The judge leaned his head toward the prosecutor and rubbed his chin thoughtfully. "Well, Mr. Fuller, I'll order the jury to disregard the witness's last sentence, but I daresay there's a bit of truth to it. It's closing in on noon, and I'm awful hungry. How far are we from finishing this up?"

"I don't have any more questions of the witness, Judge."

Wise decision, Serena thought. She rose and addressed the judge. "Your Honor, if it would please the court, I need to discuss some matters with my client. Could we meet in the conference room off the hallway during recess? I've arranged for sandwiches and coffee from the Chuck Wagon."

The judge looked at the sheriff, who was standing near the exit. "Is that a problem, sheriff?"

"No," Sheriff Mallery replied, "I can assign a deputy to the door."

50

THE TRIAL WAS going badly for the prosecution. The Nemesis had expected Locke's cleverness, but this nigger bitch was slick— stepped up there just like a white man and took over the goddamn courtroom. What was the matter with those idiots on the jury? Couldn't they see through the smokescreen? Max's evil slut was going to walk out of there, free as a bird, while Max rotted in his grave. He just felt it.

And where was Father? He hadn't appeared since the trial commenced. Had he been abandoned by the only one he trusted? From time to time Father had absented himself for stretches as long as three or four months, but never when his counsel was so desperately needed. The demons were consuming him, the lust for vengeance unstoppable. But he must be patient and await the verdict. Or must he?

The two women exited the courtroom, followed by his friend, Deputy Dagenhart, who nodded a greeting as they passed by and turned down the empty hallway. He could smell the fragrance of the women, and he thought he would like to take them both before the kill. But their meeting in the hall could be no coincidence. This was a clear message that the time had arrived, and he could not wait for another opportunity. He caressed the pearl-handled straight-razor in his trouser pocket, assuring himself that it was ready. The loaded

Colt pocket revolver was nestled in his waistcoat.

He heard Dagenhart say, "Somebody from the Chuck Wagon left a pot of coffee and sandwiches in the conference room. The judge says court starts up in an hour and a half. You got to use the outhouse, Brannon, I can take you out back. I'll be outside the door here. You ain't to leave without my say so."

He waited until they turned the corner, and, casting his eyes about the hallway, assured himself it was empty, the observers and officials having vacated to search out lunch or an outhouse, whichever they found most urgent. There would never be a better opportunity. He slowly and softly walked the course his prey had taken down the hall.

When he turned the corner he noted that he had entered a stub hallway that accessed only two rooms and had a door that likely opened to the back of the building and the privies at the rear of the lot. Perfect for a quick escape. He could do this. Deputy Dagenhart leaned against the wall adjacent to one door, rolling a cigarette. The Nemesis approached casually.

"Hello, Gid, can I get to the outhouse through that door at the end of the hall?"

"Yep. Like to take a piss myself, but the sheriff put me on watch for the Brannon bitch."

The Nemesis edged closer. "You don't like her?"

"Smart mouth. Bossy. I'd say Max is better off where he's at than livin' with her."

Dagenhart bent over and struck a small Lucifer on his boot heel and then straightened up and puffed deeply on his cigarette. The smoke didn't have time to reach his lungs before the Nemesis slipped behind him and yanked back his head and the straight-edge blade drug into his throat. The Nemesis eased the limp body to the floor as blood soaked the front of the deputy's shirt.

51

KIRSTEN AND SERENA sat across from each other at the conference table, silently eating the shredded beef sandwiches and drinking the coffee that had been delivered by the Chuck Wagon delivery boy. The warm bread reminded Kirsten of the fresh-from-the-oven sourdough delights the old trail cook used to serve up on her father's Missouri ranch, and she was struck by a wave of nostalgia for the times she shared with her father, Ben Cavelle, the one person who had been a rock in her life. He had always been on her side, even when she was foolish or made terrible mistakes. Everybody needed such a person in their lives. It made the road far less lonely. She wondered what her father would have thought about the mess she was in now. It wouldn't have mattered; he would have stood with her.

Kirsten was pulled abruptly back to the present by Serena's whispered voice. "Did you hear that?"

"What?"

"There were voices in the hall. Then it sounded like something fell on the floor." Serena quietly slid her chair back and grabbed her bag and moved to the far end of the table. She remained standing, her eyes fastened on the door.

Kirsten remained in place, but she was stricken with the same uneasiness that something was not quite the way it should be, and her senses leaped alive. The conference room door inched slowly open, and a man with a gun in his hand stepped in, his glazed-over eyes fixed first on Kirsten and then moved to Serena and back again. He pushed the door shut behind him. Out of the corner of her eye, she saw Serena's hand inch into her bag. Surely not?

She recognized the man, who was staring at her now. The banker. What was he doing here? And why the gun? This made no sense whatsoever.

Finally, the banker spoke, "I'm your Nemesis, bitch. Max was my friend, and you were his disobedient, obstinate wife. You made his life miserable, and then you took it. Today you pay."

He cast another look at Serena, as he moved deliberately toward the table, stopping directly across from Kirsten. "And you, nigger wench, you're going to make payback double."

Serena said nothing, but Kirsten could see the silent determination in her eyes. Kirsten's hands slipped under the tabletop and pulled sharply upwards, tipping the table over. It struck the man's legs and sent him stumbling backwards.

Two quick thunderclaps roared in the room, and the invader's legs collapsed, as twin bursts of scarlet appeared on his chest. He went down, still clutching his weapon and trying to aim it at Serena, but Kirsten had clambered over the fallen table and was on him now, both hands latched like vises on his wrist. Her teeth sank into his forearm, and the pistol clattered to the floor. Kirsten held on until she could feel the strength ebbing from his body.

Suddenly, the door flew open, and Sheriff Mallery appeared in the doorway. Cam Locke crowded in behind. She looked over at Serena who had not moved but stood there, seemingly calm, with the gun hanging loosely in her hand.

Mallery stepped in. "What in the hell happened here?"

Kirsten scrambled up. "He came here to kill me, Sheriff . . . and Serena."

"Dagenhart's dead. He took him out with a straight-edge, it looks like." The sheriff knelt and looked at the dead man. "This here's Corbett Avery from the Manhattan Bank. Why in the hell would he try to kill you?"

"I don't know. He said he was a friend of Max's. Something about being a nemesis. First, Nigel Baker's testimony, and now this . . . I guess I'm not real popular at the bank."

Cam stepped up beside the sheriff. "Somebody was following Kirsten before her arrest . . . the snake at the jail. It's a pretty damn good guess, Sam, that this is your guy."

"It just don't add up."

"I think you'll want to track this guy back a ways. I'd bet this isn't his first time." Cam turned to Serena, "Good shooting. Are you okay?"

"I'm okay." She spoke to the sheriff. "Here's my gun, Sheriff, if you need it. I'd like it back, though."

"No need. I'll talk to the county attorney. This'll be wrapped up fast."

Kirsten could hear the excited noise of a crowd gathering outside the room.

Cam said, "You ladies have had a busy lunch recess. Shall I ask the judge for a continuance for a day or two?"

Kirsten's eyes locked with Serena's. "What does my lawyer say?"

"I didn't get to finish my sandwich. I'd like another before I call my next witness."

Kirsten smiled. "Me, too. And a fresh pot of coffee."

Cam whirled and brushed by the sheriff. "Two sandwiches and a pot of coffee coming up."

52

SERENA'S CLIENT LOOKED only a little disheveled after the recess altercation. The blood had been wiped off and did not show much on the black dress. Certainly, there was nothing in Kirsten's cool demeanor to reveal that she had not had a restful lunch break. They had faced death together and probably saved each other's lives. They had acknowledged as much while they ate and regrouped, and Serena knew they had established a fast bond from shared combat both in and out of the courtroom.

Examination of the other early witnesses had gone quickly. Serena had decided to set forth the narrative in sequence. She had only briefly called Chet Grisham for the purpose of verifying Kirsten's physical condition when he first encountered her and the fact she had never stated she killed Max, only that he had "died."

Pilar Locke had been a helpful witness, describing Kirsten's condition in nearly every gory detail, including the breast mutilation, which Serena had skirted during Chet's testimony. She, again, confirmed the defendant's strange reference to her husband's death. Fuller had found efforts to trip up Pilar during cross-examination futile.

Dr. Hiram Robinson, as the only other physician to examine Kirsten's injuries, had been called to give his evaluation and opinion of the extent and likely cause. He expressed his shock at the damage inflicted. "I've never seen a person, man or woman, that beat up who lived to tell about it," he had testified. Serena suspected his words might have been a bit of an overstatement, but she did not discourage the thought. Cam had exercised astute judgment in having his poker-playing friend take a look at Kirsten soon after injuries.

Thad was Serena's only remaining witness, and he would be switching hats from physician to photographer during his testimony. This would have to be finessed with some care. He was insightful, though, and she was confident in his effectiveness as a witness. They had rehearsed most of her examination several times, and their rhythms of poignant pauses and appropriate nods and phrasing were excellent. Fortunately, she was adept at compartmentalizing, and she had been mostly able to set their common past and the unpleasant conversation that faced them out of her mind.

"Miss Belmont, did you hear me? I said you may call your next witness." It was Judge Whitmore's voice.

"I apologize, Judge, I was distracted for a moment. The defense calls Dr. Thaddeus Locke."

As Thad sat down in the witness chair, Serena observed that he appeared somewhat tense, but not excessively so. This was not particularly a problem. Her stomach still churned before the commencement of every trial, and she had come to recognize the feeling as her friend. Even now, she was a bit anxious but knew the feeling would disappear after the first question. She commenced. "Would you state your name for the judge and jury please?"

"Thaddeus Jacob Locke."

Serena led him through the questions relating to his medical qualifications, taking particular care to elicit the fact that he had graduated from an elite and respected medical school, and that, although he was a veterinary surgeon by choice, he occasionally treated human patients. Furthermore, he kept abreast of human medical developments, because medicines and techniques often equally applied to others in the animal kingdom. She also questioned him about his interest and background in photography, carefully laying the foundation for introduction of the tintypes into evidence.

"Dr. Locke. How did you come to be at Mrs. Brannon's home the night of Max Brannon's death?"

"My brother Cameron's son showed up at my home and said his dad wanted me over at the C Bar C right away and that I was to bring my photographic equipment with me. Myles . . . that's my nephew . . . indicated something terrible had happened to Kirsten."

"By 'Kirsten,' you mean Mrs. Brannon?"

"Yes, I didn't actually call her by her first name at that time. I had only met her on a few occasions when I was at the ranch performing veterinary services."

"So, you proceeded to gather your things and went to the ranch?"

"Yes, I have a habit of responding promptly to my brother's requests. He can be unpleasant when he's ignored."

Serena noticed understanding smiles on the faces of some of the jurors, a few of whom probably had older brothers. She began to pick up the pace, reviewing the events of that night, which had already been largely established by Pilar's testimony. He responded in kind with quick and brief answers.

Then she asked, "Doctor, did Mrs. Brannon ever say anything to you about her husband?"

"Beyond identifying him as the source of her injuries, she only said he had died and was in the bedroom. At some point I entered the room and confirmed this to be the case."

"Did you determine cause of death?"

"It appeared he had a bullet wound in his head, but I didn't make a thorough examination. There was nothing I could do for the man, and I had been told that Cam had sent for the sheriff."

"Mrs. Brannon said nothing about how her husband died?"

"No, she did not."

"Did you find that strange?"

"Yes, but she had suffered severe head injuries, and anything she said would not have been too surprising."

"Tell me, is it medically possible for a person who has witnessed a horrific event to not recall the incident?"

"This does happen. I listened to several medical school lectures on the subject. The most documented cause is brain trauma, resulting from physical damage to the head. The term that is beginning to be used to identify this phenomenon is 'amnesia.' With this condition, a man may lose all memory of his past . . . even his name. Or only a brief span or moment in time may be blocked from memory. Some doctors working in the new field of psychology suggest the same symptoms may result from emotional shock. I would be the first to say I am not competent to render an opinion on that possibility."

"You heard Pilar Locke's testimony . . . and that of Dr. Robinson . . . regarding the injuries incurred by Kirsten Brannon?"

"I did."

"Did you find their description of Mrs. Brannon's injuries substantially accurate?"

"I did."

"And do you have any documentation that might tend to support those descriptions?"

"Yes, I have a number of tintypes I took of the injuries."

"Just to clarify, Doctor, is it your practice to photograph all of your patients' injuries?"

"No, of course not. I have never done this with human patients before or since. I occasionally photograph injuries and conditions of animal patients for a book I am working on."

"So, why did you make an exception in this case?"

"My brother's request and Mrs. Brannon's consent."

"Did this request bother you?"

"Only because of my concern for Mrs. Brannon's dignity. Some of the tintypes are very personal."

Serena returned to the counsel table where Cam placed a stack of tintypes in her outstretched hands. She, in turn, delivered the photographs to the judge's bench. "Your Honor, we have taken the liberty of numbering each of these tintypes. With your permission I would like to deposit these with you and then remove them one at a time for identification by Dr. Locke prior to passing them among the jurors."

The Judge looked at the prosecutor. "Counselor, take a look at these and get your objection out of the way."

Fuller joined Serena at the judge's bench and began shuffling through the tintypes. "I object, Your Honor. These are inflammatory and prejudicial."

"To who?" the Judge asked.

"To the prosecution, of course."

"Well, Mr. Fuller, it's usually the defendant we give the leeway to on such things."

Fuller stammered, "Well, irrelevant then. This has nothing to do with the defendant's innocence or guilt."

"Overruled. Proceed, Miss Belmont."

After Fuller was seated, Serena showed Thad the first exhibit, and he verified he had taken the photo and then described the facial and head wounds displayed. After a tintype was handed to Thad and described by him, it was passed to the jurors for inspection. The jurors examined the tintypes with somber looks on their faces. Several grimaced, and the young storekeeper gave a look of horror. Finally, they came to the photographs of the mangled breast, and Serena asked Thad, "Doctor, please explain this tintype, Exhibit 8."

"It's a tintype of Mrs. Brannon's breast wounds. She testified her husband bit her breasts. You can see from the picture that this is an understatement. It looks like she was attacked by a wildcat. The lacerations were deep and ragged, extremely difficult to suture."

"And Exhibit 8 was taken after the surgery. Is that correct?"

"Yes, at least an hour later."

Serena delivered the exhibit to the jurors, and as they passed them from man to man, there was a shaking of heads and several grunts. One elderly gentleman turned pale and broke out in a sweat. When the tintypes reached the storekeeper, he stared at the object in his hands for a moment and then vomited.

As the bailiff cleaned up the vomit, Serena continued. "Doctor, I have just a few other questions. Did Mrs. Brannon have any injuries not shown in the photographs?"

"Yes."

"Tell me about them."

"She was badly bruised between her thighs and about her labia area?"

"For clarification, you are speaking of a woman's private parts?" She doubted some of her jurors would know what a "labia" was.

"Yes, that is correct."

"No other questions."

"The judge looked at the county attorney. "Your witness, Mr. Fuller."

"One moment, Your Honor." Fuller turned to his deputy, and they engaged in an animated, whispered conversation for several minutes. Finally, the prosecutor turned to the judge and stood. "No questions of this witness."

The judge pulled out the pocket watch from his vest pocket. "It's almost five-thirty. Would it be alright if we started with your next witness tomorrow morning."

"Not necessary, Judge," she replied. "The defense rests."

Judge Whitmore returned a big smile. "Very well, then. We'll start with closing statements in the morning and then toss this case to the jury."

53

CAM SLUMPED IN the oak arm-chair in front of his father's desk. It was late morning, and the energy had been suddenly sapped from his body. Post-trial downslide, Pilar called it.

"The case has gone to the jury?" Myles asked.

"Yeah, about half an hour ago."

"How long do you think they'll be out?"

"God knows. Two hours or two days. Anything can happen with a jury."

"I know. That's why long ago I decided to stay away from them."

"But some of us can't help ourselves."

Myles chuckled. "I understand. How'd closing go?"

"Serena asked to give the closing, and I deferred. She's quite brilliant you know."

"Yes, I've come to see that."

"She didn't give up on the possibility someone else might have killed Max while Kirsten was unconscious . . . reasonable doubt, you know, but a pretty big stretch. Then she pointed out that justifiable homicide is a defense, even if it she did shoot him. Of course, the statutes say 'justifiable' means self-defense or something akin to it. Serena seemed to subtly add 'killing a mean son-of-a-bitch' to that category. She pretty much convinced me. At least she gave the jurors plenty to latch onto if they're looking for excuses to acquit."

"And what do you think?"

"She's not going to hang. First degree requires willful, deliberate and premeditated killing. Frank didn't come close to proving that. I think he risked blowing his entire case by overcharging. Logic says she gets convicted of second degree. The sentence is a ten-year minimum, and the sky's the limit. Whitmore likely gives her the minimum."

"She's an exceptional woman. I'd hate to see that."

"Back east a few states recognize a 'temporary insanity' defense, but our statutes don't provide for that, and it's rarely successful where they do. Truth is that's probably what we've got with Kirsten."

"Where's Serena?"

"She's sitting in the jail cell with Kirsten. They seem to have formed a fast friendship during the course of the trial." Cam smiled wryly, "Of course, Serena's got a notch on her gun now, too. Men better treat that pair right."

"How about lunch and coffee on the old man?"

"I'm ready."

54

It was nearly five o'clock in the afternoon, and the jury had been deliberating a day and a half, when Reva knocked on the door of Serena's makeshift office in the Locke building. "Come in," Serena replied.

Reva opened the door. "Jury's been called in by the judge," she said. "Cam's out at his ranch, but I've sent a rider to give him the word. But you're on your own. Good luck."

Serena hurried to the courthouse. She had just left the jail and assumed the sheriff or his deputy would be escorting Kirsten to the courtroom. She could feel her heart racing and assumed it was from anticipation of the verdict, but there was always that nagging concern whether another attack of her illness was imminent.

When she arrived at the courtroom, Kirsten was already seated at the defense table. She returned Kirsten's nod as she sat down, but neither spoke.

Judge Whitmore entered, and as he was taking his chair, motioned to the lawyers, "Counsel, would you approach the bench?"

Serena joined the county attorney in front of the judge, who said, "I'm just forewarning you, counsel, the jury may not reach a verdict."

"What do you mean, Judge?" Fuller asked.

"A hung jury?" Serena interjected.

"It appears so. The foreman has requested instructions three times because of apparent deadlock, and I gather there's more than one holdout . . . maybe three or four. I've asked the jury to come in and report in open court. If the foreman declares they are unable to reach a verdict, I'll declare a mistrial, and it will be up to Mr. Fuller to decide if you're going to start all over."

Fuller sighed heavily, and his face turned glum. Serena thought the diminutive county attorney shrank a few more inches. "Judge, if the jury can't reach a verdict, I'd like to have them hash it out one more time."

"I'll see what the foreman says, but I'll warn you, I'm thinking this show's about over, and I don't have a lot of enthusiasm for an encore performance. If you're going to pursue this, Mr. Fuller, I'd strongly suggest you drop the first degree charge. That's not worth a cow shit pie . . . pardon the expression, ma'am. Second degree, I wouldn't be insulted by, but I wouldn't be disappointed if this whole thing would go away. I seriously doubt if you're ever going to seat a jury that doesn't have a few folks who think justice has already been done."

Serena said, "Your Honor, if you declare a mistrial, I will have a motion to submit."

"I suspected as much. You will have that opportunity. Now I'll call in the jury."

A few minutes later the jurors filed in from the anteroom and took their seats. Serena had only a moment to inform Kirsten that a possible mistrial was pending, but she did not have time to explain the significance.

The judge gaveled the court to order. "Mr. Bascomb, would you stand, please?"

Bascomb, a white-haired professor from the Kansas State

Agricultural College, who had been elected foreman by his fellow jurors, stood.

"Mr. Bascomb, has the jury reached a verdict?"

"We have been unable to reach a verdict, Your Honor."

"You understand that the verdict must be unanimous? Do you think that further deliberation may result in a verdict?"

"I do not. It is my opinion, which is shared by my fellow jurors, that we are hopelessly deadlocked."

"You may be seated, Mr. Bascomb. I thank the jurors for their service in this matter." The judge paused and tossed a look at each of the attorneys. "I declare a mistrial in this case."

The judge's eyes fixed on Serena. "I would entertain a motion, Miss Belmont."

"Your Honor, I move that Mrs. Brannon be released without bond at this time. The evidence has clearly established she is a person of property with roots in this county. She is not a flight risk, and certainly should not be incarcerated further pending the prosecutor's decision regarding any further action in this case."

The judge looked at the county attorney, who just shrugged. "Motion granted. The defendant is released from the custody of the sheriff pending further order of this court. The jury is discharged. Adjourned."

The reporters raced for the door, and the few other spectators and jurors meandered out of the courtroom. Serena caught a glimpse of Cam in the hallway. He had evidently cornered the jury foreman, who Cam had mentioned was a fellow Freemason.

Serena started gathering up her notes and trial books and Kirsten remained silent and solemn for some moments. "You seem a bit subdued," Serena remarked.

"What just happened?"

"I'm sorry. I should have explained. Everything turned to chaos so quickly. You do understand that you are free to go now?"

"Yes, I understand that."

"And when we leave here, you're coming with me to stay with Vedette and Myles overnight. It's too late to ride out to your place, and you need some time to get your thoughts together. I promise they'll love to have you, and they have plenty of room."

Kirsten nodded, although her eyes betrayed uncertainty. "But, if I understand correctly, we may have to go through all of this again."

"That's possible. Since there was no verdict, you don't have constitutional protection against double jeopardy. It's in the hands of the county attorney. The judge won't take kindly to his going after you again on the first degree murder charge. But second degree is still an open question."

"When will we know?"

"There's no specific deadline, but I don't think he will want the speculation to continue in the press very long. I'd be very surprised if we don't know by the first of the week."

"You said yesterday that you hoped to start your trip back to Washington on Monday. Does that mean you won't be able to help me in a second trial?"

"If you want me involved, I'll return."

Cam suddenly appeared in front of the table. "Well, ladies, would you like to hear what happened in the jury room?"

Serena smiled. "I saw you talking to the foreman. I can't wait."

Cam picked up one of the spectator chairs and placed it across the table from Serena and Kirsten, and sat down. "There was not just one hold out . . . there were six. There were only two votes to convict on first degree, and after voting three times, they gave up on that. The first vote for second degree was eight to four to convict.

They argued and voted on that all day and finally ended up deadlocked with a tie vote. They just ended up further away from the unanimous verdict they had to have."

"Did they have an acquittal vote?" Serena asked.

"They did, but the other side wouldn't vote to acquit either. The foreman was with us, and that didn't hurt. The young storekeeper was with him all the way, and in spite of his weak stomach, spoke up very forcefully during the deliberations."

"So what does Fuller do?" Serena asked.

"He's going to talk to some jurors, too . . . then he very quietly caves and dismisses the charges with as little fanfare as possible."

Serena turned to Kirsten and gave her a hug, and Kirsten gave a sigh of relief, as the tension seemed to melt from her body.

55

SERENA SAT AT the breakfast table enjoying a morning cup of coffee with Vedette. Kirsten had departed a few minutes earlier, planning to pick up her horse and gear at the livery and return to her ranch house. She had shrugged off suggestions she might want someone to accompany her after all that had taken place there. She had work to do, she insisted, and Chet and the new hired hand, Asa Morgan, she was sharing with Thad were both staying on the place.

Vedette and Myles had graciously opened their home to the surprise guest, and they had spent the previous evening chatting about everything but the trial. Kirsten had excused herself early to one of the spare bedrooms, and she looked well-rested when she departed this morning. Serena promised Kirsten they would get together as soon as Serena returned to the Flint Hills.

"So you're leaving Monday?" Vedette asked.

"That's my plan. Before I left the courthouse, I spoke with Cam and asked him to get a message to Thad to meet me at a place I call the 'medicine wheel' . . . it's actually on Thad's property. I could tell Cam was curious, but I just couldn't tell him more. He'll know soon enough, I guess. I'm to meet him at noon, and I'm going to pick up some sandwiches at the Chuck Wagon to take with me."

"I could make something."

"No, that's not necessary. I have to walk downtown to rent a horse, and the café is just across the street."

"So you're going to tell Thad today?"

"Yes, and after that I'm going over to my folks. I promised I'd spend the night there and go to church with them tomorrow. I'll head back here after Sunday dinner with the family and impose on your hospitality one more night, if that's alright."

"Of course, it's alright. It hasn't been an imposition. You've been a joy to have here. I can't wait till you return to Manhattan to stay."

"I'm looking forward to it. I've been wrong to deprive Ned of the Locke side of his family. It's despicable. I can't excuse it. I'm getting the shakes over having to tell Thad about his son." She hoped that was what the slight chills that had started during the night were about. Facing a jury was nothing compared to what she had to deal with now.

"It's got to be difficult, I know, but Thad may be the kindest, gentlest man I've encountered . . . next to his father. As I've told you, he's very controlled and thoughtful. He'll listen, and he won't judge harshly. They're not religiously devout men, but I always thought Myles and Thad instinctively take to heart the words found in Matthew . . . 'judge not, that ye be not judged.' If only more so-called Christians would heed them."

"I'll pray that your opinion holds true today. Do you have some riding clothes I could borrow?"

"The trousers may be a bit long, but we'll put something together."

56

THAD DISMOUNTED CATO and led the horse toward the young woman standing next to a sorrel mare at the base of the bluff. She appeared tired, and she was a shade too thin. Attired in faded denim trousers that were rolled up at the ankles and fell to the top of her moccasins and a checkered flannel shirt that she swam in, she looked something of a poor vagabond. But she was still stunning.

"Thad," she said, remaining next to her horse. "I'm glad you're here. I was afraid you might not come."

He moved closer. "I'm curious, so I took the bait. Cam said you wanted me to meet you here, although he had no clue where the 'medicine wheel' was. I think he was a little annoyed when I just told him it was a spot on the Rickers place."

"I brought some sandwiches, but all I've got to drink is water. Shall we go to the top of the mesa?"

"Sure, give me your saddle bags with the food, and I'll carry."

He took the bags and grabbed his canteen after tethering the horses and followed Serena, who had a head start up the trail. He quickly caught up after she stopped and sat down on a slab of limestone that had evidently ended up next to the trail after some past rockslide. Her breathing was labored and she was sweating profusely, which he thought was strange for such a young woman on a balmy day.

"You must be spending too much time in the office these days," Thad teased.

She returned a wry smile. "I do, I'm afraid, or I'm on a train to somewhere."

"We're not quite half way. Do you want to turn back?"

She gave him a horrified look. "No, we can't."

Thad tossed his canteen strap and the saddle bags over his shoulder and suddenly bent over and scooped her up in his arms.

She struggled for only a few moments. "What in the hell are you doing?"

"Just be quiet. I'm your train."

She couldn't weigh a hundred pounds, he thought, as he plodded up the trail. It was nice to have her in his arms, and he savored the scent and closeness of her. When they reached the top and stepped over the lip of the bluff, he let her slip out of his arms.

"I'm embarrassed," she said, "I didn't realize how I'd let myself go."

"Don't worry about it," he said. "I'm glad I could be useful."

She strolled over to the medicine wheel. "It's just the same as when I last saw it."

"I don't think anybody comes here. I suspect only a few know about it."

She turned to him. "Do you come here?"

"Yes, sometimes. Just to think or when I want to be alone."

"And now you own it?"

"I do. And you can come here anytime you wish."

She walked slowly around the circle as if scrutinizing each stone, and then she focused on the cottonwood. "It's grown."

"Trees do that, you know. Why do I think you are avoiding something?"

She sighed. "Because I am. Let's eat first, and then we'll talk."

They sat on the lush grass under the gently-swaying cottonwood branches and ate dried beef and cheese sandwiches made with fresh-baked wheat rolls, topping their lunch off with some original spice cookies Charlie had concocted. Neither spoke until they finished eating, and then Serena broke the silence. "Now we can talk."

"You said we needed to talk, and it's all sounded quite ominous."

"I suppose it is a little ominous as far as I'm concerned."

She took off a kerchief that had been tied about her neck and began dabbing at the perspiration on her face.

"Are you okay?" he asked.

"I will be," she said. "For now."

"You're speaking in riddles."

She looked away from him, gazing skyward, as she spoke softly and matter-of-factly. "I have stories to tell, and they will eventually merge into one story that involves both of us."

He decided to say nothing.

"I've been told that I'm dying. The last physician I spoke with said I won't be alive two years from now. That's one reason I'm coming home."

He felt like a sledge hammer had struck him in the gut. Bile surged in his throat. "What was his diagnosis?"

"He said I have a cancer in my internal organs and that it's eating its way from the inside out."

"How does he know this?"

"I don't know. My symptoms, I guess."

"And may I ask what your symptoms are?"

"They come and go. They started a little over two years ago. I had this terrible pain in my muscles and abdomen, as well as vomiting, and then got a terrible fever and the chills. Between chill episodes, I'd get the sweats and an excruciating headache. I'd have spasms in my chest. I was in a coma for several days, and when I woke up the symptoms lessened over several days until I pretty much recovered. "

"You said they started two years ago. I take that to mean that you've had other episodes?"

"I had another three months later . . . but no coma . . . and I continued to suffer the attacks every three or four months after that. It's been nearly three months since the last one. I'm due."

"Have you seen other physicians?"

"Yes, but the doctors who will see colored people in Washington are limited," she said with some bitterness in her voice. "One doctor said I had a poison in my system and wanted to start a bleeding procedure. I got up and walked out."

"Yes, that's nonsense. They helped kill our first President with that. But it was an accepted medical practice for some years . . . they even used leeches."

"Another doctor said I have consumption and that I'll eventually die from it."

"Consumption might mean anything. Many physicians apply the term to what we now call tuberculosis, but others apply the term to anything they can't find an explanation for. Do you have a chronic cough or anything like that?"

"No."

"Any blood when you do cough?"

"No."

"You're not carrying any extra weight, that's for sure. You were like carrying a goose-down pillow. Are you losing weight?"

"I lost ten pounds when I had the last attack. I never gained it back, but I haven't lost any more."

"You can have night sweats and a fever with tuberculosis, but it wouldn't usually be dormant for long periods of time and your decline would be fairly consistent and continuous. Your lungs obviously aren't at full capacity, which is a concern, but that could be from limited use. Talking doesn't build up your lungs."

She turned to him now. "Thad, I appreciate your interest in my case, but you're talking like this is a damn doctor's visit. That's not what I wanted to talk to you about."

She sounded annoyed, just like she was when they first met all those years ago. "Sorry, I'm just concerned that you're not doing everything you can to get the answers. You sound like you've accepted the verdict . . . a death sentence. That isn't the person I saw in the courtroom."

"Look, I haven't given up. I'll work until I die. That's why I've taken a position with the Locke firm. But I'm a realist. I know I don't have good health, and there's a distinct possibility I'm going to die sooner rather than later . . . maybe very soon. That's what drove me to right some wrongs."

"Wrongs? What's that got to do with us?"

Her dark eyes fastened on his like they were trying to bore into his soul. "Thad, you have a son. You and I have a son."

What in the hell was she babbling about? He tried in vain to sort out her words, to make some sense out of what she had said.

"That's not possible. How?"

"Good God, Thad, you're a doctor. Do I have to draw you a picture?"

She was irritating him now, but he subdued his anger. "That's not what I meant, and you know it," he said evenly. "Just explain."

"Our son is ten years old. He was conceived right where you

and I are sitting."

He could feel his heart racing and a mix of emotions—anger, regret, sadness and, yes, joy stirring in his mind. "And you've never told me during all of these years. I can't believe it. Did your parents know?"

"Yes, Mama begged me to tell you, threatened to do it herself, but I told her she had no right. But I wronged her, too. She's carried the burden of a silent lie all of these years. It hurt her terribly to keep this from you."

"But why didn't you tell me? I had responsibilities. I would have met them. I loved you. There's no way I wouldn't have been there for you both, even if I had to move back east. I would have married you in the blink of an eye. You know that. I asked you to marry me before you left."

"That's precisely why I didn't tell you. I loved you then, Thad, but you didn't fit into the life I was driven to, and Aunt Clara was there to help me raise a child. Besides, you would have hated it in the East. You probably wouldn't have got your education. This is where you belong, doing exactly what you do."

"That doesn't change the fact that somehow I could have been a part of his life all of these years."

"I know. I'm sick about what I've done."

"What's his name?"

"Edward Thaddeus Locke. He goes by 'Ned.'"

"He carries the Locke name?"

"Yes. I asked Mama to enter it that way in the family Bible. I was going to tell you, but each year it got harder and harder."

"And if you hadn't determined you are dying, I would have never known about my son?"

"That's not true. He's been asking too many questions about his father. I had decided I couldn't wait any longer. I was going to bring him back to meet you and then we would talk about how you would see each other."

"I have no doubt you intended to do that, but pardon me if I'm skeptical that this would have ever happened if you hadn't been concerned about your health."

"I can't blame you for thinking that."

"What does he know about me?"

"I've told him where you live and about your family. For years I told him that you couldn't come see him because you were so far away and so busy. He seemed to accept that since he had never known a life with a man in the house. But then a year ago he started to hammer me with questions and demanded I take him to see you. It was then I told him the truth . . . that you didn't even know about him. He became very angry and belligerent, and then he turned sullen and quiet. This normally loving and enthusiastic boy grew distant and wouldn't open up to me anymore. When I left on my speaking tour on my way to Kansas a month ago, I told him I was going to tell you about him and that we would probably be moving to the Flint Hills to be near his father and his grandparents. He was thrilled but, understandably, a bit disbelieving."

"Tell me about him."

"Well, he's got the Locke gray eyes. Very tall for his age. I guess, by the standards that prevail, he'd be considered colored, but he's even lighter-skinned than I am. He has a beautiful, friendly smile. Sometimes, he's too serious. A very kind boy. His teachers tell me he's smart as a whip, and he reads all the time."

It stung Thad that he had missed out on this boy's life, and thoughts of the things they could have shared flashed through his mind. He was nearly overwhelmed by a black melancholy. He stood up and extended his hand to assist Serena to her feet. "I don't think we have much else to say to each other about this," he said. "I need to think."

Serena faced him, "I understand."

"I want to see him soon."

"We'll be back within six months, probably sooner."

"I can travel to Washington and spend a week or so. We can get acquainted."

"I'd rather you didn't come. I'm afraid it would be disruptive. School's starting, and I have my affairs to wind up there. Please, give me this time to prepare him. I know I don't deserve your consideration, but, please, let me do this my way. When we return, I promise I'll do everything I can to bring him into your life."

"But I've already missed all these years."

"Please."

"I'll have to think about it," he said noncommittally. "Now you'd better be on your way. Do you need help getting down the trail?"

"I'll be fine. But there's one other thing you should know. I had your father make out my will. Everything goes to Ned. Your father is executor, and I've named you Ned's personal guardian. You and your father will be co-trustees of a trust to handle Ned's money until he's twenty-one."

"The Judge knows about Ned?"

"Yes, I put him in a very difficult position. He insisted I tell you immediately. I convinced him to wait until the trial was over. Besides, at that point he was bound by attorney-client confidentiality. He and Vedette are the only persons outside my family who know about Ned."

He shook his head in disbelief. A will. She did believe she was dying. She didn't look well, but this had been a difficult reunion for both of them. What more could he say, though? She had made it clear she wasn't interested in his medical opinions.

Serena looked at him expectantly, as if waiting for him to respond. He did not, and she turned away and walked unsteadily toward the trailhead.

57

HENRY, WHO HAD not yet returned to the home of his mistress, woke Thad up when he leaped on his chest and began to give his nose love nips, a clear signal it was time for breakfast. That meant it was precisely five-thirty this Monday morning, for Henry was as reliable as the best timepiece. Thad tossed back his covers and reluctantly climbed out of bed. He had just pulled on his trousers and boots, when he heard a feeble tapping at the exterior door of his office at the opposite end of his small residence. He slipped into a shirt and buttoned it on his way to the single-room office area.

When he opened the door, he was surprised to find Elizabeth Belmont standing there, her eyes wide and glistening with tears. "Elizabeth," he said, waving her into the room, "come in. What's the matter? More trouble with the hogs?"

She began sobbing, stopping intermittently and taking deep breaths as she spilled out her story. "It's Serena. She's dying. She's been sick since Saturday night and keeps getting worse. Old Doc Robinson came out yesterday afternoon and said she was dying. He left laudanum to help with the pain."

Thad was struck by a wave of regret about the cold parting he and Serena had experienced Saturday. Her illness had remained very much on his mind, however, and he had spent most of the afternoon and evening searching his limited medical books and journals to ferret out fragments of information that might help.

"Sit down, Elizabeth," he said calmly, offering her one of the captain's chairs before he pulled up another and sat down facing her. "Tell me, why did you come here?"

"Mama sent me. She said you should be there, and she told me she's been praying you might help."

"Tell me about Serena. I want to know her symptoms . . . how she's acting."

Elizabeth had composed herself now. "She has the shakes . . . awful chills. And she sweats and sweats and hurts all over. A lot of the time she's out of her head."

"Delirious?"

"Yes. That's the word . . . delirious. And she goes into these trances where she doesn't hear anybody talking to her. She was like that when I left. Mama called it a coma."

Thad leaned back in his chair. He should head for the Belmont place right away. He needed something from Smith's Drug Store, though. He was hesitant to send Elizabeth on the errand. Ebenezer Smith was rumored to be a part of the hierarchy of the local Klan. Thad wasn't sure what kind of reception a young colored girl might receive there. "Elizabeth, do you know where Kirsten Cavelle lives?"

"The C Bar C? Sure."

Thad slid the chair over to his desk and pulled out pencil and paper and began to write. When he was finished, he handed a folded sheet to Elizabeth. "I want you to ride over to the C Bar C and tell Miss Cavelle what's happened and ask her to have Asa take this note to Smith's Drug Store. I've instructed Smith to put the medicine on my account. When he gets the drug I've requested, he is to bring it to me at your parents' house. Can you do that?"

She gave her first smile and nearly leaped from her chair. "Yes, sir. I'm on my way."

58

WHEN THAD ARRIVED at the Belmont farm, he was met at the door by Rachael, who latched onto his arm and guided him into the parlor. Her face was sober and drawn, and he thought she had aged ten years since he last saw her.

"Thad, I can't thank you enough for coming. Dr. Robinson gave us no hope. Quincy is crumbling. He's out back, praying his heart out for a miracle."

"Elizabeth should be along soon," he said, "I sent her to relay a message to Kirsten Cavelle. Has Serena's condition changed since Elizabeth left?"

"Not really. She's asleep, and I can't wake her. I can tell she has a terrible fever."

"Where is she? I'd like to see her."

"She's in one of the upstairs bedrooms. Clarissa's with her." She moved toward the stairway. "Follow me."

When they entered the bedroom, an obviously frightened Clarissa slipped out of the bedside chair and, without a word, scurried out of the room. Thad took her place and sat there for some moments, studying the young woman clad only in a sweat-soaked cotton nightdress. The wet fabric clung to her like a second layer of skin and her body shook like a feather fluttering in the wind. Her teeth rattled noisily. He placed his hand on her damp forehead and felt fire. She was teetering on the edge of death. "Serena," he said. "Serena." There was no response.

He turned to Rachael. "We need to fill a tub with fresh well water. Can you get the kids started on that?"

"Of course, we've got a large claw-foot bathtub in a closet off the kitchen." She disappeared from the room,

Thad watched Serena helplessly, wishing he could take back the cold, harsh words he had tossed at her during their meeting at the medicine wheel. They had to pull her out of this crisis. He prayed for a chance to make things right with her. What's done is done, he decided. Forgiveness purges the bitter soul. They would go forward from here, not likely as a couple, but as a team working for a good life for Ned. If he was right, her condition was mostly about fever. One of his medical school professors had always preached, "treat the symptoms, and let the disease take care of itself." Thad had always followed that precept in his veterinary practice and had come to accept it as faith.

Soon, Rachael returned. She was nearly breathless. "The tub's ready. I got Quincy off his knees, and it didn't take long."

Thad stood and bent over the bed and lifted Serena's lifeless form into his arms. In a moment they were in the kitchen where Quincy stood, looking deeply chagrined and helpless. Thad was pleased to see Elizabeth had returned. She could be helpful now. "Elizabeth, did you get the message to Miss Cavelle?"

"Yes, and she took it herself. She was off like the wind before I even started back."

Thad had asked for Asa because he feared Kirsten, in light of her recent history, might also encounter resistance at the drugstore. On second thought, however, he shrugged off his concerns. How many men or women were tough enough to stand up to Kirsten?

Damn few.

He carried Serena over to the tub. "Rachael and Elizabeth, when I let Serena down next to the tub, I need to have you help me slip her out of the nightdress and get her into the tub."

In a few minutes Serena was submerged to her neck in the cold water. It worried him that her body did not noticeably react to the water. "Elizabeth," he said, "would you find a washrag and just keep washing your sister's face with the cool water? We'll do this for about half an hour and then get her into some dry things and back in bed."

"Yes, Doctor, I'll do that right now." She left the room for a few minutes, returned with a cloth and was soon kneeling next to the tub ministering to her sister. The young woman wanted to be a veterinary surgeon. She had the raw material to make a good one, he thought. Thad watched Serena's face intently. Her eyes fluttered, and he moved next to the tub and got down on his knees for a closer look.

"I saw it, too," Elizabeth said. "Her eyes."

Serena's eyes blinked several times, but that was the extent of her response. After Thad decided it was time to remove her from the tub, Rachael and Elizabeth dried Serena's body and maneuvered her into a fresh nightdress, and then he carried her back up the stairs and returned her to the bed. He felt her forehead. Still hot, but not the raging burn. Her shivering seemed more subdued. But she stayed locked in the coma.

"Hi, Doc. I've got your medicine."

Thad started at the sound of Kirsten's voice and turned to find her only a few feet behind him. "You didn't waste any time."

"I rode like a bat out of hell." She handed him a paper-wrapped bottle. "The magic potion?"

"I hope. But I can't give it to her while she's asleep."

Kirsten stepped to Serena's bedside. "My grandma was like this once. She had some kind of lung fever where she coughed and hacked and had a terrible fever, and everybody thought she was dying. I was just a little girl and I remember the family gathered around her bed and started to sing hymns to send her on a peaceful trip to the hereafter. She woke up all at once and scared the hell out of some of the singers." Kirsten pulled a chair up next to the bed. "Any better ideas?" she asked.

Without waiting for an answer, Kirsten sat down and took Serena's hand in hers. Thad and Rachael stepped back, but Elizabeth continued applying the wet cloth to Serena's face and forehead. Kirsten began to sing softly and clearly, with a voice that was incredibly beautiful and so unexpected from this tough-talking rancher woman. She sang non-stop for nearly an hour, from time to time squeezing Serena's hand as if trying to pump life into her body. Her repertoire of songs ran the gamut from "Aura Lea" and "Listen to the Mockingbird" to "Camptown Races" and an inspiring rendition of "Amazing Grace."

And then Serena's eyes opened slowly and she turned her head and looked at Kirsten, who still gripped her hand firmly. "Kirsten, what are you doing here?"

Kirsten smiled. "I was just running an errand for Doc here and thought I'd come by and wish you my best."

It suddenly occurred to Thad that sometime during the singing, Serena's chills had subsided significantly. "Rachael," Thad said, "I need a small glass or cup."

"I have a little cordial glass, but don't tell Quincy. He's a teetotaler . . . I'm not. I'll fetch it."

Thad noticed that Rachael's mood had lightened quickly with

Serena's return to the living, but he was certain this was simply a brief cease fire in the battle ahead. He moved in next to the bed and looked down at Serena.

"We need to talk about your illness. Are you thinking clearly?"

"I'm a little confused about you and Kirsten being here, but I know I've been more or less unconscious."

"More rather than less. I wasn't sure you'd make it back."

"I heard music. I thought I was in heaven."

"Kirsten was your angel. Your mother sent for me. I'm your doctor, if you'll let me be for a while."

She gave a weak smile. "You did a good enough job with my ankle one time. Yeah, you can be my doctor."

Rachael returned with a tiny glass, and Thad unwrapped the druggist's package and pulled out a large bottle embossed with the drug store name and nearly brim-full with a clear liquid. He plucked the cork from the container and took the glass from Rachael and poured no more than an ounce. He turned back to Serena and observed the perspiration forming on her brow again. She was on the brink of another attack, he thought. With his free arm he reached down and propped her up so she could drink. "I want you to take all of this . . . just sip."

"What is it?"

"Drink."

She obeyed, and then he lay her back down. "We need a few more pillows. I don't want her lying so flat. Her head and upper body should be elevated some. Now, this may make you a little drowsy, and that's okay. It's a good sleep. I gave you some quinine."

"Quinine?"

"It's a drug that's been around for a long time. It's processed from the bark of the Cinchona tree, generally found in South

America. It's used as an antipyretic."

"Oh my God," Kirsten chimed in,"how can you go wrong? You've got a horse doctor that uses big words." There was a soft tittering in the room, and even Serena smiled.

Thad cast Kirsten an annoyed look. She never let him get too full of himself, he had to admit. "An antipyretic is a drug that fights the fever. It's very effective, but you have to monitor the dosage and determine just how much it takes to get the results. Your fever was coming back. We'll wait an hour and probably try some more. It's the fever that will harm your body and, quite frankly, cause the complications that could be fatal."

"You know something. Tell me."

He tossed a look at Kirsten. "Anyone who doesn't want to listen to a medical lecture, possibly with a few big words, may leave." Nobody left.

"I don't *know* something for sure, but I *suspect* something. I think you have malaria. The fever, the chills and the fact it goes into remission and comes back. It's been called bilious fever, miasmal fever and any number of names. The name comes from Italian words, *mal* and *aria* . . . bad air. There were all kinds of suspected villains over the years, but about five years ago, a French physician discovered that it's caused by a parasite in the blood."

"Not a pleasant thought," Serena said.

"No, I guess not. We don't know how the parasite gets in your system, but we know that the disease has something to do with the parasites, and they apparently go through different stages and die and then come back again. That's why you have recurrences."

"But you can't get the varmints out?" Kirsten asked.

"That's the bad news. The good news, Serena, is that this isn't a death sentence. Control the fever and you control the disease. When the symptoms start to come on, you commence taking quinine and do anything else that helps to reduce the fever. You can head off the disease before you get so ill. That doesn't mean you won't have some unpleasant episodes, but you can live a normal life span. I would strongly suggest taking better care of yourself . . . getting more rest and physical activity, for instance. Build up your endurance."

Tears began streaming down Serena's cheeks, and Rachael began to sob. Kirsten moved to embrace the ecstatic mother. Elizabeth stayed at her post with the cool washrag and water bucket.

Thad moved closer to the bed and took Serena's hand. "You're going to live to see Ned's children, probably his grandchildren."

"Yes, thanks to you. And you're going to see them, too. I'm not changing my plans. I'll head back to Washington as soon as I can. But I'll be back. I promise."

"And I'll give you the time you asked for. Now go to sleep."

59

MYLES FRANKLIN LOCKE stared at the sheaf of papers on his desk but saw nothing. His mind was disconnected from the project in front of him—a rare occurrence for a man of his discipline. But he worried about what Thaddeus had in store with the changing events in his life.

His youngest son had just left the office after seeking his counsel about the feasibility of setting up a corporation for the company town he was seeking to establish with his business partner, Kirsten Cavelle. They planned multiple business ventures on a parcel of land adjacent to a projected extension of railroad service to Randolph, lying some twenty miles north of Manhattan. Their project would lie at the midpoint between the two towns, but it would take money, and that would require other investors. Myles had explained that control of a corporation required ownership of fifty-one percent of the shares. Thad could not leverage that much ownership by himself, so he could not acquire sole voting control. He and Kirsten could probably accomplish it together, but there was risk. What if they had a falling out? What was his level of trust that they could maintain their business relationship? Myles had professed his fondness and admiration for Kirsten, but relationships change, he pointed out—sometimes for the better and not uncommonly for the worse, much worse. Regardless, they needed an escape hatch, a contract provision that would set out a mechanism for resolving differences and assuring that one could buy the interest of the other if they determined they could no longer pursue business together.

This was a huge risk for Thad, but risk-takers had built America and would continue to do so for many generations, he hoped. And he thought Thad had an extremely competent partner, but such commercial undertakings between a man and a woman were unheard of. Thad and Kirsten were indeed pioneers.

He had few reservations about Kirsten's trust of Thaddeus. He had not been at liberty to tell his son that, prior to the trial, Kirsten had named Thad as executor of her will and trustee of a trust created by its terms. The will canceled Thad's note to Kirsten for the Rickers land purchase and gave him the Red Angus cow herd. It also provided Thad would hold all the land in trust for thirty years with the right to rent it during that time and to pay rentals to the Kansas State Agricultural College to build a fund for establishing a veterinary school. Upon expiration of the trust, the land would go outright to the college. For some reason Kirsten Cavelle had decided Thaddeus Locke was a man she could trust. Myles did not think for a moment that her trust was misplaced, but he found this instant trust rather strange for a woman of Kirsten's business acumen. It would be interesting to watch how this venture played out.

And then there was Serena returning to the Flint Hills and bringing a new son to Thad's life—and a grandson to his own. Thaddeus had two full plates, Myles decided. His thoughts were interrupted by a soft tapping on the door. Without waiting for a reply, it opened and Cam sauntered in and took a chair across from Myles.

"Well," he said, "I just left Serena at the railroad station. She'll be headed east in about fifteen minutes . . . said she'd be back in six months, hopefully less."

"She's a week later than she'd planned, but she seems to have recovered from her illness. I understand she can expect future attacks, but she should be able to carry on her work without much problem."

"Yeah, I assume she told you she's going to try to convince the Bill of Rights society to let her continue her work from here. She says we're almost dead-center in the middle of the country. She's going to argue that travel convenience would help carry on their work nationally. She can still take cases with our firm, but we wouldn't have to worry about carrying any financial load at all."

"Yes," Myles said. "On the contrary, she could make a nice contribution to overhead. We'd discussed it at home last night, and I was going to tell you about it this morning. I'd bet she wins her argument and our office becomes headquarters for the Bill of Rights Society."

"Little brother did himself proud in diagnosing her illness."

"Yes, he did. He gave her hope for her life. We all need that."

"And he's got a son. In my wildest imagination I'd have never dreamed that up. And here I always thought my young brother was boring as hell. And now he's got a woman moving back here with a child he didn't know about . . . a colored woman to boot. I don't know what that brings with it. Then he and crazy Kirsten have some wild-eyed scheme about development along the railroad. From my viewpoint he's got two wild women in his life. Trust me, one's about enough."

"I'll let him deal with the women . . . but I think they have the railroad project well thought out."

"I sure as hell hope so. Kirsten's talked Pilar into ten percent of the stock and a seat on the board of directors. We had a little unpleasantness over it, but I knew I'd lost that battle before it started, so I made a hasty retreat. I'm sort of a kept man, I guess. Pilar has her own money from her family's holdings in Texas, and I don't have any say about what she does with it."

"Pilar's a good woman. She's perfect for you."

"I know."

FALL 1885

60

THE SUN NEARLY blinded Kirsten as she stood near the edge of the mesa and looked eastward over the Big Blue River Valley this mid-November morning, and she tugged the brim of her hat down to nearly cover her forehead. Her eyes surveyed the brown, dormant grass that blanketed the landscape for acres and acres between the mesa and the river, and in her mind's eye, she saw the ribbons of steel that would start threading their trail northward and parallel to the river's course next summer. She could envision the buildings rising from the earth, one by one: the auction barn with its adjacent stockyard, a large general store, and Quincy Belmont's blacksmithing and metal works with an adjacent smoke house.

Negotiations were underway for both a sawmill and flourmill to be built on the northern outskirts of the central complex. There would be a small company office with the auction barn. They had not initially planned for residences on the site, but when the realization came that employees living nearby could be more available and productive, they began to rethink the plan. Managing the stockyards, for instance, was more than a daytime job. Thad had already decided to build a new home with a large attached clinic building somewhere on the site. The house would include several additional bedrooms to accommodate guests. He obviously intended for his son to occupy one of those rooms as often as possible.

A noticeable wind had suddenly started biting at her ears and neck, and she turned away and started meandering back toward the medicine wheel. This was her first visit to the spot. She knew about it, of course, and in a vague way she understood it had meant something special to Thad and Serena. Thad had suggested several times that she view the commercial site from the bluff but had not offered to accompany her. That was fine by her. She had little interest in visiting people's pasts. To Kirsten, life was now and the future.

As she studied the medicine wheel again, it occurred to her that some knowledgeable person should take a look at it before the table top of the mesa was overrun by civilization. There might be something to learn here, and it should probably be preserved. She would broach the subject with Thad. That wouldn't be difficult; he was always approachable and seemingly unflappable about anything she might bring up. She found him receptive to her opinions but firm when he disagreed. But not once in the some three months since the trial had their differences burst into angry words. Somehow, they always worked their ways to a common decision without even knowing which one had given ground.

As the wind picked up, she looked skyward to the west. Dark, menacing clouds rolled her way. Such was November in Kansas, a warm, balmy day one minute and a bitter ice storm the next. She decided she had better head home. Thad was riding over to the C Bar C early afternoon to finalize plans for organizing the new land company, and she should clean up a bit and straighten up the house.

It suddenly occurred to her that she hadn't given a damn about her appearance for anybody until a few months back when she started replacing some of her threadbare shirts with some new ones and picking up a few fragrances at the Manhattan shops. She had rationalized that she needed to appear more the businesswoman in her new enterprise and even bought a few professional-looking dresses for meetings with prospective investors. But it occurred to her now that Thad's opinion had come to count for something with her.

61

THAD SAT AT the table in Kirsten's ranch house, a stack of papers scattered out in front of him. Kirsten was brewing coffee, which he knew would be bitter and grainy. Maybe that's why she generally offered to add a thimble of whiskey, an offer he routinely declined while she added it to her own cup. He had shared light meals at her home when they were working and quickly learned her cooking was little better than her brewing. She had not protested when he gradually started helping her with the food preparation. He was glad, because it was the only way he could get a meal that wasn't burnt to a crisp.

None of this mattered anyway. Her enthusiasm for the company town had been contagious, and he was caught up in the planning, but he had lately come to realize how so much of what he looked forward to in their meetings was less the project than whom he was meeting with. She had somehow inched her way into becoming his best friend. He guessed that wasn't saying all that much, since, outside of family, he was a man of few, if any, close friends but many acquaintances.

Kirsten sat a cup of steaming coffee in front of him and joined him, taking a chair on the opposite side of the table. The wind howled like a prairie wolf outside, but the crackling fire only a few paces away was keeping up with it. The room was toasty and comfortable.

"I didn't offer you any whiskey this time . . . passed on it myself," Kirsten said. She took a sip of the coffee. "Having second thoughts, though." She smiled and he grinned back and gamely tried his own.

"It will keep us awake," he said diplomatically. "You've been doing some work on your house."

"You're very observant, considering it's been finished for two months. Yes, I've repainted all the rooms. Cleaned everything out of the bedroom and replaced the bed . . . I had to sleep on the floor till I got that done. I don't find anything creepy now. I miss Killer, but ever since that night he's taken up residence in the bunkhouse with Chet and Asa . . . only visits during the day. And, of course, Henry's abandoned me."

"I brought him back."

"Yeah, and the next day he was back at your place."

"I'm sorry. We've got to be pretty good friends."

"I'll find me another more appreciative cat sooner or later. I do like having a cat around." She abruptly changed the course of the conversation. "I visited the medicine wheel this morning."

The remark caught him by surprise, and he was uncertain how to respond. It wasn't like she had trespassed on a sacred temple, or at least it was sure as hell time for him to quit thinking of it that way. "What did you think?"

"The view was stupendous. You'll be able to see every detail of our development from there. In fact, it gave me an idea for the name of the company. Your father says we need to come up with a name for what he calls the 'umbrella' company. What would you think of 'Medicine Wheel Properties'?"

Thad did not respond immediately, running the name through his mind several times and repeating it out loud. "I'm okay with that."

She handed him several sheets of paper. "Here's what I've figured out for the stock based on cash and property contributions. You'll deed forty acres of river bottom to the corporation in exchange for twenty percent of the stock. I'll put in twenty-five thousand dollars for twenty-five percent of the stock . . . I can get that with a mortgage on my land now. Pilar will take ten percent, and Quincy wants fifteen. John Cooper from the Riley County Bank is in for ten percent. Your uncle El and aunt Nancy want ten percent. The other ten percent will be split four ways among the ranchers we talked to."

"No one person's got voting control."

"No, but if you, Pilar and I hang together, we've got the votes to run the company, and everybody can see that. I'm sure your aunt and uncle would stick with us, too."

"And if we don't hang together?"

"The whole thing blows to shit anyway."

"I don't want to run the thing day to day once it's set up. I've got my vet practice to look after, and we've already agreed I'm selling off my Herefords and going into the Red Angus business with you."

"I'll manage the company if you and Pilar will support me for president. I thought we'd put all the shareholders on the board to get their active involvement. Pilar could be vice-president and you'd be secretary-treasurer."

"Damn, you had this all figured out, didn't you? I don't know why I came over." He was relieved, not angry. Kirsten had the vision for the project and the management skills. He would not have been involved if he had not been confident she would take the project and run with it. The other investors had understood the pecking order, and after they met Kirsten, that's why they signed on. Conservative

Uncle El had been totally smitten, and Aunt Nancy, an astute judge of men and women, had given her enthusiastic blessing.

They spent the rest of the afternoon reviewing Kirsten's sketches of the site plans. Here they had to hammer out some differences over building locations, and there were issues over whether the lots would be platted and sold to business operators or whether the company would build and lease. They agreed to hire a surveyor to divide the land into platted lots and then decide on a case by case basis whether to sell or lease. They had concluded it might take too much borrowed money to be everybody's landlord. Certainly, Thad would own his own tract and bear the cost of constructing his home and clinic. That was one reason he had elected to take fewer shares.

Dusk was settling in by the time they had exhausted their ideas for the day, and Kirsten had already lighted a few kerosene lamps to brighten the house. Thad went to the window and peered out. "I probably need to get on my way. It's spitting snow. Henry's been confined to the barn this afternoon, and he'll bitch if he has to mouse for his supper."

"I know Henry won't starve, and he's no doubt curled up in the hay. And this is Asa's day for chores at your place. Stay for supper."

He hesitated. "On one condition."

"What's that?"

"I cook."

She stuck out her tongue at him. "I've some of Quincy's smoked sausages and the fixings for flapjacks."

He walked into the kitchen. "That sounds good, I'll get to work. Do you have some eggs?"

"I do. Fresh. Chet dropped some by this noon. I can make the coffee."

He gave her a warning stare.

"I guess I'll just add a log to the fire and sit."

"Do that."

After supper, Thad and Kirsten silently cleaned up the dirty pans and dishes together. They had barely spoken since he put supper on the table, but that was one thing he enjoyed about their friendship. They could be quiet together for long stretches without compulsion to break into each other's thoughts. Thad chided himself for eating too much, although Kirsten had out eaten him by far. She was slender as a young willow branch, and how she did it eating like that, he couldn't imagine. On the other hand, she had to eat her own cooking most of the time, he guessed.

When the dishes and pans had been put away, he looked outside again. "Oh, God, it's snowing and blowing like hell out there. This could get serious. I'd better get out to the barn and get Cato saddled up."

"Wait for it to blow over."

"And if it doesn't?"

"Sit down with me in front of the fireplace. We need to talk."

She did not wait for his reply but scooted the settee closer to the fire.

"We've been talking all afternoon," he said.

"About business. This isn't business."

They sat down together, just inches apart, and took in the warmth of the fire. He decided to let her set the agenda.

"How do you feel about what happened eight months ago," she asked.

"What do you mean?"

"Does it bother you that I probably killed my husband?"

"You weren't found guilty. The county attorney dismissed the charges the Monday after the mistrial was declared."

"Yes, but that doesn't change the facts. We both know I shot him. But, for what it's worth, I truly don't remember it. I didn't make that up. The terrible thing is, I don't even feel remorse. Isn't that sad? What does that say about me? I know Cam calls me 'Crazy Kirsten' sometimes. Do you think I might be insane?"

Thad laughed. "That isn't what Cam means. It's an affectionate label. He thinks you're crazy like a fox. He's never seen the likes of you." He paused and turned to her, lifted her chin and kissed her very softly on the lips. "The truth is I've never seen the likes of you, either. But I sure as hell like what I see."

She gently pushed him back. "Then all of that . . . with Max . . . it doesn't matter?"

"It doesn't matter."

"Another question."

"I feel like I'm back on the witness stand."

"Then tell the goddamned truth. I generally keep my distance on your personal business, but I'm breaking that rule tonight. What's going to happen with you and Serena? She's moving back to the Flint Hills and she's bringing your son with her."

He had thought a lot about that and he was prepared to respond. "I am going to become an important person in my son's life. We've got a lot of time to make up for. I believe her when she says she will do everything to bring me into his life. We talked when I made follow-up visits during her malaria recurrence. We have no intentions of taking up where we left off more than a decade ago. I have forgiven her for what she did with our son, but I haven't forgotten, and a part of me will always resent it, I suspect."

"She and I connected during what we experienced. I think we will continue to be good friends."

"That doesn't concern me. I asked Serena to marry me. But we were kids. Some kids marry and grow old together, and mature love evolves. I've seen it happen. But Serena made a wise decision when she turned me down. People have separate dreams, and if they can meld them into a shared dream, life is good. If they collide, they turn into a nightmare, and I fear that's how Serena and I would have ended . . . in the middle of a horrible nightmare. But who knows? And it doesn't matter now. What's done is done."

Now Kirsten reached behind his neck and pulled him to her, pressing her lips hungrily against his. He responded and his body told him what he wanted more than anything at this moment.

"I think you should stay the night," she whispered in his ear.

"Probably should," he agreed.

She led him into the bedroom, sat down on the bed and began pulling her boots off and slipping her faded denims down long, seemingly endless, legs. "You'll probably want to check my scars."

Thad started shedding his own garments. "Probably time for a follow-up exam," he said.

And when they tumbled naked onto the sheets, Thad learned that "Crazy Kirsten" was as innovative and enthusiastic in the bedroom as in the boardroom.

SPRING 1886

62

THE CALENDAR TURNED to the first of March with a strong suggestion of an early spring, although Thad well knew this could be one of Mother Nature's false promises. The winter's snow had thawed to mere isolated patches, and as Thad led his venerable Appaloosa into the yard, the sun warmed his back and made him drowsy. He hadn't been getting enough sleep this winter, he chided himself—thanks to Kirsten Cavelle. He'd found too many excuses to trek over to the C Bar C on a cold night to discuss some contrived Medicine Wheel business, and if he didn't spend the night, he stayed well past the time any company business was resolved. And if he was absent a few nights, Kirsten found her way to his place, for their lust ignored the clock. One afternoon she had even stopped by on the pretense of visiting Henry, but Henry had been left yowling outside the bedroom door.

In spite of the distractions, the Medicine Wheel project moved forward, and the critical structures would be up and in business by the time the new railroad line was constructed. The merger of their cattle operations would be accomplished after spring calving, when Thad would try to sell his Hereford cow-calf pairs to local breeders for summer pasturing.

He knew that the personal relationship with his business partner was playing with fire, but there was no use trying to shut it off at this point. There was nothing stressful about it, and somehow it all seemed perfectly natural that he and Kirsten end up in bed together after a hard day's work. Beyond that, he had decided he was not ready to analyze it all. He had other personal challenges on the horizon.

As he neared the barn to unsaddle and tend to Cato, he heard a horse's distant whinny from behind him, and he turned to see two riders passing through the gate. He paused and watched as they moved his way. As they drew closer, his heart raced. It was Serena, and the other rider had to be Ned. He wasn't prepared for this, but he led an uncooperative Cato toward his visitors.

"Hi, Thad," Serena said, as they rode up to within a half dozen paces of him. His eyes were fastened on the other rider. Tall for his age and skinny, dark but even lighter-skinned than Serena, he had flawless skin and steel-gray eyes. His face had a sober expression, just a tad short of fear.

"Thad," Serena said, "I've brought somebody out to meet you."

Thad smiled. "I see that. This is Ned, of course." He moved closer to the boy's Pinto gelding. "I've been waiting all winter to meet you . . . your lifetime, actually."

The boy returned a weak, tentative smile.

"Ned, why don't you get down and shake your father's hand?"

The boy hesitated a moment and then gracefully dismounted. He stood in front of Thad, who wasn't sure what his next move should be.

Ned solved his dilemma. "Are you really my dad?"

"I sure am, Son . . . and proud of it."

The boy suddenly flew into his arms, locking his own arms about Thad's waist as if he were holding on for his life. He began to sob uncontrollably.

And then Thad started to cry as he folded his arms tightly about the shoulders of Edward Thaddeus Locke. He looked up helplessly at Serena and saw that she was crying, too.

ACKNOWLEDGMENTS

I must first express sincerest appreciation to Leafcutter Publishing Group, Inc. for making my novels available via its Poor Coyote Press imprint. I have been well served by the quality of my publisher's final product and the effectiveness of the company's marketing.

My editor, Mike Schwab, who has the last word on the manuscript, started me down this road with the suggestion some folks out there might enjoy reading the stuff I was writing, and then he figured out how to make it happen.

Bev Schwab has assisted immeasurably on the early edits and is my constant sounding board and cheerleader.

I highly value Kim Schwab's editing contributions and Cole Bauer's manuscript assistance. Rick Leeson read the raw manuscript to see if the story line made sense, and let me know when it didn't. Judge Linda Bauer reviewed the court scenes to help me stay within the bounds of literary license, and kept a sharp eye out for other inconsistencies.

Special thanks is owed to my world keeper, Diane Garland. This novel presented unusual challenges (mostly created by the author), and she sorted out the timeline problems and character inconsistencies with great skill and professionalism.

Finally, I must send my love and gratitude to my large extended family for their continuing support and encouragement—and for providing inspiration for a character or two from time to time.

ABOUT THE AUTHOR

Ron Schwab is the author of *Night of the Coyote*, *Sioux Sunrise*, *Paint the Hills Red*, and *Last Will*. He is a member of the Western Writers of America, Western Fictioneers, and Mystery Writers of America.

For more information about Ron Schwab and his books, visit the author's website at www.RonSchwabBooks.com.

Made in the USA
Lexington, KY
27 November 2016